THE MANOR MYSTERY

AMARA TRAVEL MYSTERIES

Book One: The Manor Mystery

THE MANOR MYSTERY

MURDER ON THE FOOTHILLS OF MOUNT KENYA

An Amara Travel Mystery

THANDI NOAH

ISBN: 978-9914-9406-4-0
First edition

For information about the author and future releases, visit:
https://thandinoahauthor.thandishaven.com

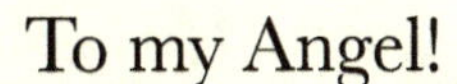
To my Angel!

The truth will out!

— *William Shakespeare, The Merchant of Venice*

ACT 1

Chapter 1

A sense of unease hung in the air as morning approached. The calm before the storm lay heavily upon the farm, as though the land itself anticipated a day's reckoning. Somewhere in the dark, the watchmen made their silent rounds. Those men never really slept. Neither, it seemed, did the truths hidden in this rural world.

He splashed cold water on his face at the outside tap. It stung him awake immediately. The air was crisp and thin. Back in his room, he pulled on his work clothes, slung his rucksack over his shoulder, and began his early morning journey. His heart was steady. His mind was full. He was ready for whatever secrets the day might reveal. He walked slowly but with purpose around the back of the buildings and into a grove of trees. He walked along a small footpath that led gently upward, getting steeper as he climbed. Shadows of stones, huge mounds amid the trees, dotted the path. He knew every step.

This was his quiet ritual, his sanctuary before the world awoke. From up there, he could see everything: the sleeping farm below, the distant roofs of the manor, and beyond them, the dark silhouette of Mount Kenya keeping its silent watch. Today felt different. Anticipation tingled in his chest, though he couldn't pinpoint its source. The air, charged with the promise of revelation, the day held mystery. The family's arrival disrupted the quiet routines. Miss Amara's return, the person who had opened his eyes beyond the farm, heightened his anticipation. Yet tension lingered, signalling imminent change and a shift in his usual balance.

He walked faster as the path steepened, careful on the damp stones. His "journey" led to the crest of the grassy mound, not quite a hill. He liked sitting there on the carpeted grass. He arrived slightly out of breath, having hurried the last bit. He did not want to miss it. He took the last few steps up and waited. Slowly, he began to see the first light of dawn along the horizon. The sky lightened. Slivers of the sun's rays reached around him. He held his breath. Up on this hill, hidden by the grove, he felt like the only person on earth. Standing still, he listened. He smelled and felt the dawn: fresh, new, full of hope. A new day had begun.

He sat, closed his eyes, and felt. The first rays reached him, warming his hands, resting on his knees. The sun kissed his face. In that moment, he was happy and blessed. Quiet and calm, he knew the day would begin in full force soon enough, but for now, it was him and nature. For a moment, he felt completely at peace , unaware that this dawn, carried within it a shadow. He held onto that peaceful feeling. Then he opened his eyes, took his book from his pocket, and began writing. He recalled yesterday, noting everything he had seen and every detail he wanted to remember. He filled pages, reviewing and questioning anything interesting or odd, marking arrows, question marks, and lines until answers came. Later, he would upload this to the computer Miss Amara had given him.

He'd already collected so much information. Little things: the small plants in the vegetable garden, weeds, or edible? The pink sow's piglets were growing faster than the black-and-pink sow's. Milk or genetics? The barley shoots on row seven, shelf twelve, were not growing like the rest. Light, water, or soil? The river stones, why were some dark and smooth, and others not? Always questions. Always the need to know. He included pictures, voice notes, and recordings of observations and even conversations he had overheard. All of these he had begun to compile into content for his future blog. He got excited just thinking about it. Miss Amara was right! Observe, document, observe, record, observe, upload, then organise. He had all the content at his fingertips.

He uploaded files each time he went to the manor, where Wi-Fi was strong. Each day, his phone synced to the cloud file he had made. He would share it with Miss Amara. Today, when he carried eggs and milk to the manor before the guests arrived, he would upload the last bits. It was a wonderful day when he first met her at "his rock" one morning. She was kind, helpful, and encouraging, giving him a laptop and guiding him in recording his observations. She felt like the older sister he never had. She was coming today; he had much to show. He was sure she'd be proud. Though he did not speak with her often, when they did, she was always full of encouragement. She had promised to spend time while in Nanyuki helping him set up the blog properly and start publishing. He was looking forward to her arrival and all he had to share.

He loved his job. Being a farmhand meant work changed every hour, every day. He moved across the farm, sometimes to the manor house over the river. Some tasks lasted hours. Others took days. He never knew what would come next. When work called for the manor side, only trusted hands went. He had always been trusted. More often than not, they sent him. From his first day, Madam, the matriarch, had put faith in him. He worked both sides: muddy chores in the pigsties. Careful tasks by the house. He liked it. Felt at home, almost as much as at his mother's. They treated him well. He was well fed and paid. Accommodation was comfortable. The work was hard but fair.

Lately, the farm was changing, though not for the better. The new manager started well. At first, he was fair and just. Things improved. But over the course of six months, he changed. Now he walked on edge. Nervous and jittery. That nervousness rubbed off on others. Eruya noticed the tension. He kept his distance. He noticed lies. He overheard the manager telling the owners the tractor was broken and that money was needed for repairs. Minutes after the manager's call, he filmed the tractor in use. He got the licence plate number. He watched as the manager asked for additional feed, equipment, and more money. Each lie Eruya heard made him watch more. He documented everything: times, dates, amounts. The owners were being conned.

But the manager's dishonesty ran deeper than money or equipment. There was the matter of the piglets. At first, it seemed ordinary. Births monitored. Mammas tended. Piglets counted. But over time, a pattern emerged. Sixteen to twenty weeks after birth, piglets were missing. The manager would take crates of piglets out of the compound, never to return with them. One day, he discovered the manager's piglet book, left on a corner. Notes included dates, schedules, and numbers. He photographed the pages. Then he slid the book back exactly where he found it. That book, those records, was proof.

Eruya kept his journal with him at all times. He continuously asked questions. Checked feeds and water. Counted piglets when he could. At night, he compared records and noted the discrepancies. He was patient, gathering facts beyond any doubt. At the Manor House, he noticed the judge, Lauren's boyfriend, rifling through family documents on a prior visit. He recorded it with his small camera. He had also seen Naomi the niece/adopted daughter, and the judge several times, in compromising positions; he recorded what he could, including dates and timestamps. He planned to show it all to Madam during the audit.

Eruya remembered now how he had come to this point —what started him off on his observations and investigations. Thinking back to that day just before dawn, everything became clear. The memory took him back in time.

He heard her before he saw her. Footsteps, soft on the path within the copse of trees.

He didn't know who it was at first; he only felt a flicker of irritation at being disturbed in his ritual, his early-morning peace.

Then he saw her, Miss Amara. He sighed in relief.

Amara was a family friend. He liked her. She was kind and spoke to him as an equal, not a servant. She often asked questions about the kitchen garden. She had even come to the pigsty once, curious to see how things were done. He'd been proud to give her the tour.

She had arrived yesterday evening, alone. Rumour on the farm was that she had come before, alone. Very quiet and sad. Something had happened to her. She had come to the Manor to escape.

He thought perhaps he should leave and let her have the hill to herself, so he stood, ready to give up his space.

"Oh," Amara said softly. "Sorry, thought I was the only person who used this place." When he stood to leave, she reached out, stopping him with a gentle hand. "Please don't go. I'm happy to share, if you are?"

He nodded and sat back down.

"Morning," Amara said softly, lifting her thermos. "I'll trade space for coffee?"

He smiled back. "Morning, Miss Amara," he replied.

Do you always bring coffee when you come to sit here?"

"Always," she replied, and offered him a cup.

He took it with a shy grin. "I—uh—I wanted to ask you something."

Amara tilted her head, encouraging him to go on.

"I see how you write online… about your travel, places you've been, people you've met. How do you notice everything?" he asked, voice tentative.

She smiled. "By paying attention. Always watch, listen, and even touch. Then write down what you see. Don't worry about style initially. Worry about truth."

He frowned. "But I don't have a proper notebook. Or… anything."

"You do," she said, nodding toward his small phone. "Start there with what you have. Take photos, videos, and make short voice notes. Capture the day, even simple things. How the soil smells, how the sun hits the hill, the cows returning to the barn."

He considered this, eyes brightening. "So… I can record and eventually show the world my farm?" he asked.

"Yes," she answered gently. "Your farm, your experiences, your view. Nobody sees it as you do, and no one can tell it like you do."

She paused. "I have an old laptop at the Manor," Amara offered. "You can come and pick it up. Charge it, and tomorrow morning I'll help you get started. We'll set up a shared folder. You upload everything there, and I'll help organise it. One step at a time, until you're comfortable and have gathered a lot of information. Then I'll show you how to organise it. I will guide your progress and help you structure it. Deal?"

He looked stunned, then thrilled. "Deal!"

In the weeks that followed that morning with Amara, Eruya started The Hill Diary; clips of fields, notes about workers, small observations about machinery, weather, and even casual conversations he overheard. From that morning on the hill, after his talk with Miss Amara, everything changed. Inspired, Eruya began noticing everything and recorded as much as he could. What began as curiosity soon became something more important.

The bell for the morning briefing snapped him out of his thoughts and back to the present. He fed the chickens, replaced sawdust, and gathered eggs. At the farm office, he washed his hands before the manager and others arrived. Tasks were assigned: morning in the kitchen garden, afternoon assisting at the manor.

A wave of excitement flowed through him, the family was arriving for a week's visit. Though in his excitement, he could not help but feel some dread. Madam had called for him to meet with her and an external auditor she had brought from Nairobi. She had noticed discrepancies as well and needed clarification. He liked Madam. She trusted him. He did not want to cause pain. But he owed the farm and the family the truth.

He was excited to see Miss Amara and to start working on his blog. As he was going home, he had several days to upload and begin. He hoped that tomorrow morning, at the crack of dawn, he would meet with Miss Amara,"their rock." He had finally decided to share it with her.

He mulled over who else would be present: the master. Julius, with his lazy entitlement. His vulgar wife. Her own schemes. Lauren, Naomi, and the judge. He had recordings of conversations. Photographs. Timestamps, evidence.

Though brave, he felt a cold edge of unease. Julius had looked at the boy strangely during his last visit. Had the manager recognised the boy's persistence? He had noticed the manager exchanging looks with Julius. When Madam saw his proof, everyone's schemes would crumble. Was it worth risking himself? This was not even his family. Still, his loyalty and moral compass drove him. He remembered his mother's advice: "Don't ever fear doing right." The memory steadied him, gave him courage. He remembered Madam's faith in him. Her trust that he would share whatever she felt in her gut was off, and he had evidence to back it up. Then he remembered Miss Amara and her encouragement; she thought he could do great things. He straightened his shoulders. No. He would see this through, no matter what. Besides what's the worst that could happen? A small smile on playing on his face he walked on now, determined. Perhaps the family would see his loyalty and courage. Perhaps they might even "adopt" him in some sense, reward him beyond a thank you?

With those thoughts driving him on, he collected the milk and eggs, shouldered the crate, and began the walk to the river, towards the manor. A quiet satisfaction tugged at him. He was doing this for them. Yes, and it was okay to expect something in return.

Chapter 2

He hated these mornings. The bell rang. The workers gathered. He had to look them as though he were in control. Some watched him too closely. That boy, Eruya, especially, the one with the habit of writing things down. He didn't trust him. Always quiet and polite, but with eyes that missed nothing. It made the manager's skin crawl.

He hadn't begun this way. When he came to the Manor, he meant to do things properly. The owners liked him, and Madam had learned to trust him. For 6 to 8 months, he tightened everything: fired useless workers, stopped petty theft, turned the farm around. For the first time in years, the place ran smoothly.

But working as an honest farm manager didn't pay off debts. And debts had a way of piling higher than the maize granaries. He started small, a little skim off feed deliveries, a few tools gone. Easy. The owners were rarely around, and he always had numbers ready to explain. A broken tractor here, an expensive repair there, nothing too out of the ordinary. He could talk with confidence, and they believed and more importantly trusted him.

Then the pigs had given him an idea. Piglets were quick money. There were always willing buyers waiting to start their own pig farms, looking for stock. Piglets were easy to sell because in the books, he would "kill off" four to six piglets at each birth. It was always believable, too small to survive, or the sow might lie on them and crush them. So in his ledger, they were gone. In reality, they were alive, weaned, and fed until he could arrange for their sales.

That was where the discrepancies began. Madam, while checking the feed inventory, noticed they were buying far too much feed for the number of piglets on record. He was stealing feed and pigs, a perfect duo, hidden in plain sight.

The boy started to notice. He saw him once, notebook in hand, eyes moving from sty to sty, lips counting, calculating. The boy was trouble. Always asking, always recording, always poking around.

"Everything tally up, sir?" the boy had asked once, politely yet…too casually, eyes still on the pen.

"You worry about cleaning the muck, not the math," the manager had snapped.

Lately, the manager had noticed him watching more closely, even when he thought he wasn't being observed. The boy had a way of appearing where he shouldn't, near the office, by the storerooms, the pigpens, just as deliveries were being loaded.

He also noticed that the boy had formed a friendship with Lauren's friend, Miss Amara. He had seen them a few times chatting together, and one of the watchmen had told him that they often walked and sat on the rock at dawn, having coffee. He wondered how much the boy had told Miss Amara. She was not family, but she might as well be. Friends with Lauren, the daughter of the manor, treated by the master and Madam as one of their own. And one thing he knew about Miss Amara was that she did not miss a beat. Sharp, observant, impossible to fool. If she got wind of anything remiss, she would blow the whistle without hesitation. So far, he got nothing but grace and friendliness from her whenever they crossed paths, but he feared it was only a matter of time. That friendship between her and the boy was dangerous. The boy looked up to her, trusted her, and might well share what he suspected.

His wife didn't make it easier. She had taken to hanging out with the boy, laughing at his serious manner, asking him questions about the animals, the feed, the piglets. The manager worried she might inadvertently reveal details of his schemes or further motivate the boy. Sometimes she lingered too long, smiling, as if she enjoyed those little exchanges.

"You like talking to him so much?" he had growled once.

"He's polite, that's all. Not like the others," she'd replied, her tone light but her eyes defiant.

The manager felt the heat of jealousy rise in his chest. The boy was harmless, yes, but the attention he received from his wife was maddening. It added to his nervousness. These days, his hands shook sometimes when he lit a cigarette. He was drinking more. He barked at workers who whispered as he passed. He imagined them plotting against him. Waiting for him to slip.

Julius, the son of the manor, didn't help. Lazy and entitled, but liked easy money. They'd made deals, small equipment sales, minor thefts. Julius couldn't be trusted; he talked too much after a drink, boasted about things best left unsaid. If the boy overheard… God help them.

And the housekeeper. She was dangerous, sharp, and greedy. She knew his schemes, introduced him to buyers, and collected her cut from stolen piglets. She could be trusted if he remembered who held the real power. But she was cunning, unpredictable, and if she decided to betray him… he'd be finished. He wasn't completely afraid of her. He had dirt on her as well, including clear records of every time he had paid her cut. If he went down, he could take her with him. A fact she knew only too well. She was a force to be reckoned with, he felt, and he steered clear of her.

The main problem lay with the boy. Today, the family was arriving. Madam had spoken of looking deeper into the books. He felt the ground shifting beneath his feet. If the boy spoke to her, if she saw that damn notebook…. No, he couldn't think about that. He needed to focus on staying ahead of the truth. He needed to control the story before it controlled him. He could not let fear win!

Nevertheless, the weight of suspicion pressed down on him. Every noise on the farm seemed louder than it was. Every shadow looked like a person lurking, watching. He hated that feeling, the sense that someone, anyone, could see the truth. He forced a smile as he handed out the day's tasks. His voice shook only a little.

"The top field for you, livestock for you, deliveries later…"

His eyes slid to the boy, and for a moment, he let the smile fade.

"Take the eggs and milk to the house on your way to the kitchen garden," he added, tone deliberately casual.

The boy nodded. "Yes, sir."

Yes, the boy was watching him. Always watching. He had to play his cards very cautiously; he had to play them right. He watched the boy carrying milk and eggs, heading toward the river and across to the Manor.

Chapter 3

The housekeeper's attention snapped to the pounding at the kitchen door. It was the boy from the farm, delivering the milk and eggs.

"Good morning, Ma'am. I've brought the milk and eggs for the family."

"Place them on the small table over there. And be sure to watch for any cars that come in, the family is arriving, and I'll need help with their bags."

"No problem. "I'll be working in the kitchen garden if you need me."

"Thank you, boy. That will be all for now."

He walked away toward the garden, and she watched him, before returning inside.

Morning at Manor House always began with careful contemplation. Today was no different. She moved through the kitchen, barely wiping countertops. Her movements were slow, deliberate, a performance of diligence for the staff. In truth, she only ever did the bare minimum. The Manor House was far too large for one person, she had explained to Madam, and had been allowed to take on a few extra staff, some permanent and some as needed.

Her thoughts turned to the linen cupboards. Tablecloths, duvets, napkins, so many, all within reach. If she remained discreet, no one would ever notice a few missing. If they did, she could blame a member of staff or invent another plausible reason. She would have time to hide her tracks, after all, the owners lived three hours away in Nairobi and always announced their trips to the Manor in advance.

She listened from the kitchen doorway as the staff moved about, each absorbed in routine. Their loyalty to the family was unmistakable. Yet she, as their boss, knew their weaknesses. She could manipulate or exploit them. Worse, she could abruptly fire anyone who defied her. A raised eyebrow here, a quiet threat there. She governed them all by small, constant fear. Most of all, she guarded her personal schemes to herself, never willingly giving anyone power over her.

She recalled the unforgettable incident at the market. A friend had betrayed her, threatening exposure of her schemes. She hadn't hesitated. She drew a knife, striking before the girl could react. The girl survived, barely, then vanished from town. The authorities were fooled. The housekeeper claimed self-defence, and they believed her. Violence was not always needed, she thought. But when it was, she wielded it with precision and without hesitation.

Then there was the farm manager, an ally, though hardly honest himself. When she'd caught him and her old boss exchanging piglets, she confronted him boldly. She was motivated to silence by a desire for control and extra income. He confessed and agreed to give her 10% of every sale. She had smiled, knowing she now had leverage over him. And income. She kept a careful track of the sales and her share. She also relished the control and the pleasure of knowing that one word from her could destroy him.

She pulled herself back to the present. The family was arriving for the week, more work, more deception. She would play the part: visible, efficient, indispensable, while doing as little as possible. That was what the rest of the staff were for. Nothing was going to change for her with their presence.

Madam and the master were coming. The master was quiet, unreadable and disengaged from day to day household matters. Madam, however, was no fool. On her last visit, She had asked the housekeeper for a few items that the housekeeper "could not find." They were already sold at the market. Madam dropped the subject, but she had watched her closely. The housekeeper had felt those eyes, she knew suspicion was growing.

Lauren was arriving too, along with her Nigerian boyfriend, the judge, this made the housekeeper smirk. Another avenue for profit. She knew a lot about the judge and Naomi, the niece/adopted daughter of the family. They had both been reckless and careless. She'd caught them more than once in compromising situations around the estate. Especially on the farm. A word here, a subtle threat there. She could bend them to her will. Their combined fear of exposure was perfect. Blackmail would be easy. This weekend was rife with opportunity.

Lauren was harmless, oblivious. Foolish not to see what was happening right under her nose. The housekeeper saw Lauren's ignorance useful. It kept Lauren from interfering with her plans. Better that way, the housekeeper thought. The less Lauren knew, the more the housekeeper could use her ignorance to her own advantage.

Julius and his wife were another story: both lazy, useless, self-important. Shame they had nothing worth exploiting.

Once, she'd caught the wife photographing the silver cutlery. At first, she thought the woman meant to steal it. She was just "taking inventory," preparing for the day she and her husband would be master and Madam of the manor. The housekeeper had worried then; had the wife photographed anything she had already sold? But no, her own "goods for sale" came from storerooms the wife had no access to. As long as she kept to items tucked away, she was safe.

Then there was Miss Amara. That one unsettled her. Quiet, watchful, impossible to deceive. Amara had once asked about a brass figurine that had gone missing from the end of a hallway. The housekeeper had initially pretended not to know which one she meant. Relentless, Amara produced a photo of it. Panic had nearly undone the housekeeper. The figurine was hidden in the back store, waiting to be sold. Luckily, she had not yet taken it to market. The next day, she retrieved it, claimed she'd taken it away to polish it with Brasso, and the gleam showed. Amara said nothing but placed it back in its original spot. A close call.

Since then, the housekeeper avoided anything that would be easily noticed. She stuck to linens, napkins, sheets sets and duvets. Though this meant smaller profits, it was safer. Amara's watchful eyes missed nothing. "What a cow," the housekeeper muttered. "And she's coming too." She would need to be very careful this week.

As she moved through the Manor, her work was cursory. A dust here and there. Her mind measured risk and opportunity. She anticipated the opportunities for her schemes that would be available this weekend. Her thoughts drifted to Eruya. He'd been watching her. She was sure of it. Once, he'd even caught her selling a few items at the market. She'd spun a convincing story then. He had seemed to accept it, though not entirely. He was always watching, documenting, and being in places he shouldn't. She remembered catching him coming out of the back store, phone in hand.

"What were you doing in there?"

"I left some tools inside." "It's dark, I was using my phone for light. The bulb's blown; it should be replaced."

She'd forced a smile. "Thank you. I'll get you a new one."

When he left, she changed her hiding place. She didn't trust him. He was always taking photos and notes in that stupid little notebook he carried around in his jacket pocket. Always watching. She believed he wanted something, perhaps to catch her. Let him try. She was smarter. If he ever became a threat, she had ways to deal with it, she'd done so many times before. That girl at the market had not been her first, nor if required, her last.

The Manor would soon be full again: family, guests, servants, secrets. She was ready. Every glance. Every whispered word. Every instruction could be turned to her advantage. No one would ever see her for what she truly was. A very dedicated and hardworking housekeeper. That was the story she sold to the staff. A loyal servant was the mask she wore for the family. But beneath it all, she was selfish. Ruthless. Greedy. Dangerous. She would stop at nothing to protect herself, her schemes, and her secrets. The house was hers, in the ways that mattered. Nothing, not the family, not Miss Amara, not that upstart of a boy, would take that from her. Not without paying a price.

Chapter 4

The car ate the distance from Nairobi. As they approached Nanyuki and their destination, the country air came in through the half-open window, a promise of what lay ahead. The Manor waited. They had arrived. The car rolled up the long, winding drive, gravel crunching beneath the tires.

The judge adjusted his tie, smoothed the slight crease on his shirt, and kept his smile fixed. Eyes forward. Polished. Perfect.

Beside him, Lauren chattered lightly about the week ahead, radiant, trusting. He smoothed his tie again, met Lauren's eyes as she laughed at his comment, and rested his hand gently on her leg. This place, these people: all were pieces on a chess game he was playing.

"Imagine it," he said softly, coaxing the future between them as if it were already theirs. "Quiet mornings, you and I reading books on the lawn and tea, the garden kept just how you like it, a game of golf in the afternoon, quiet evenings by the fire. We'll have the right housekeeper as well," he caught himself with a smile and said it softer, "and a cozy place in the city for when we tire of the quiet. Think of it. Us, together."

She glanced at him, bright-eyed and trusting. He gave his best, most loving smile. She believed him. He had spent years learning: the right pause, the look, the laugh, the movement through a room, and the predicting of people. He made himself a man people trusted implicitly. The consummate con.

He had always been wicked. Reckless and completely self serving as a boy. He was expelled from school at sixteen. One disgrace after another. Tired parents, shutting their door forever. Survival on the streets, unprotected and alone, forced him to learn other lessons. Lessons that would assure his future.

He chose the law. Since he had resigned himself to always being on the wrong side of it, he might as well be a step ahead by mastering it. Always wanting the best, believing he deserved nothing less, he had chosen not just to be a lawyer but a judge. However, he was unwilling to take the time it would have taken to get there the typical way.

He possessed a sharp mind. He recognised it, wielded it to drive himself toward ambition. He went where lawyers went. Observed. Imitated. Became. Then he did the same with judges. Scrutinised their mannerisms. Absorbed the language, the subtleties. Anything for credibility. He watched judges in court until he knew the rhythm of their sentences. He learned what respect earned you, how a title was a coat that could be tailored. Clothes, speech, posture, each a calculated move in a new game.

He'd bought books on probate law, real estate law, and any law that might affect him as a con. He learned the loopholes, manipulating paperwork until it blurred into ownership. He even impersonated a judge. Since then, each role, lawyer, judge, or landlord, let him impersonate someone new, collect hefty sums, and store away the profits. His current life is financed by these ongoing deceptions.

Now, years of practice had a purpose. The papers he'd felt under his fingers in the study, the old, yellowed titles, the ledgers that meant more than money when you knew how to read them, those were his map.

Not marriage, though that's what he let this family believe, dangling the promise without commitment. He had no intention of marrying Lauren. He only needed proximity, familiarity, and the kind of casual trust that allowed him to slip things from desk to briefcase without drawing attention.

Now the pressure was mounting. He had one week to work his magic, take advantage of familiarity, Lauren's love, and her hope of a match. One week. Seven days to copy, to arrange, to send. A company name here, a forged signature there, an account offshore, and willing buyers waiting ready on the sidelines. The Manor would be a victim of a theft so quiet it take them a while to notice the absence, and once discovered, it would be too late for this family. Another victim of "The Judge."

He had partners. The man in Nairobi procured forgeries, soft copies, connections to the Lands Department, the man who knew where to tap a source, where to push a file through. Partners were convenient, until they weren't. "Convenience" had teeth when a partner wanted a bigger cut.

He smiled at Lauren again as they rounded the final curve of the drive. He noticed the boy from the farm, the one always lurking where he shouldn't, drop a sack in the kitchen garden, wipe his hands, and move towards the parking lot. The boy handled the land as though it belonged to him. Diligent, observant. Quiet. What did he know?

The judge understood the risk of discovery from the moment he first slipped through the master bedroom door. He wondered whether any staff had observed his reconnaissance the first time, when Lauren left for the farm, and he roamed the Manor to identify opportunities. He was uncertain whether anyone had witnessed his activities, especially later in the study. He wondered if his phone calls to his partner in Nairobi about their plans were ever overheard, though he always took care to make them far from prying ears. The recent suspicion in the boy's gaze now made him question his earlier confidence.

He thought of the partner and his increased pressure to get more, thought of him in the same balanced way he thought of men who served his ends: useful, replaceable, but for the moment essential. The partner had assured him the documents would be arranged, the copies smuggled out, the "company" paperwork ready to present to the Lands office. The partner had been the one to find a buyer who would move quickly, offshore, untraceable, hungry.

He remembered how he had arrived in Kenya, the cunning it had taken to get this far. The fake credentials and recommendations, the endless practice of mannerisms. The charm he rehearsed in private golf clubs, hotels and board rooms from Lagos to Nairobi. Every handshake, every polite nod, every pause carefully studied, rehearsed and duly executed. He had lied, had seduced, manipulated, and stolen. Reputations had been destroyed, and fortunes lost at his hand. Now here he was again, calm and composed, poised to do it all over, his smile and charm hiding the predator within.

The car drew up to the door. As he jumped out and ran around to open the door for his "beloved," he said, "Here were are my love! Welcome home!" He held her hand as she stepped out and gently brushed her cheek with his lips.

"Thank you, kind sir," she said in mocking laughter as she hugged him, laughing at his charm.

Out of the corner of his eye, he saw the housekeeper and noted her glance. The tilt of her head and knowing look in her eyes, that had seen him in the past, when he had been less careful. She had seen him and Naomi together in private, totally compromised. She had eyes that saw what others didn't, and she was the kind of woman who remembered the smell of secrets. She would be useful, or dangerous. He had a plan for any eventuality.

As he returned Lauren's embrace with a smile, he noticed the boy hurrying up to help with the bags.

"Welcome, miss, sir! Let me get the bags, please, you go on in," he said in an easy, friendly manner.

Lauren grabbed her handbag from her seat, said a warm hello to Eruya, and started inside. The judge nodded in acknowledgement and moved to open the boot.

He watched the boy carefully. Though he seemed so friendly, so easy, he watched him. That efficiency, that friendliness, that vigilance, that loyalty to the family… dangerous. He noticed how the boy looked at Lauren with genuine fondness, and at him, the judge, with a guarded glance. This boy definitely knew something, and like the housekeeper, he was a threat, possibly more so. A threat the judge needed to deal with.

The boy, the housekeeper, and even Naomi would all be bent or neutralised. Persuasion would come first. Tonight, he would seek out the boy: flatter him, offer comfort, dangle the promise of safety, perhaps even payment for silence. A favour, a distant opportunity, whatever was needed. He'd blended bribes with threats before. Most people were pliable; it was just a matter of finding their trigger. The housekeeper's greed made her easier. Naomi, already close, would be easier still. The boy? He would find out tonight.

He moved towards the entrance, the plan maturing as he went: a private word, a small envelope, a promise. He noted again the young man carrying their bags, moving toward the side entrance. Observing. Silent. A twinge of irritation ran through him, and he swallowed it.

Upon entrance into the house, the housekeeper's practiced courtesy greeted him, voice trained for subservience.

"Welcome, sir," she said, and for a moment, he saw her calculations in that look she gave him. A reminder of a memory of hands that had been too adventurous, in situations that could not be misjudged as something else. He had let his guard down once, twice, numerous times. The housekeeper had witnessed his indiscretions. He gave her a small, agreeable nod, almost in promise of something in exchange for her silence.

Inside, Lauren chattered, oblivious, delighted at the comfort of home. He answered with the right words and feigned interest, making a note to himself to keep the study door unlocked tonight, where he had left some of the documents carefully set aside, ready for the first part of his plan.

He needed time alone to execute and be rid of all the pretence.

As he moved further into the house, he noted the young man again, carrying the bags inside. Observing. Silent. Efficient. That boy had begun to understand too much. He would have to act. Soon. Tonight.

He reflected, almost absentmindedly, on past successes. Lagos. Abuja. The associate who had stumbled upon his schemes and had an "accidental" fall. It was ruled an unfortunate mishap. The widow, whom he had persuaded to sign over control, in her vulnerability, on the pretext of protection. He had later abandoned her penniless for her efforts. He remembered the tension, the cold thrill, the perfect calm he maintained as chaos unfolded around him. No need for an answer for the authorities, who believed his lies, veiled behind his position. He felt no remorse for the trail of tears following in his wake. It had always worked before. It would work again here.

But the stakes were higher now. The Nairobi partner, intoxicated by greed, was threatening exposure. Initial documents needed within a few days, to keep the buyers interested. The family's continued trust for one more week was necessary. Naomi, clever and watchful, her insatiable desires and ambitions a subtle pressure on him, but pressure nonetheless. And that boy. Always watching.

The air seemed heavier, even though the afternoon sun was sharp on the manicured lawns. Everything looked serene, controlled; he noticed it all. Yet the tension beneath it was palpable. However, he was the Judge; he would control this and manage it. As he always had, again he would bend the pieces to his design.

But then a small, cold fact intruded on his thoughts: he had tried his partner's number in the car on the way up. The message should have been routine: send the copies through tomorrow. There was no message, so he was forced to call. He checked the number gain and called. He heard nothing familiar. No voice, no garbled line, only a curt electronic recording that sat at the edge of his patience.

He tried again, and again. Then a recorded voice telling him the number is unavailable. He felt a prick of ice at the base of his skull. and tried to shake it off.

"Bad reception," he lied to himself. Though he told a thousand half-truths on long flights and in dim bars, and when executed, they tasted like champagne. But it was usually to others. Now he was trying the same on himself. In an attempt to shake the growing doubt and fear, he told himself the partner was tied up with paperwork and that his phone was off, charging. So he tried the emergency line, a text, an ultimatum in a single sentence: Call me. Now. still nothing.

His hand tightened on the armrest of the chair until his knuckles blanched. An image intruded into his mind, the partner leaning close, a week back at a routine meeting in Nairobi, his whisper grey with threat:

"I want more, or…" a dead pause "After all," the partner continued, "I'm the one taking all the risks. I'm the Kenyan. You have no standing here, a foreigner." He sneered. "I need a bigger cut or…"

The judge had laughed it off, agreed easily, offered a larger slice of the take, and reassured the man that he understood the risks and that they were in it together to the end. He'd planned to see him on return, to sort the numbers. He needed to complete his part and then…. But he could not ignore the silence. It gnawed on him, and he admitted to himself that he felt unsure.

"All okay, darling?" he asked smilingly as he walked up to his girlfriend and lightly kissed her hand, his voice smooth and casual.

She smiled back. "You hungry?" she asked. "You want to freshen up, and then we can eat?"

"Starving," he acknowledged. "Give me five minutes, sweetie." He headed to his room, entered, and closed the door behind him. Trying the number once more.

The line answered with the same terse statement: *"Mteja hapatikani kwa sasa"* *the mobile subscriber cannot be reached.* This normally happened when a person's phone was off, or was out of reception, and he tried to reassure himself.

Panic was not an elegant emotion on him. It narrowed his perception and made his breath thin. He was not given to trembling generally. Yet, in the washroom, he found his fingers were not steady when he smoothed his tie. The plan that had been a clean line was now fragmenting.

He shook off the doubt, washed his face, and composed himself, reminding himself who he was and the mission at hand, he plastered a smile on his face and left the room. He walked back to the main living room. "Where is that food you promised, sweetie? I really am very hungry, lead the way." He reached for her hand and allowed her to lead him to the outdoor patio, where a table had been laid out in preparation. He pulled her chair and then sat down across from her, ready to begin their meal. All appearances maintained. Perfect. The final game had begun.

Chapter 5

The long drive up from Nairobi had left her and her husband in silent reflection, each minute stretched their nerves tighter as they awaited the uncertainty of the coming week. As always, her husband deferred the details to her, his trust both a comfort and a weight. The three-hour drive was not just a journey, but a steeling of hearts, bracing for tensions. It had been too long since all their children had gathered under one roof for more than a fleeting moment, and the anticipation left her both yearning and anxious.

"You've planned everything, haven't you?" he asked, his voice assured but laced with fatigue. He had had a trying week in Nairobi, and it showed in every part of him.

"As much as anyone can," she replied. "It's the people's behaviour I can't plan for."

He gave a small, indulgent smile. "You mean our children?"

She didn't answer, instead turning to look out the window as the hills rolled past, her expression reflective as memories surfaced.

As the familiar landscape rolled past the car window, the trees and the grasslands drew them closer to their destination. This gave her a tug of both pride and unease. They had built this life carefully, accumulated wealth through a lot of patience and intelligence, sprinkled with a carefully calculated amount of risk.

Though her own fortune had once outweighed her husband's, their shared trust and love had consolidated their assets into a legacy neither could have built alone. The fruits of her business acumen and foresight, and his connections and influence, were evident in the abundant wealth they had amassed. The Manor stood as the crown of their estate. Order and prosperity were etched into every stone and field.

The car entered the gates, along the drive, and turned into the final bend towards the house.

Their daughter Lauren ran out as soon as they parked, arms open, face bright, her laughter carrying. Her boyfriend lingered at the door, already adopting the air of the Manor's lord.

"Mum! Dad! You made good time!"

"Three hours exactly," the master said, stepping out.

He embraced his daughter, breathing in the scent of home. "It's good to see you, sweetheart."

"And you too, Dad," the girl said, beaming, then turned and ran towards her mum, giving her a big hug and kiss, which was warmly returned. There was genuine love evident between the two women.

Madam's gaze shifted toward the judge leaning on the door at the entrance. "You're here early," she said, her tone polite but cool.

"I wanted to make sure everything was ready for your arrival," he replied smoothly. making no effort to leave his perch at the door.

Of course he did.

Seeing her daughter filled her with comfort; seeing him, with caution. He had ingratiated himself thoroughly, too thoroughly maybe. And with the others still to arrive, she was reminded that this gathering was far from a casual visit. It was a convergence of family, ambitions, and hidden agendas.

This would be the first time in years that they would all be under one roof again. Normally, it was one or two at a time, for a long while, Lauren with Amara. Now, it was Lauren and her boyfriend who came most often.

She shook that thought off and drew a slow, steadying breath. The young man from the kitchen garden appeared and hurried to greet them, smiling as he took their bags.

"Karibu Mzee, *welcome, sir.* The master nodded in acknowledgement of the welcome and shook his hand.

"Karibu, Madam," Eruya said warmly.

"Thank you, my dear. How have things been?" Replied madam.

"All well," he said, eyes lowered with quiet respect.

His presence steadied her. She liked and trusted him, recognising his quiet reliability. She expected much from him in the coming days and believed he would deliver.

In her mind's eye, she envisioned her son with his wife: the son, lazy and entitled; the wife, always loud crass and disruptive. Her attention then shifted to Naomi, her husband's biological niece and their 'adopted' daughter.

"Where are they?" she asked her daughter quietly. "Your brother, his wife and Naomi?"

"On their way, I guess, Mum," her daughter replied with a shrug.

Madam nodded, though tension coiled inside her. This week would bring more than an audit; it would unearth old resentments, long-held rivalries, and truths too long ignored. Envy would surely rear its ugly head again.

Her stepson, difficult, lazy, entitled, obviously hated her and constantly tested her patience. Despite her attempts to teach him responsibility, his arrogance and his father's indulgence undermined her efforts. Lauren, in contrast, was quiet, kind, and respectful, creating mutual love between them.

Naomi, whom they had raised as their own, brought back memories of the waif they had taken from the village at age 8. Raised as family, she became ambitious, calculating, vindictive, and envious, always ready with subtle malicious games. Naomi never liked her and made no effort to hide it. She manipulated, knowing who to charm and where to push. Naomi, resented her, but her goal was clear: to benefit from the family's wealth, she was a mixture of both a false sense of entitlement and opportunity.

And finally, there was Amara. Thinking of her softened Madam's features. What a lovely, composed young woman Amara had become. She had known her for years. Amara and her daughter had attended school together as teenagers and forged a friendship that remained into adulthood. In many ways, she considered Amara one of her own. The young woman had standing permission to stay at the Manor anytime she wished, alone or with friends. Madam trusted her implicitly.

"Has Amara arrived yet?" she asked her daughter.

"Not yet," her daughter replied. "She'll come this evening."

"Good," she murmured. "She always brings balance."

Amara was intelligent and discerning, a quiet observer who never sought attention. Unlike many of her generation, she needed no spectacle. Madam admired that. She valued the friendship between the two girls; it grounded them both, made them better. Yet lately, she sensed a subtle chill between them.

She suspected Amara disapproved of the judge. She shared the sentiment. Amara didn't trust him; that much was clear. At gatherings in Nairobi, Madam had noticed Amara watching him. Not in admiration, but in scrutiny. The girl's sharp intuition was one of the things Madam valued most.

Amara's presence would bring balance to the impending storm. She had a way of softening tensions. Perhaps it was because she stood just outside them, trusted but not entangled. She respected everyone and never took sides, though her loyalty to Lauren, and her love for the family was unquestionable. Madam looked forward to her arrival. Later tonight, she planned to pull the two girls aside and speak to them about her concerns about the farm and the planned audit. She needed their ear and feedback.

So deep in thought, she didn't notice the housekeeper approach until the woman was almost beside her, quiet, deferential, her false humility practised to perfection.

"Madam, welcome back," the woman said slyly, smoothly.

"Thank you," Madam replied, giving her a penetrating gaze.

Madam's smile tightened. She knew that duplicity well. She had glimpsed the deceit behind those watchful eyes, but for now, she needed the pretence of loyalty until she had proof enough to cast her out. This weekend would clean out more than the accounts, she thought grimly. This weekend, she told herself, would clean out all the rot.

The housekeeper moved to the back of the car, feigning her desire to help with the luggage. Madam knew better; where this woman could escape any physical effort on her part, she did. She saw her sliding bags around in the boot, making no effort to lift any of them out or carry them.

The young man reappeared to carry the last of the bags. He caught her eye again, and she felt a small surge of relief. Loyal, diligent, steady, he was one of the few she could depend on.

"Do you want these at the front entrance, Madam?" he asked, pointing toward the personal items in the car's boot. Madame glanced as the housekeeper slipped away, noticeably carrying nothing.

"Yes, please," she said gently. "And thank you, for everything."

He nodded, he understood, and left to take the rest of the bags.

As she followed the others into the house, she paused to look around. The kitchen garden to her right was coming along nicely under Eruya's care. To the left, the manicured lawns stretched into the little orchard grove with its wooden benches among ordered rows of trees. She heard at a distance the familiar hum of the farm on the other side of the river. Everything looked and sounded as it should. But beneath it all, she sensed something was seriously wrong.

The pigs, her pride and joy, had started losing litters, four, sometimes six piglets at a time. The farm manager called it unforeseen. Sometimes the sows crushed them, or they were too weak to survive. It had happened before, but never this often. Feed records didn't match usage. Too much feed for too few piglets, abased on the official reports. Even the chickens were producing less, more breakages, more spoiled eggs. The numbers no longer added up.

Inside the Manor, a lot of small things were going missing, too. Tablecloths, napkins, sheet, even one of her cherished dinner linen sets; gone one day, and when questions were raised, found and returned miraculously. The loses had become too many for mere coincidence. She felt in her gut that something was wrong. She was determined to get to the root of it all this week.

The Manor gleamed in the afternoon light, its beauty masking the slow decay that she alone seemed to sense and feel compelled to act upon. They had neglected this place for far too long, she thought sadly. She thought of all the years of building, investing, of ensuring every asset they owned contributed to their comfort and their legacy for their children. They had made this home the heart of the family, a retreat from the bustling world of Nairobi. Now, looking around and knowing what she suspected, she realised that it was not enough to amass wealth; it needed nurturing, and for this place, barely any had been invested in recent years.

At the threshold, she paused once more, taking in the life she and her husband had built, their project, their pride, now, their burden. Despite the fact that she was the one to actually make it happen, her husband's support had always been steadfast. She was not going to give it up without a fight. She would figure out what was wrong and who the culprits were, and turn them out.

She would rebuild the manor and farm to even more than it had ever been. The children were older and would be asked to step in and help protect their legacy. Tomorrow, the auditor would arrive, and with him, hopefully, truth. But for now, she bore the quiet weight of doubt. Feeling every strained relationship and unspoken grievance in the manor and the surrounding grounds.

Once she stepped inside the house, the smiles came easily, but her eyes missed nothing: her daughter's genuine warmth, the judge's curated charm, the housekeeper's sly watchfulness. She saw them all for exactly who they were.

Interrupting her observations, the young man passed by again, distracting her gaze as he set down the last bag before heading back out again. His presence assured her that in the midst of the fog, there was genuine light.

Their eyes met briefly. He smiled. She returned it, genuinely hoping that what he knew would set the auditor on the right course. And in that moment, she felt the full gravity of what had already begun, and the quiet fear of what might yet unfold. She was home. And for tonight, that was enough.

Chapter 6

Another overcast, dreary day in Nairobi, the kind that makes you want to stay indoors with a blanket, a hot drink, and a book, forgetting the world beyond your couch. The weather was like a spoiled child, grey one minute, pouring the next, then grey again waiting, as if exhausted by its tantrum.

Looking out, Amara imagined the sky as a child sulking in a corner, uncertain whether to cry or thrash about, causing havoc. What a day to begin her latest quest: she was fated to drive through this angry, ephemeral weather. Three hours on the road lay ahead, to the foothills of Mount Kenya.

Her destination: Nanyuki, the sleepy, almost forgotten little town fondly called Mwisho wa reli, *the end of the railroad.* The name fit; when the railway was first built inland from Mombasa in the colonial era, it ended here and never extended farther north.

Amara would spend seven days in this town and, from there, travel through the surrounding area for her tourism market study.

In her mind, Nanyuki existed only because the railroad ended there. Passengers are forced to continue northward by other means. Though started long ago, the track has not moved. Nanyuki remains, literally and metaphorically, the end of the line.

But the town has grown. Once sleepy, now it hums with life under Mount Kenya, Kenya's tallest mountain, Africa's second tallest. The magical town sits astride the equator at zero degrees, which adds to its allure.

Climbers and dreamers flock to Nanyuki now. Nairobi's restless use it as a weekend playground. For adventurers, it's the last stop before the semi-arid north. Their last chance to stock up, check vehicles, and gather courage before vanishing into the wilderness.

The British army keeps an outpost there, using the northern terrain for their "war games." The land beyond offers the same arid harshness as faraway battlefields, perfect for practice, if not for peace. When they return, Nanyuki welcomes them with bars, hotels, creature comforts, fresh air, and mountain rain.

It carries its history lightly, aware of colonial ghosts yet too busy living to mourn. Full of promise and opportunity, the place draws you in. Beneath Mount Kenya's watchful gaze, everything seems to grow. When the mountain appears, it steals your breath. No matter how often you see it, the mountain surprises, always different, always striking. Known as Kirinyaga to the Agikuyu people, it is the silent guardian over Nanyuki's daily rhythm: the rise of tourism, the hum of trade, the promise of new industry.

Amara thought of all the times she'd stayed in Nanyuki, sometimes for work, sometimes to rest. Hotels, Airbnbs, and best of all, the Manor, the family home of her friend Lauren. Though she would never admit it openly, the guaranteed solitude in that place was always a welcome gift and reprieve she'd give herself when the world overwhelmed her.

After her engagement ended, a heartbreak whose echoes she still hears sometimes, she needed space to breathe, to remember who she was before the relationship that almost became her forever. Nanyuki was her refuge.

Amara would wake before dawn, wrap up for warmth, and, armed with her journal, walk out into the early mist. The air was cool and clean, with the scent of dew and hope. Even before the farm stirred, she'd be awake, coffee thermos in hand, crossing the little bridge to the fields. She would walk through a grove of trees beyond the fields and clamber up a steep outcropping of rocks and settle down to watch the first light spread across the mountain's slopes.

This became her morning ritual and therapy. The stillness healed her, one sunrise at a time. She drank her coffee, cried, laughed, cried some more, wrote, sat in silence, and it helped. Mount Kenya listened and whispered back, in sounds, scents, and rays of sunshine. Amara learned it was okay to grieve and to be thankful; the experiences proved she was alive. The home gave her space to regroup. In the cool mountain breeze, she found hope for another day, another love.

By the time she left Nanyuki, Amara could hold her head high again. In Nanyuki at the Manor, the world did not demand anything of her. It simply allowed her to exist, to hurt, to heal, to hope.

That's what the manor meant to her. Peace, even in its greyest weather. Solace, even when the mountain hides behind the clouds. She knew it would always reappear even more splendid!

Amara was headed there today, despite the weather in Nairobi. Excitement filled her as she tossed her bags into the car, jumped in, put on her seat belt, and drove away from Nairobi and its weather tantrums.

As she drove out of the city, the rhythm of rain on the windshield was like applause. If she'd known what awaited at the drive's end, she might have faltered. Instead, butterflies in her stomach propelled her towards Nanyuki, the end of the railroad!

Chapter 7

He hated coming back to the Manor. Every visit reminded him of the weight of expectation. Silent disappointment from his father, the cold glance from his stepmother. The silent judgment she never even tried to hide anymore. Her manner with him made him feel like a useless boy. But he was already a man. She was right, but it wasn't her place. She wasn't his mother and had no business standing over his father, running things with that cool, calculating manner. He despised her for it. Deep down, he feared her. She was everything he wasn't: strong, brave, razor-sharp. Her love for his father and his children, himself included, baffled him, especially given how badly Julius had always treated her.

Bracing himself for arrival, Julius clenched his jaw and turned the car to the gate. He drove through. Greeted the guard and headed up the drive.

He knew the farm manager would be waiting. His only "ally" here. Each trusted the other. At least as much as two men with shared secrets could trust each other. Their arrangement was simple. A subtle "adjustment" here, resulting in discreet profits there. Neither his father nor stepmother needed to know, let alone suspect anything. Who would notice if the books didn't tally? Or if goods slipped out? What would it matter if they did? The family was wealthy. The farm was thriving. Julius certainly did not care.

The farm manager had always been cunning, maintaining books that passed cursory inspection. No one questioned his record-keeping. But lately, Madam had been querying his decisions, and Eruya's gaze lingered too long over the ledgers. At least this is what he confided to Julius. Eruya was watching. He had begun to notice patterns and take notes. That silent, observant boy with a spotless conscience.

The information Eruya was gathering might be a threat, one neither man had considered prior. Julius felt a sting of unease. He remembered the way Eruya watched on his last visit. Julius and the manager huddled, speaking in hushed tones. He began to wonder if the manager was right.

The manager feared Eruya was starting to put things together. His observations might not be so easily dismissed as Julius initially thought. Maybe there was something in this, something that needed attention. Julius bristled. The idea that Eruya could threaten everything he and the manager had built, even if it was against the farm's interests, unnerved him.

What did Eruya know? And if he knew, what proof did he have?

The car slowed and crunched to a stop at the front door. His wife leaned forward, eyes gleaming at the sight of the house.

"Still as beautiful as ever," his wife said with a little sigh. "I can almost see myself out on that Veranda with morning tea. When this place is ours...."

"It's not ours yet," Julius cut in, his voice sharper than he meant to.

"Not yet," his wife repeated, smiling thinly. "But one day it will be. Your father isn't getting any younger."

Jaw tightening, he said roughly, "Don't say those sorts of things here, and so loudly. The walls have ears."

She laughed scornfully and retorted, "Oh, please. Your stepmother's the only one who listens in this house, and she's too busy pretending to be queen, lording it over us to care what I say."

He was the eldest son, the "heir," now seen as a wastrel. With a wandering eye, idle hands, and a warped moral compass, he robbed his own family to bankroll a lifestyle beyond his means. Julius had not turned out as expected, and he was well aware of his failings. But he had his reasons, his grievances, and felt no need to change.

His wife only exacerbated matters. She was brash and common, latching onto him after glimpsing the Manor during a weekend trip with friends. Knowing who his parents were, her desire sharpened, and she rushed the marriage. She knew exactly what he was: a lazy, indulged son who had never done an honest day of work in his life, living solely on handouts from his parents. But he was the eldest son, the one who would inherit the wealth (so she believed). That was enough. She wanted this rich lifestyle, and so, by marrying Julius, she had it.

He stepped out of the car, stretched, and forced himself to stay composed. Looking up, he saw Eruya standing by to greet them and help with luggage. Always there. Always watching. What did he know? Probably too much.

He walked up and said, "Hi, Eruya, how have you been? Everything okay on the farm?" The boy smiled and shook his hand.

"I am well, thank you, nice to see you." Julius opened the boot.

"Get the bags, will you?" he said, then turned to his wife. "Come, let's just get this over with." They walked up the steps together.

The housekeeper stood at the door, her head bent in mock humility. She, too, knew of Julius's failings, but he was the son of the manor, so...

"Welcome, sir," she said, her voice polite. "Madam. You've had a safe journey?" Interesting how she made the word madam sound like something vile she had stepped on inadvertently.

"As safe as one can be with my husband driving," his wife quipped, offering a brittle laugh.

The housekeeper's lips twitched, but she didn't smile. "Welcome home, sir."

The house smelled of polish and roses, his stepmother's touch in every corner. He loathed her.

"My big brother is here!" Lauren said brightly, getting up from her seat and moving to the entrance to hug her brother. "Glad you are here, it's been too long. "Funny," she chided, "how we rarely see each other, yet we both live in Nairobi."

Her gaze flicked to his wife. After a frosty "hello," she turned back to her brother. "Still spending money as though it grows on the trees out back?" Lauren asked in jest.

His laughed. "Someone has to keep the economy going."

The judge stood and walked up to them, all poise and polish. He extended a hand. "Good to see you again," he all but ignored Julius' wife.

Julius shook it briefly, studying the man. "Likewise. How are you?"

"Well," Julius's wife interrupted the judge's response, "isn't this lovely? A real family gathering. How long has it been since we were all under one roof?"

"Too long," Lauren said. "I hope things will be more pleasant this time. Last time... "she shuddered at the memory of the drama that had transpired when they were all gathered at the Manor.

Julius smirked faintly. "That depends on how we all choose to behave, doesn't it?"

He looked at the judge, the air tense, a test between men: the judge versus the heir.

The housekeeper's voice broke the tension. "Your rooms are ready, sir."

"Good," Julius said, forcing a genial smile. "It's been a long drive."

He noticed Eruya lingering in the doorway with the bags. Unease returned. Eruya was always watching. Julius had to discreetly find out how much Eruya knew and whether the manager could handle it before anyone else noticed.

"Welcome home, Julius," Lauren said to her retreating brother. Begrudgingly, she added "you too" to his wife.

Julius turned to his sister and smiled. "Thanks, sis. Nice to be back," he lied. He followed his wife to their rooms, a smile fixed; he was home.

Chapter 8

She stepped out of the car with practised grace, the faintest lift of her chin in pride, as if the gravel drive itself might recognise and acknowledge her arrival. The Manor rose ahead, familiar and imposing, and her mouth tightened slightly before she smoothed it into a smile. She had learned long ago that her smile made people underestimate her.

She saw all the cars already in the parking lot; hers was the oldest, and the smallest. She could not ignore the gnawing, rattling under the bonnet, signalling just how old the car was. The family all drove brand new four-wheel drives; even the judge had a beautiful SUV. Why was it that her car was just an old Toyota Corolla? Second-hand; a hand-me-down from Lauren when she got her new car. It made her bitter. She could only get second best. This was the way she was treated all the time: she was family, but not quite.

She caught Lauren's laughter carried by the evening breeze. The sound grated. Always her, always the precious one, always the one who got what she wanted without trying. Naomi got the leftovers.

That disrespect had to end. She would have her revenge on the "perfect" daughter and on this family. She would have the last laugh. She would take her cousin's man. She would take the life that was hers, no more hand-me-downs, no more fake acceptance of all the crumbs she got off the "big table." The judge would be hers.

The Judge. So self-assured, so polished. She remembered his intimate smiles and soft whispered words full of promise of escape to a better place. Away from this family that would never truly claim her. He would give her her own "big table". He would make her feel as though she belonged. It was only a matter of time.

Her thoughts were interrupted by movement near the car. Eruya was walking towards her, smiling cautiously, but he did not quite look her in the eye. Always so diligent, always so correct. Madam doted on him, and everyone else followed suit. He carried himself as if his diligence and honesty were a halo. He walked as if he carried virtue itself on his shoulders. It irritated her.

He had seen too much. She knew it. He'd seen her, she was sure, with the Judge, in those foolish, reckless moments when desire drowned out sense. Since then, he looked at her differently, never quite able to keep the contempt he felt for her out of his eyes; he wasn't rude, but he also looked at her with accusation. As though he judged her for them. That look had stayed with her, cold and measuring.

Let him look. He was only a worker, though favoured. If needed, he could be undone; she had ruined better men with a word to the right person.

"Get my bags now, please, and bring them to the house right now," she said haughtily. "Hurry up, I don't have all day." She walked off towards the house.

The housekeeper appeared, wiping her hands on her apron. That woman: another one always watching. Always pretending to know her place. another one who had seen far too much. Naomi regretted her and the judge's carelessness in their indiscretions. The housekeeper was definitely aware of their affair. She didn't doubt it. The woman's eyes said everything her mouth never did. It was only a matter of time before she tried her hand at blackmail in exchange for her silence. Naomi pursed her lips.

"Good evening, Miss," the housekeeper said with mock deference. "Welcome home?" The housekeeper stepped aside and let her in.

Naomi heard Lauren's laughter, her "man" still talking near the veranda. He was looking her way now. Her way, not Lauren's. For an instant, the corners of her mouth curved. He remembered. He always would. Even in Nairobi, they met frequently. Not in public. He could not get enough of her; she made sure of that.

"The family is getting ready for dinner; your room is ready, miss," the housekeeper continued.

Naomi started up the stairs to the suite of rooms she and Lauren always shared.

"Oh no, not that way, miss," the housekeeper said. "You'll stay in the small room. Miss Amara is expected and will share with Miss Lauren. Madam's instructions: You stay downstairs."

How humiliating. Even an outsider got more respect than she did. Miss Amara, indeed. She thought of how she hated her and them. The family always made her feel less. She could not wait to see their faces. Soon, she and the Judge would tell them all: they were going to be together. He would not marry their precious daughter.

Naomi followed the housekeeper, pausing just long enough to take in the familiar scent of the place. Walking to the little musty, mildewy room under the stairs, she imagined their faces when they learned the truth. She smirked. "I will get the last laugh!"

There would be a reckoning soon. Things could not go on as they were. She had decided that even before driving to the Manor. She would no longer be ignored or set aside. The Judge had promised time, a future; she would make him live up to them. As they gathered and the house filled with old resentments and hidden fears, she would have her triumph.

She had already decided she would not wait until morning. Tonight, she would have it out with him. The Judge. There were things that needed to be said. She would not risk him slipping away again behind his smooth smiles, his possible lies. They would meet across the river, on the far side of the farm, where the trees closed in. No one came after dark. There, away from the prying eyes of the Manor and its faithful servants, she would make him listen.

She stepped through the doorway to “her room.” This little, mouldy room was mostly used to store luggage and rarely used items. This would be her room for a week? Never! By tomorrow, she would be leaving The Manor with her Judge. She would have no apologies to make. By tomorrow, everything would be changed.

Chapter 9

It was early evening, dusk, when Amara pulled into the gate of the Manor. The guard opened it; she had been expected.

"Karibu *welcome*, Miss Amara!" he called out as she drove through.

"Asante," *thank you* she responded with a big smile. It felt wonderful to be home again.

The car strained forward, matching the excitement in her heart. Oh, this beautiful, lovely place! Amara thought. She loved it, every moment she had ever spent here. The Manor was her place of healing, a place that made her feel whole and complete. She thought about how much she loved it and the family who owned it. They were like her own. The excitement built inside her; she could not wait to get inside and see everyone again.

The staccato sounds of the car tires as they crunched over the gravel drive matched the excited racing of her heart. It had been too long, she thought.

Upon reaching the parking area, she noticed many cars already there, a rare sight now that the family seldom gathered all at once. Raising her eyebrow, she wondered how the week would unfold, finding herself genuinely curious. Amara ran through the list of attendees in her mind: the master and Madam, Julius and his vulgar wife, her dearest friend Lauren with her boyfriend, the enigmatic Nigerian judge. Amara frowned slightly, instinctively feeling unsettled about him. Naomi's complicated deviousness. She thought, this mix would surely make for an eventful week, perhaps more than she bargained for.

She shook off her thoughts as she drew closer to the house, her long journey finally at an end. Turning off the car and stepping out, she stretched, feeling the miles in her bones. The drive had been long: rain and thunder marked the first half, the last two hours blessedly dry. Behind the mountain, a stunning sunset finished her day. Beautiful.

She stretched again and noticed someone hurrying toward her, Eruya.

"Hey there! How are you? Come here and give me a hug!"

He came smiling shyly and gave her a warm hug.

"Miss Amara, it's so, so nice to see you! I have so much to show and tell you!"

She smiled at him fondly, noting his eager face. What a pleasant young man, she thought. If she'd ever had a younger brother, perhaps he would have been just like Eruya, someone she really liked.

In him, she saw promise, a future laden with success. The family was lucky to have him, though she doubted he'd remain a farmhand for long. He had far too much potential. She was certain the master and Madam saw that too and would help him advance. His time here was a test. One he had passed with flying colours.

"What are you doing here so late?" she asked.

"I was waiting for you, Miss Amara! I wanted to be the first to receive and welcome you.

"Well, except for the guard at the gate. You're the first! And I didn't give him a hug," she added cheekily.

They both laughed.

"So," she continued, "what have you been up to? Have you been making good use of the laptop I gave you and the advice I consented to share with you?" She wagged a playful finger at him.

He raised both his arms above his head in feigned surrender. "Yes, Miss, I've done a lot. I have collected a lot of information!" He looked around, then lowered his voice. "I think you will be very interested in what I have gathered. May I show it all to you tomorrow morning? At our usual spot, same time?" he asked.

"Yes, of course. I look forward to seeing everything you've been up to. I hope you haven't been neglecting your duties in the process, though?"

"No, Miss Amara," he said quickly. I have been doing all my work first, as I should." he paused "I know that this project is only to be done on my own time."

Amara nodded and continued.

"And I hope you haven't been poking your nose into other people's business?" she looked at him, "The kind that might get you into trouble?" she said, half-teasing, half-admonishing.

Little did she know how close she was to the truth.

"I only write what I observe, Miss, as you taught me. He said earnestly, "And I make sure my personal work doesn't interfere with my duties. You know I wake up at dawn every day, so I have at least two hours before everyone else wakes up to do my personal work."

"Good," she said approvingly. "I look forward to seeing it all tomorrow morning. I'm sure it will be wonderful. Just remember me when you become a world-famous blogger."

"Thank you, Miss!" he said excitedly. "I'll never forget you, no matter what."

"Okay," she smiled, "let me go inside, I am sure they are waiting for me, and I'm sure you're tired too, after working all day."

He took her bags and headed in through the back way into the house. Amara watched him go, her heart full of gladness. Some people reached your soul simply by being themselves. Eruya was one of them, reserved yet warm. Honest and curious. She felt grateful to know him and honoured by his trust. She was already looking forward to their dawn session and hearing all that he had discovered since their last talk.

With a smile on her lips, she walked toward the main door. Just as she was about to ring the bell, the door opened, and there stood her bestie, Lauren.

Lauren had heard a car crunching over the gravel. She looked up from the veranda, where she'd sat with the Judge. The engine's low hum was familiar, too familiar. She smiled instantly.

That must be Amara. Her heart lifted. At last, someone who would make the evening bearable. She stood up hurriedly. As she tried to excuse herself, the Judge rose too and caught her hand.

"Where are you going in such a hurry? Are you not enjoying my company anymore?" he teased, not letting go.

"Excuse me," she said, laughing lightly. "I think Amara's here, I heard the car in the drive. I was just going to meet her." She tried to pull away.

The Judge still held her hand. "In a minute, Miss," he said softly. "Right now, I want to kiss you. Is that what you want too? I won't get many chances tonight, so I must take my chance now."

He kissed her full on the lips. She laughed, hugging him back. "You are the sweetest man."

He hugged her tightly, faking warmth as part of his act, then released her hands.

"I think I'll go and freshen up before dinner," he said, "and I have a few calls to make."

"Okay," she smiled. "See you at dinner, sweetie. I'll tell Amara you said hello."

She barely waited for his reply before hurrying into the house, her skirt brushing the stone steps. The sound of Amara speaking outside quickened her pace. She opened the door with genuine warmth, lighting her face.

"Amara!" she cried. "Welcome home! I've missed you so much!" She enveloped her friend in a warm hug.

Amara laughed, hugging her back. "I missed you too, darling, since earlier this week!" She winked, teasingly.

Amara, with a glint of mischief in her eyes, continued. "Finally am here! I thought I'd gotten lost halfway down that endless drive," she said, laughing.

Lauren chuckled. "You and your dramatic entrances! Welcome to the Manor."

Amara looked up at the grand old house. Her half-smile was tinged with reminisce. "I've missed this place," she said, voice soft. "There's a peace and happiness here that settles my heart, even when I can't say why.

She paused and looked at Lauren, "You being here doesn't hurt either," she teased.

Lauren poked her fondly in the ribs. "I hope my company does more for you than this pile of rocks, grand though it may be."

Amara laughed. "Okay, true, but only just."

They walked into the house as Eruya brought in Amara's bags and keys.

"Here are your keys, Miss Amara," he said, handing them over.

The housekeeper entered from the kitchen, greeted Amara, and took the bags upstairs to the room she was to share with Lauren.

Amara looked around, pleased. The house she loved still felt alive with memory and warmth. She caught sight of the Judge heading to his room and made a mock curtsy.

He returned it with a mock bow and wave before disappearing down the hall.

"Come, let's go upstairs," said Lauren. "Mum! Amara's here!" she called loudly, up the stairs.

A door opened above, and the master and Madam appeared just as the girls reached the top landing.

"Amara! How lovely to see you!" said the master, hugging her warmly. He genuinely liked this young woman. He was glad his daughter had such a loyal, dependable friend.

"Darling Amara, come here and hug me properly," said Madam. "It's been far too long since I last saw you."

She drew Amara into a fond embrace, kissing both cheeks.

"Mum, Amara can't breathe!" said Lauren, laughing. "Are you trying to smother her to death?"

Amara hugged Madam back. This lady was like a mother to her, and she loved her deeply.

Her husband laughed as he walked back into the room. "I can't compete, Amara see, you at dinner!"

Madam held onto Amara's hand, took her daughter's with the other, and led them both to their suite. "I just want to make sure everything's ready for you girls," she said. "If it's not, heads will roll!"

Inside, she inspected every room with her usual keen eye.

When she finished, she found the girls whispering and giggling. "What are you two talking about, pray tell?" she asked with mock suspicion.

"Nothing, Mum, at least nothing appropriate to share with one's mother," her daughter replied cheekily.

Madam grinned. "Hmm. I'll wager that very little you could tell me would shock me. Remember, I was a girl once." She winked, and both girls burst out laughing.

"Now, girls, I'm going to need your help with something," she said more seriously. "Later tonight, after dinner, when everyone's settled, I'd like to discuss something with both of you. I need your advice. May I count on you?"

Each woman placed a hand in hers.

"Of course you can, Mum," said Lauren.

"Absolutely," added Amara. "We'll help anyway we can."

Madam nodded and smiled, reassured. In response to the anxious faces looking at her, she said. "Please don't be alarmed, your father and I are fine. It's to do with the farm. I'll explain later. And please, don't mention our meeting to anyone." She paused. "You'll understand why soon."

She smiled gently as she reached for the door. "Girls, I'm so glad you're here. You both give me strength."

The door closed softly behind her.

Amara and Lauren hugged again.

"Okay," said Lauren, "you've got just enough time for a quick shower and change before dinner."

Amara set her handbag down, looking around approvingly. "It's always so beautiful," she breathed, inhaling the sweet scent of flowers that Madam had instructed be placed throughout the suite.

"Being here makes my heart sing." Thanks for the invite." She gave Lauren a hug, which was returned with warmth.

"You know you don't need an invite to come here, Amara. This is your home, too. "

She tilted her head slightly in contemplation and continued. "It's home, yes. Beautiful, again yes, but I fear it has not now a happy home. At least not like it used to be when we were little children," Lauren mused, remembering her childhood.

Amara looked intently at her. "You mean…."

Lauren hesitated, then nodded. "Yes. When we were young, there was always laughter and happiness in this house. As we got older, the tensions began, and sadly, even now, though we are all here, I know that all is not well," she paused. "Even mum alluded to it." Amara nodded.

They fell into a companionable silence, both deep in thought. Through the open window, they heard the laughter from the garden. They recognised Julius's voice, alongside the Judge's deeper tone, and the sharp, deliberate laughter of Naomi. Though they did not hear Julius's wife's voice, they assumed she was there as well. Everyone was gathering on the Veranda for the ritual cocktail before dinner.

Amara caught her friend's eye. "It's going to be an interesting week, isn't it?" She was equal measure amused and alarmed.

Lauren looked at her and, half-smiling, half-nervous, said, "You have no idea."

A soft knock came at the door. The housekeeper's voice floated through.

"Dinner will be served in twenty-five minutes."

"Thank you," Lauren called back.

Amara picked up her bag and walked into her room. She turned, grinned at her friend, and said, "Shower time, I've got to wash the Nairobi grime off me!"

Lauren smiled back and retorted cheekily, holding her fingers up to pinch her nose,

"Yup, it's definitely Shower time, for some people." She said, laughing as she moved quickly to her own room before Amara could throw something at her.

Chapter 10

Lauren entered her room, breathing in the scent of lilies and jasmine, her mother's touch. Softly humming, she felt genuine pleasure at Amara's presence. The Judge might propose this week. She was uncertain about it. It seemed too soon. Perhaps if she agreed, a long engagement would help. She liked him, but did not love him. Besides, Amara seemed wary of him. Lauren would talk with Amara this week. She needed to understand her friend's thoughts and hesitation.

Amara was a fantastic judge of character and would be objective. She also knew how much Amara loved and protected her. As she moved around her room, freshening up, her thoughts drifted back to her first meeting with Amara and everything they had shared. She remembered Amara's broken engagement and how she had been there to comfort her. Seeing her friend in such pain from a failed promise, hurt. She hated Amara's ex-fiancé for his infidelity, and breaking her heart.

Lauren had always been the classic girl next door. Attractive in an understated way, with a calming presence, people warmed up to her and trusted her. She quarrelled with no one and maintained quiet patience. Well-mannered, she was the kind of daughter every parent would wish for.

Her elder brother was a wastrel, drifting through life oblivious to anyone's needs but his own. Selfish, self-centred, and yet fundamentally harmless. She loved him, though liking him at times was very challenging. She had learned the value of diligence early on. Having her stepmother serve as her anchor and role model from a very early age taught her that.

Yet, regardless of how progressive her stepmother was, they lived in an old-fashioned society. Her role was to marry well, so little effort was made to expand her mind beyond what would make her "proper marrying material." She had gone to university, but even her degree was a safe choice; English in a liberal arts college, selected with her marriage prospects in mind. Home Economics first, to learn decorum and domestic skills, then English, to polish her manners and make her suitable for polite society. She did not dislike it, though; she did not have the mettle for tougher things.

She had returned home, taken a role in administration at her parents' company, which she enjoyed, and settled into the life they had mapped for her. A flat, a car, a steady job, she was content and quietly accepting of her lot. Marriage would come in due course, and she would acquiesce.

She was not her stepmother or Amara. She was softer, more yielding to societal expectations, and she felt comfortable there. Only with her stepmother or Amara did she become truly brave. Amara often laughed at her for being such a nice girl, and that was okay. Lauren knew the laughter was not from a place of malice. Maybe that was why they were such good friends, despite their differences. They shared the same values but differed in how they acted on them.

Lauren and Amara were opposites. Amara was bold, mischievous, outspoken, someone who lived fully and unapologetically. Through Amara, Lauren glimpsed a world of spontaneity, adventure, and new acquaintances. Together, they brought laughter, mischief, and infectious fun to even the dullest moments.

It was this side of herself that led her to invite Amara to the golf tournament celebrations, as she had done many times before. Lauren loved the game. The social aspect, however, could be stuffy and tedious. Some members were rowdy or crude; she preferred to have with her, a trusted companion. Amara's boldness and hospitality always made these evenings more enjoyable.

That night was lively and fun. They sat at a table with the Judge and other guests, exchanging polite conversation. She noticed the Judge immediately, handsome, polished and confident. At first, though, he seemed more interested in her friend. Amused, Lauren watched as he tried to draw Amara into conversation.

"Your charms are wasted on me," her friend had said, brushing off his attention with a playful grin.

"I'm not interested in men right now, thank you very much."

Lauren had laughed quietly at the exchange, though inside she felt a small spark of curiosity, was Amara ever going to open herself up to date again? The Judge unperturbed, soon turned his attention to her, especially after overhearing their talk about the Manor. He asked around discreetly. When he learned she came from a wealthy family, he forgot his initial interest in Amara.

She thought fondly of her friend in the adjoining room and smiled. Lauren felt a thrill about the coming week, not only for the quiet moments at home, but also for a chance to see Amara in action: daring, bold, and effortlessly, herself.

Maybe Amara would let her tag along on her tourism research project that week. She always went to such cool places.

This would be an exciting week for many reasons. Her entire family was together under one roof, and sparks were sure to fly. With her adopted sister Naomi and all her mischief-making, and her brother's vile wife, there was bound to be drama. She only hoped the Judge would not be discouraged by family tensions and antics.

This would be a chance to see him through her family's eyes, to see how he fit in. Would he propose? Would she accept? He thought she was smitten, and though she liked him, she was not naive enough to miss the furtive behaviours she had observed, unbeknownst to him. His behaviour with her adopted sister hadn't gone unnoticed either. Nothing concrete, but she had seen looks exchanged, times she had walked into a room to find them both there, sensing that all was not well.

She had a lot to consider. She was glad her friend Amara and her mother were there to offer counsel; they were the two people she trusted most. They would never let her make a mistake in choosing a partner. If it came to that, they would lock her in a tower and throw away the key before letting her marry the wrong man.

Was the Judge the wrong partner? The verdict was still out on that.

Shaking all of this off, she went to her bedroom door and called out loudly,

"Amara! We need to get downstairs! Come on, girl, exactly how dirty were you then?"

She laughed at her own little joke. Grabbing a jacket, she stepped into the sitting area. Amara stood there, freshly ready and smiling warmly. Linking her arm through Lauren's, she replied,

"Very dirty."

"You clean up well then, miss! Come on, let's go meet the rest of the tribe."

They left the room together, heading toward the Veranda where the family gathered for cocktails before dinner. Their laughter floated ahead. Lauren kept a smile of excitement on her face. The first step to the weeks drama. This would be fun and with Amara by her side, she looked forward to it, even if it pulled her out of her comfort zone. Little did she know what she was wishing for, and how much of it she would actually get!

Chapter 11

As the two girls traipsed down the stairs hand in hand, they were met by Naomi coming out of her room.

"Hiya," Amara said, her voice warm as she reached in for a hug. Naomi recoiled sharply, her eyes icy, a silent wall slamming between them.

Naomi offered a cold handshake. Amara shook it, recognising the snub.

“Hi, Amara. "You're here?" Naomi said flatly, her dislike obvious.

Lauren cut in. "I told you she was coming when you messaged me this morning."

Naomi shrugged. "Anyway, I need a drink." She brushed past them to the Veranda.

Amara and Lauren stood, looking at each other.

“Sorry, Amara,” Lauren said softly. “I don’t think she likes you very much.”

Amara shrugged. "I don’t like her that much either. I was only polite because I thought it would make things easier. Since it doesn’t matter anymore, I won’t bother!” Lauren smiled uncomfortably.

“Come on, girl,” Amara said, “I think we’re the last ones to get here.”

They walked outside to the Veranda, and were greeted by a flurry of voices. Amara was intercepted by Julius, who offered her a drink and began grilling her about her recent trip to the Maasai Mara. Lauren, meanwhile, Lauren was led by the hand to the far corner of the Veranda by the Judge.

"Took you long enough," he said. "You left me to your family's mercy."

"I was settling Amara in and catching up on stuff," she said with a smile.

"Stuff? What stuff?" he asked curiously.

"Girls' stuff," she teased. "Wouldn't want to confuse you on an empty stomach." She grinned, released his hand, stuck out her tongue at him, and went to speak to her mother.

Moments later, the housekeeper announced dinner. Everyone began moving inside toward the dining room.

Then Amara heard Naomi call the housekeeper back. "Can you carry my drink inside? That's what you're supposed to do."

The housekeeper clenched her jaw briefly, then her usual mask of perfect composure returned. "Of course, Miss," she replied evenly. Then, to the master and Madam, "Would you like me to take their drinks to the table?"

Both declined, as did everyone else, except Julius's wife, who said, "Well, since you're asking, I could give my hands a break." She handed it to the housekeeper and walked in.

Amara watched the exchange with a faint smile of amusement. Such divas, she thought. I wonder which one will win the Queen B.. award this week.

Catching the Judge's gaze from across the veranda, she walked toward him.

"Hello, sir. How are you? Nice to see you, it's been a while."

He smiled politely. "Hello, madam. Nice to see you too."

"I bumped into someone who says he knows you from Lagos," Amara said casually. "A Mr. O'Brien Onifade. Ring a bell? Maybe from your judicial circles?"

She noticed the Judge start ever so slightly. He quickly regained his composure. She smiled, spotting the crack in that practiced facade. She was pleased; rattling him was exactly what she wanted. Good, she thought. He is way too smug.

"Onifade is a common name," he said smoothly. "Not sure, I know him. How did you meet?"

Amara smiled innocently. "You know, I don't actually remember. What I do recall is that he asked about you, said he knows you well. He told me to say Double O if you didn't remember." She paused for effect. "Anyway, no matter. The next time I see him," she added lightly, "I'll be sure to get his contact and pass it on to you. He seemed anxious to catch up with you."

She told this lie with a straight face. Double O had, in fact, given her his contact, but she wasn't going to let that on. Not yet. She had noticed his reaction, and it made her curious; she wanted to know more.

She touched his arm. "We'd better go in; they're all waiting." She walked ahead.

The Judge stood for a moment, unsure what had just transpired. He needed a moment to comprehend it. Then he walked into the house. Lauren had just come out of the dining room and met him in the hallway.

"Come on, sweetie, we're waiting," she said, offering her hand.

He touched it lightly but did not take it. "You all carry on. I'm sorry, I need to grab something I forgot in my room," he said with as much lightness as he could muster. "I'll be right there. Start without me, please."

With that, he turned and walked rapidly to his room. He entered, shut the door, and leaned heavily against it. His heart was racing.

Onifade? O'Brien Onifade? Double O?

Oh, he knew him well. From Lagos. The odds of two? None. He knew what this meant. Things were escalating. He had to rein it in before everything fell apart.

He quickly tried calling his partner again. Again "Mteja…!"

He threw the phone angrily onto the bed. His temper boiled. Deep within his gut, the anger churned. He took a few breaths. He paced, forcing himself to calm down.

There was a sudden knock on the door.

"Hi, Judge. Are you okay?"

Naomi. He knew that voice well. She followed the knock by turning the handle and slipping in, shutting the door behind her and locking it.

"Hi, darling. Have you been avoiding me? I've missed you so much since last week. I'm craving you!"

She launched herself at him, kissing him. He barely had time to react and soon found himself in a passionate embrace, hers fuelled by desire, his by anger.

He was not gentle, but she didn't mind; she liked it rough.

He released her and stepped back, breathing hard. "We can't do this, not right now. Maybe later?"

She looked disappointed but hopeful. "Okay. Let's meet at our usual spot across on the farm. Eleven p.m.? I want you, and I refuse to take no for an answer."

He nodded absently, already thinking of Double O.

She said hurriedly, "Don't disappoint me. No excuses."

He grabbed her by the arms, pulled her into another embrace, and kissed her hard. "No excuses. I want you too, more than you can imagine."

She smiled. "I'll go first. Give it time, then follow."

At the door, she glanced back. "See you later, lover."

She walked out and closing the door behind her.

He went into the bathroom, smirking. She would take any lie he gave, anytime, anywhere. She was a pawn, putty in his hands, and he felt nothing for her, beyond animal lust.

He washed his face, and walked back into the bedroom. Picking up his phone from the bed where he had thrown it, he tried his contact again.

Once more, the message: *"Mteja wa nambari hii hapatikani kwa sasa."*

He turned and walked out of the room. As he headed toward the dining room, he saw a shadow in the darkness, the housekeeper.

How long had she been there? What had she seen?

Another one he would have to manage. But this one was easy. He could smell her weakness from a mile away. Greed. Easy to handle.

Later tonight, he thought, or tomorrow.

He drew a deep breath, fixed his charming smile, and walked into the dining room.

ACT 2

Chapter 12

After dropping off the bags and watching the housekeeper carry them upstairs, Eruya stepped out of the manor. He checked his phone. 6:45 pm, plenty of time to reach the farm mess hall for the 7 o'clock dinner. He smiled. He genuinely loved this family especially Miss Amara; they were his hope for the future. Having everyone together felt wonderful. Tomorrow, after his meeting with the auditor and Madam, he had planned a short trip to visit his mother. He would be away only three nights. He would be back before the family departed.

It was a dark night. Without his torch on and the moon behind the clouds, Eruya could hardly see his way as he walked. He heard a soft clang from the direction of the little gate into the kitchen garden. He knew these grounds well. Even before his eyes adjusted to the dark, he walked towards the sound and to the gate. He had been so sure that he had closed it. In the rush to meet and greet Miss Amara, he might have forgotten. He closed and latched the gate. Suddenly, he caught a movement out of the corner of his eye, which startled him. Someone was moving in the shadows. He froze.

"Who's there? Can I help you?" Gathering courage, he started walking towards the shadow, fumbling in his pocket for his phone.

The person quietly said, "Please don't turn on your light. It's me, the judge. I mean you no harm; I just wanted to talk."

Eruya relaxed and started walking toward the voice, wary. He did not trust this man at all. What was he doing lurking in the shadows? Always in the shadows. Always hiding his actions from light and plain sight. Eruya felt strongly that this man was up to no good.

Within a few paces of him, Eruya stopped. The moon emerged, casting a blue hue on them both. He shivered, seeing the judge watching him.

"What are you still doing here at this time? Are you supposed to be here?" the judge asked authoritatively. "I thought your work here was done?"

Eruya looked at the judge. He knew this man had no right to question his comings and goings. He was not restricted anywhere on the farm. Did the judge think he was family? The next master of the manor?

He stopped and stood to his full height, tilting his face upward to look up at the judge. He was not normally a disrespectful young man. But he did not like the judge, and at that moment, he felt the judge had overstepped his bounds.

"I was doing what I am supposed to be doing, and where I go on this farm is none of your business," he responded defiantly.

A slow smile spread on the judge's face, but it did not reach his eyes. He eyed the boy, calculating his next move. Angering this boy would not do. Not now. He needed him pliable. Amenable. He needed to find out exactly what the boy knew. With those facts, he would know how to act.

"My apologies," he said with a mock bow, never taking his eyes off the boy. "I was only concerned because you have not had your supper yet, and you have been at work all day and must be tired. I was concerned about you. Are they overworking you?"

Eruya visibly relaxed, and though he did not take his guard down completely, he breathed out a small, sigh of relief. He did not like being rude to anyone, and this was Lauren's boyfriend; if he married her, he would be part of this family. He had also been raised to give all his elders respect, whether they deserved it or not.

He did not trust the judge. He knew of his negative intentions toward this family. He sensed the danger more than he understood it. This made him even more anxious to share his work with Amara tomorrow. He hoped she could help him figure it out. It was bad, he felt. He just did not know how bad it was.

He shook his head and managed a small fake smile. "Thank you for caring for me, sir! I was just latching the gate on my way back to the farm. I am done for the day, except for a few light chores at the farm."

The judge returned the fake smile and said to the boy, "So your day is not completely done, then? You still have chores?"

The boy replied, "Well, if you want to call it that. I'm heading to the farm for dinner. They serve at seven for all residents. After, I'll shower and change, then check the chickens and pigs to ensure they're secure. Then I'll head to bed. My day is done; those are easy chores. Good night, sir."

He started to walk past. The judge reached out and held his arm as the boy walked by. As the boy started to pull his arm away, the judge's grip tightened, forcing the boy to turn towards him in surprise and annoyance.

Maintaining composure, the judge looked down at the boy, standing two inches taller. He fixed the boy with a cold, intimidating stare, then gradually loosened his grip and released him.

A smile on his face, he said, "Wait. I wanted to ask you if we could speak later. I have watched you work and seen your character whenever we come here, and I would like to help you if I can. Can we have a chat later, after dinner, maybe before you sleep?"

Putting on his most persuasive smile, the judge turned in the boy's direction and draped an arm over his shoulder. Suddenly gentle and congenial, his tone shifted to disarm. He expertly switched from pressure to charm.

They started walking.

"So, what do you say? I also brought you something from Nairobi, and I want to give it to you later. Will you spare me some time?" His questioning smile seemed open, almost sincere.

"Uh, okay," stammered the boy. "Thank you, sir, for thinking of me. I will see you later tonight, then? I finish my chores around eleven thirty at the pigsties. Where would you like me to meet you?"

The judge stopped, smiled, and, looking at the boy, said, "I will find you around that time; no need for you to stop your work. Also, I would prefer we do this in private. I would not want the farm manager or the other farmhands to think you are getting preferential treatment. You know how tongues wag around here. Let's keep a low profile, shall we?"

With that, the judge said softly, "Eleven thirty it is, then, tonight around the pigsty. Remember," he said, holding a finger to his lips, "mum's the word." He turned and faded back into the shadows.

Chapter 13

Eruya stood there for a moment, trying to wrap his mind around what had just happened. One moment, the judge had seemed so dangerous and menacing; in the next, he was kindness itself. He even supposedly brought a gift from Nairobi. Still, he did not trust this man.

He shrugged off his feelings. The night was still. He heard a distant cowbell on the farm across the river. It was time to call it a day. He started to walk down to the river. A sound, something, made him turn around suddenly. Was the judge still there, silently watching him, following him? Or was someone else there, witness to all that had just transpired?

"Who's there?" he called out. Silence.

Then he laughed at himself. Why was he so jittery? How many times had he walked this compound after dark? He did not even need a torch now; the moon, emerging from behind another set of clouds, shone brightly. The whole place was bathed in the silvery light, except in the shadows, where the light did not reach. Why was he so afraid? What was he so afraid of?

“Don’t be an idiot,” he told himself sternly. “All is well. You have a difficult task tomorrow, but after that, everything will change, everything.” He shrugged off the fear and foreboding he felt, and continued walking down to the river, towards the bridge that divided the manor and the farm. As he approached, he thought he saw a shadow shift on his side of the bridge. He stopped abruptly. Was he seeing ghosts tonight?

He remembered a story he had heard about this bridge and how, in the past, a leopard used to travel along the river from Mount Kenya Forest. Farm workers and night watchmen said they would sometimes see the leopard resting on this same bridge. Maybe the leopard had returned on its solitary night walks.

Leopards were dangerous animals and could kill without provocation. But the stories never said the leopard attacked anyone not even livestock. Only that the Leopard would be resting on the bridge and, when disturbed, would get up and bound back into the dark.

He shook his head. "Now you're seeing leopards in the dark?" he chuckled and continued.

Almost on the bridge and preparing to cross, he heard a "psssst." That was not a leopard.

"Psssst, over here," he heard again softly.

He turned to his left and saw someone in the shadows of the trees by the riverbank. Surprised, he turned in the direction of the sound.

"Wewe, kijana, *you young man* come here," the housekeeper's low voice called.

What was going on tonight, Eruya thought. Was everyone lurking in the dark? What was she doing here?

He walked towards her voice. Soon, he was a foot from her. She stepped out of the shadows. As he got closer, Eruya noticed a large kitchen knife in her hand. He stopped short, his eyes on the knife, then her face. She did not seem menacing, but the knife gleamed in the moonlight.

She noticed his glance at the knife and put her hand down beside her.

"This isn't for you," she said, her eyes hard. "It's for the leopard, if he dares show himself. I know how to use it." Smiling sharply, she let the knife gleam in the moonlight.

He took a step back.

"Don't be afraid; I won't hurt you," she said as he started to turn and walk away. "I wanted to speak with you, to give you something."

He stopped and turned back around. She moved the knife to her left hand and reached into her right pocket. From there, she withdrew a wad of cash and, stepping forward and closing the distance between them, tried to hand the money to the boy.

He stepped back. "What are you doing? What is this?" He eyed her warily.

"No, nothing bad," she coaxed. "I just wanted to give you something small. You always work so hard, unlike these other useless workers; you never hide from your duties. You have been a great help today with all the family returning, and I just wanted to give you a small thank-you." She stepped forward again and reached out to hand him the money.

He shook his head. "No thanks. I don't need a tip to do my job; there is no need for this." With that, he started off back towards the bridge.

She put the money back into her pocket and, moving the knife back into her right hand, followed him quickly. She got past him before he could make it onto the bridge and stopped his movement, again, the knife gleaming silver in the moonlight.

"Stop," she said. "I need to speak with you." She noticed him looking at the knife and slowly moved it again to her side. "I told you, don't be scared. I won't harm you." Yet, even as she spoke, the knife remained foremost in his thoughts, impossible to ignore.

He heard her words, but did not believe her. He knew who she was, what she was capable of. He had seen it first-hand when she stabbed a woman at the market. He had watched her brazenly lie to the police that it had been in self-defence. This woman was dangerous, and Eruya knew it. He drew back and stopped.

She continued, "I really did just want to reward you for your hard work. I don't mean to threaten you."

The boy shook his head again. "It is really not necessary."

She continued as though he had not spoken. "Madam told me you were taking a few days off tomorrow to go and see your mother," she lied.

Actually, Madam had not told her; she had eavesdropped, as she was so wont to do, and had overheard the master and Madam speaking. "She said you were meeting with some important man in the morning, then heading home for some well-earned rest." She paused and feigned a smile that did not quite reach her eyes.

"I wanted to just give you something small to aid you in your journey, or to buy something for your mother." She was all soft and maternal now.

She looked up to the manor and said to him, "Think about it, and later, after dinner, when the family is settled, I will come and find you and give you the thank-you. I also wanted to give you a few dresses to take to your mother. Madam has given me some of her old clothes to give away, and there are two or three that I think would make your mother very happy. They may have to be altered, but..." She trailed off.

Then without waiting for him to respond, she continued. "Anyway, I will see you later tonight. I need to go and sort out dinner. I see them gathering on the Veranda for cocktails. Remember, I will come to look for you. I will be bearing gifts."

With that, she brushed past him and swiftly, almost in a run, headed back to the manor.

Chapter 14

Eruya stood frozen. His pulse hammered. His heart deep in his stomach. What just happened? He shook his head, recalling the knife flashing in the housekeeper's grip. He rubbed his sore arm, still feeling where the judge had grabbed him as he passed. Whoever claimed the full moon brought out madness was right.

"If I see the leopard tonight, I will not even be surprised. This is all too crazy."

He stepped onto the bridge, paused to check both directions for the leopard, then started across. Seeing nothing, he wondered if the animal had already been there and left, possibly frightened away by the housekeeper or himself.

The night air felt colder here, carrying the scent of damp earth. Water gurgled as it rushed beneath his feet. He heard the distant cry of a wildcat. Shivering suddenly, he rubbed his arms. Everything looked ordinary. Nothing felt right. He continued across the bridge.

Once over the bridge, he paused, surveying the familiar farm sprawl. To his left, the pigsty's low roof glimmered in moonlight. Beyond it, acacia trees cast long shadows just beyond the garbage area. He wrinkled his nose, recalling the stench of wastewater from the pigsty's which emptied into that area. To his right, past the cowsheds, the mess hall glowed faintly, and laughter drifted, a reminder that dinner had begun.

He followed the path toward the farm buildings, listening to the faint hum of voices and the clatter of plates in the night air. Approaching the mess hall, he glanced at his phone, 7:10 p.m. Knowing dinner had already started, he paused at the outdoor tap to wash his hands, then went inside for his meal.

As soon as he entered, he saw his friends seated at the table and waved at them. They beckoned him over. He got a plate and went to the server for his share of the food: Sima Ugali, Nyeni greens, and goat meat. He took a spoon and joined his friends.

"Where have you been? We thought that you were going to eat with the family tonight," they teased.

He shook his head, laughing. "No," he said. "I was just finishing up work at the manor. Miss Amara arrived late, and I wanted to greet her and help with her bags."

He thought of all that had transpired after that, but kept it to himself. He sat down and started to eat.

"Hey, Mwangi," he asked one of his friends, "what are you doing here? Aren't you supposed to have gone home? How come you're eating dinner here tonight?"

"The boss asked me to stay. He needed help stocking goods from the late truck this evening. I was happy to help, so here I am. I'll leave as soon as work is done. We stopped to eat. Then we'll go back and finish. After, I'll head home," replied Mwangi.

"Cool," Eruya said, eating. "Need more help? I'm free till pig feeding later. Can I join?" Being busy with others keeps my mind off what happened Eruya thought to himself.

The manager, walking past, overheard the boy's last comment and said to him, "Your help would be very welcome. Please finish your food and join them. The more hands, the faster the work."

He walked away before Eruya could say, "Yes, sir."

After eating, the young men headed to the large farm store joining the others, to help offload the truck. They approached the supervisor.

"I am back boss," Mwangi said, "and I bring more help." He pointed to Eruya.

"Great," the supervisor, Okelo, said. "Many hands make light work. Okay, boys, Mwangi, you go back outside to the truck and continue getting things off the truck as you were doing before."

He turned to Eruya. "You come with me."

He started off towards the far back corner of the large storeroom. "I want you to begin stacking in this corner," he said, pointing. "The guys will bring the boxes here. I want you to pick them and begin a new stack there. Okay?"

He called out, "Karisa!"

Karisa answered, "Yes, sir," as he came around the corner.

"Can you bring your boxes this way and drop them here? Then Eruya will pick them from here and begin a new stack in that corner."

Karisa gave a thumbs-up, then moved off to start bringing the boxes. Okelo moved away. Eruya started stacking as instructed.

The offloading continued. While stacking boxes, Eruya listened to the workers' playful banter and laughed when someone called, 'Wewe, Mzee Kobe, harakisha!" *Old man tortoise*, hurry up to another.

Occasionally, Okelo checked on his progress, asking, 'You good?'

“Yes, thanks,” said Eruya.

Sometimes, Okelo would come, carrying a larger box. "Let me help you with this one," he’d say. He would bring it to the corner and add it to the stack himself. He was big, strong, and powerful.

Eruya was grateful. Some boxes were too heavy for him to carry alone.

This went on for the next hour. Once or twice, Okelo checked the stacking of the boxes and patted him on the back to acknowledge his good work.

Mwangi came in once or twice to bring boxes, saying, “I need a break from all the stooping on that truck.” He grinned and walked away.

As Eruya finished stacking one box and turned to get another, he nearly collided with the farm manager, who had silently approached and was now standing close, blocking his way. Startled, Eruya jumped back, tripping over the boxes.

“Easy there, we don’t want you to injure yourself. I was just coming to see how the work was going. Good job!” said the manager, reaching out and grabbing his hand to steady him.

The manager kept hold of Eruya’s hand. His grip was unexpectedly firm. His words were light, but his expression and tone carried an unmistakable seriousness.

He looked around to ensure no one was there, then said quietly, “I know that you know what has been going on. What I have been up to”

Eruya started to shake his head and pull his hand away, but the manager tightened his grip.

“Listen, boy, you cannot fool me. I have seen you writing in the journals, asking lots of seemingly innocent questions. I know you know what is happening, and I also know you have been keeping records of it all.”

Again, Eruya tried to release his hand from the farm manager's grasp. Again, the manager tightened his grip and said, “You don't fool me, boy! I know you know. I also know you overheard my conversation with Julius when he was here last, and the tractor disappeared. I saw you taking pictures of the tractor we sold, including its licence plate. You can't fool me.”

Eruya froze; his blood ran cold. He felt his knees giving way and had to steel himself to stay upright.

Scared, he looked around and past the manager. The manager saw his look, sneered, and said, “Don't bother looking around. All the others are outside taking a tea break. You and I are all alone in here. I volunteered to come and get you.”

Eruya knew he was cornered. He gave up, and his body visibly relaxed, or so it seemed.

“Well,” said the manager as he felt him relax, “good, you know your position.”

He let Eruya's hand go. "The housekeeper called me a little while ago. She mentioned the meeting Madam has with you tomorrow morning, with a man from Nairobi?"

Eruya started. The manager laughed. “Yes, I know everything,” he continued. “I understand you have needs, your mother has been unwell, and you are the primary breadwinner for the family." He paused then continued "I understand that. I have struggled in my life as well with barely enough food for us to eat. I was once you, a farmhand. Just like you, I was the primary breadwinner for my family, so I understand what it is to want."

He paused and looked at Eruya. His tone coaxing, more understanding than threatening.

"I want to help you. I like you and know you have a lot of potential, so I have a proposition for you."

Eruya looked up in surprise.

"Yes, I have an idea of how you and I can work together, help each other. I can ensure your success on this farm if you let me."

Again, he paused. They heard the rest of the group resuming work and said quickly, "I will come and meet you at the pigsty later tonight, as you are locking up. I want to share my ideas with you on how we can work together. There is no need for you to go to that meeting tomorrow. You can head out for your time off immediately after your early morning chores."

Hearing voices approach, he stepped away rapidly. "I will come. I know when you finish work. I will tell you my plan."

With this, he ended abruptly. "Later," he said, and walked off swiftly. He almost bumped into Mwangi, who was bringing Eruya his tea, since he had missed the break.

Chapter 15

"What Sir?" Mwangi said, as the manager brushed past, nearly spilling the tea.

"Move," the manager snapped, striding out.

Mwangi steadied himself looking at the managers retreating back. Then he shrugged turned and walked toward the back of the store. Turning the corner, he found Eruya sitting on a stack of boxes, head in his hands, and moved closer.

"Everything okay?" he asked in concern. "Kwani, what happened? I waited for you to come and have tea, Mr Okelo, said the manager had come to fetch you." Mwangi glanced down towards where he had just come from. "The manager almost ran me over coming from this direction."

Eruya looked up. He did not look at all well; he suddenly looked haggard and tired.

Mwangi started again. "Are you okay? You don't look so good. Here, have some tea. I brought it for you so you would not completely miss out. Sorry, I was not able to get you any of the bread, it disappeared so quickly you would not think people had just had dinner less than an hour and a half ago. Greedy guys," he joked, trying to lighten the mood as he handed him the cup of tea.

Eruya visibly relaxed as he took the tea from Mwangi and started drinking it.

Mwangi sat beside him, concern on his face. "Is everything okay? You look like death warmed over."

Eruya managed a little smile.

“What did the manager say?” Asked Mwangi.

Eruya shrugged. “Nothing really,” he lied. “I think I’m just really, really tired. I shouldn’t have volunteered to help you guys with this work. I still have two chores left to do before bed tonight. Also, I haven’t packed for my trip tomorrow.”

“Oh yeah,” said Mwangi, buying the lie. “You’ve had a long day. You still wake up at dawn, don’t you? You actually haven’t stopped today, have you? Did you even have lunch?”

“Yes,” said Eruya. “I had lunch over at the manor. The housekeeper was kind enough to include me in the house staff’s food.”

Then, as Mwangi stood up, he said, “Okay, man, we’re almost done. Go finish your chores quickly, pack, and get to bed. You can rest on the bus on your way home. I’m leaving as soon as I finish here.”

Eruya, finishing his tea, stood up.

Mwangi continued, ”Why not ask Okelo to excuse you? I’ll cover here so you can finish your chores. We’re nearly done unloading."

Eruya looked gratefully at Mwangi and nodded.

As they walked, towards the entrance of the warehouse, Eruya stopped him. "Mwangi, can you do something for me?"

Mwangi stopped. "Sure. What do you need?"

“Could you take a package for me and hand it to Suleiman tonight when you leave? Don’t let the watchman see you leaving with it, okay?”

Mwangi looked at him in surprise. "Stealing something?" He was shocked, not Eruya. He was as honest as the day was long.

"No," Eruya reassured him. "I just don't want them to ask questions and know that I've given you anything to take from me. I swear it's nothing stolen. I just have a few personal things that I want Suleiman to keep for me while I'm away." Eruya paused, then continued "He was also supposed to help sort out the speaker for my laptop, and the best time is when I'm not using it. You know how good he is with tech stuff."

Mwangi nodded. Suleiman was known in Nanyuki to be a wizard with anything electronic, computers, phones, radios. He was the one you took your phone to when it stopped working. Mwangi knew this well. Suleiman had once fixed his phone after it fell into a watering trough on the farm.

Mwangi said, "The guard on duty tonight is my uncle Githenji. He's cool and trusts me. He won't bother me about the package. If he asks, I'll tell him it's some mending you've given me to take to a tailor in town."

He pulled his phone out of his pocket and looked at it. "It's now 9:30. We should be done here soon. Why don't I meet you in your room, say, in 30 minutes? You shower before your final chores, don't you?"

"Yes," replied Eruya, looking happy. "I'll have the package ready. I'll also text Suleiman to expect you. Tonight or tomorrow?" He looked at Mwangi questioningly.

"I'll take it to him tonight. I'm off tomorrow, and I'm not going to wake up early for anything. Also, Suleiman and a few other guys were meeting up tonight to go out, so I'll definitely see him. Okay, so 30 minutes in your room, cool!"

They both headed towards the entrance. They approached Mr. Okelo, and before Eruya could speak, Mwangi said, "Sir, may I switch positions with Eruya? He still has chores left to do tonight, and he has helped us so much." He looked expectantly at the supervisor, a smile on his face.

The supervisor looked at the two boys and said, "Sure, and Eruya, thanks for your help. You didn't need to. I won't forget that. Go on and complete your normal chores. Okay, Mwangi," he turned to him, "go finish the stacking. I'm ready to call it a day as well. I think we're all exhausted."

Mwangi said to Eruya with a wink, "Goodnight, man! Sure, you don't want to come party with us?"

"Maybe. You guys going to Stardust?"

"Yes," Mwangi said. "Finish and join us, you know it's always fun. Just finish, shower, and take a nduthi *motorbike*, and come."

Eruya grinned. "I'll see how tired I am. Maybe I'll join." He headed out.

Okelo, had overheard the conversation, said laughingly to Mwangi, "Wewe, focus on finishing the work and not on the young women you're going to seduce later. I've heard what you guys get up to when you go clubbing. Heaven help the young women of Nanyuki."

He walked off, saying loudly, "Weee, Makau, can we finish this work quickly, and be careful with those boxes!"

Eruya walked from the storeroom to his room. He was tired, and more than that, he was scared. He had misgivings and fears all day; he remembered his feelings earlier that morning about what was to transpire tomorrow. Now, with all those encounters and veiled threats he had received tonight, he finally realised what was truly at stake.

He reached his room, grabbed his towel, and moved quickly to the shared staff bathroom, thoughts racing uncomfortably in his mind. He quickly finished his shower, went back to his room. He shut and locked the door. The shower had helped remove some of the fatigue. He still had a strong sense of foreboding. Shaking it of as best he could, he dressed quickly in clean clothes, knowing he had to go back out to complete his chores, but they were not heavy chores, and he did not need his work clothes. His final chores included; checking on the water and food for the chickens and the pigs and locking up both for the night. He folded his uniform neatly and put it on the chair. He would use it once more in the morning to finish his early chores, then drop it off at the laundry on his way to the manor meeting.

Chapter 16

Eruya could not shake the sense of unease. What had started as a wonderful day had turned into a night of threats, enticements, and fear. How had he gotten here?

He was afraid. Afraid of what was to transpire later tonight and tomorrow. Suddenly he felt fully the weight of it all. He knew what they all wanted: the judge, the housekeeper, the farm manager, even Madam.

Madam needed the information he had gathered to prove what she felt was wrong with this compound. The first three wanted his silence. They wanted him not to disclose what he knew. What he had found out about each and every one of them. They wanted the evidence that he had collected. By what he understood from the confrontations this evening, each one of them was willing to pay for his silence. For his betrayal of his beloved family. And barring that, he did not doubt that the alternative may end up in violence, towards him. Indicated in their earlier conversations with him. He knew in his gut that he had every right to be scared.

All three of them, he had seen, were quite capable. And though he was a young man and strong, he also worked and lived on a farm, and there were many pitfalls and plenty of dark corners. Accidents on farms were commonplace. It would only be a matter of time. He did not want to be the victim of "a farm accident".

The fear ran through him again. It made him pause, and sit down. He considered each conversation from the evening and the barely veiled threats. He knew he had to act, both protecting himself and safeguarding his evidence.

A lot of the evidence was already on the computer in files that Miss Amara had helped him create. Some evidence was still in his journals, his phone, and his old notebooks. He figured out a plan.

He reached into his suitcase and pulled out some spare journals he had started writing in. He picked three journals labelled Pigs and Farm, Manor, and Miscellaneous. He thought, hatching a plan, I need more time. These journals will give me more time and allow me to pull this whole thing off, protect the real evidence, and walk away unscathed. Thus resolved, he began executing the plan rapidly.

He had some spare envelopes in his suitcase, brown and yellow envelopes. The farm office clerk had given him the envelopes at his request to help him organise his papers and books. All of the envelopes were recycled from documents that the farm manager and the office had received.

He took one of the journals, slipped it into an envelope, found some cellotape, and sealed it. He found a black permanent marker and labelled the envelope 'Miscellaneous.' This envelope he planned to give to the judge.

He took the next journal and, doing the same, labelled the envelope "Housekeeper." The final one he marked "Mr Oricha"

He put all three envelopes in his jacket pockets. A different pocket for each envelope, and he memorised which was which. He though about the favour and promises the three had made. Why should I not take all they they offered? he thought. I am the one taking the risks. The extra money and gifts could go a long way in helping his mother. It never hurts to have savings. Finally, he rationalised, he was taking from bad people and using it for good. A payment for the risk he was taking to get the truth in the right hands.

He moved the bed away from the window and, taking a panga machete he kept in the room, used it to pry open a few floorboards beneath the bed, near the window. He pulled out from there all his actual journals full of evidence, his laptop still in its protective case, and a flash drive with more evidence. He placed them all on the bed.

He walked over to where he kept his "home" clothes, the ones he wore after chores and while on the compound resting, not unlike what he was wearing tonight to complete his chores. He pulled out a few old T-shirts and sweatshirts, and a couple of jackets. He placed them on the bed, placed the bigger heavier jacket on the bottom, spread out, and stacked the rest of the clothes on top of each other inside that jacket.

He placed the journals between the clothes, tucking them closer to the bottom of the pile. Next came the laptop in its neoprene case. He added more T-shirts above it. Raising the other jacket, he found an inner pocket, a small one, where he placed the flash drive and placed it on top of the entire pile.

Then he sat at the desk in the corner of the room. He took out some writing paper and wrote a few letters. One letter he sealed and, after labelling it, slid it inside the bundle. He pulled the bottom jacket over the entire bundle, zipped it, wrapping the arms to secure everything within. He took the other letter he had written, sealed it, and placed it on top of the bundle. He took the entire lot and placed it all inside a large shopping bag. Using masking tape this time, he sealed the bag. He used the tape to reinforce the bulging bag and addressed the top: "Suleiman Abdi." He put them all in an extra rucksack he had. He placed it at the edge of the bed.

He sat back at the desk, took out his phone, and sent a few texts. The first was to Suleiman, who responded immediately, inquiring why Eruya did not just call him. He replied by text:

"Walls have ears."

Suleiman responded: "Is how?"

Eruya sent a long text explaining that Mwangi would deliver a package to him. He asked Suleiman to hold the package for him until the next day. He would stop by Suleiman's in the morning to pick it up. Suleiman texted back in agreement.

Eruya then sent a text to Madam, reassuring her that he would be there by 10 a.m. for the meeting. He explained, that he would leave the compound earlier but return on time. He would not come through the farm but by the main manor gate, and would leave the same way after the meeting. He hoped that would be okay. After a few minutes, he got a thumbs-up and a *"thank you and good night, Eruya."* His response *"You are welcome and good night too."*

Hearing a knock on his door, he opened it tentatively at first, then, seeing Mwangi, he admitted him into the room. He handed Mwangi the package and thanked him. Then Eruya put on his work boots and jacket, slipped his phone inside the pocket of his jeans, and both young men walked out of the room.

Eruya closed and locked the door, placing his key into his pocket.

"Mwangi," he said loudly, "you guys have fun tonight. I'm too tired to join you."

Eruya gave Mwangi a knowing look and, quieter still, whispered, 'You know what to do. He's waiting for you. Please text me when you clear the farm?"

Mwangi nodded and said loudly, "Baadaye! *later*

The young men slipped into the darkness, Mwangi towards the gate, and Eruya towards the chicken coop.

The air felt even cooler now, and the moon had risen higher above the trees. The farm was quieting down; the laughter from the mess hall had long faded, and staff had either left the farm or gone to bed. He glanced at his phone; it was going to 10pm. Still time to finish the last of his chores before his meetings.

Eruya was busy adding food and water for the chickens when his phone beeped, a text. He stopped, pulled out his phone, and read:

"Hakuna shida, niko kwa boda." *No problem, I am on the motorbike.*

He breathed a sigh of relief. He could feel the envelopes with the notebooks rustling in his jacket as he moved. He carefully stopped and checked them again. He wanted to give the right journal to the right person.

Chapter 17

He checked for late eggs placing them in a basket, and settled the chickens for the night, moving on autopilot as he did every evening. Suddenly, he heard a sound outside the coop and stopped. Again, soft footsteps coming closer. He froze, frightened. Who could it be?

He kept completely still. The footsteps continued advancing. He braced himself and, turning off all the lights, went out to meet them. He quickly and quietly stepped out of the chicken coop. Instead of heading toward the footsteps, he hid in the corner, in the shadows, away from the bright, silvery glow of the moonlight. At least that way, he would see the person before the person saw him. Then he would know how to act.

He heard a voice in the darkness.

"Kijana, habari ya jioni?" *Young man, how is your night*

It was Githenji, the night guard, patrolling. Eruya breathed a sigh of relief and responded,

"Mzuri na yako Mr Githenji?" *Good, Mr Githenji, and yours*

Githenji nodded and moved on quietly into the night.

Eruya secured the chicken coop and walked to the pigsty. It had been a long day. The pigsty was on the north side of the farm. Situated up the hill east of the river. It was a large, low building with a single long corridor running through the centre. There were two entrances on either side of that central corridor. Inside were stalls for pigs. The south entrance opened onto the offices, and beyond them, the stores and staff quarters. The north entrance led to empty farmland with more Acacia trees in the distance. Directly northeast of the building, around the corner, was a large garbage heap where the wastewater from the sty's drained. Beyond that more acacia trees

The lower stalls (towards the river) had troughs to the left. The higher ones (away from the river) had troughs to the right. Feeding was simple: he filled the wheelbarrow with food, stored just outside the south entrance, and then dished it out with a large pitcher, alternating left and right as he advanced. In this way, he filled all the troughs by the time he reached the north entrance of the building.

He began filling the troughs. This was not a full feed so one wheelbarrow of feed was enough. As he turned to check any he might have missed, he sensed movement behind him, spun around, and jumped back.

"Hey! What are you doing? You scared me!"

There, standing directly in front of the now-empty wheelbarrow, was the housekeeper.

He straightened. "So, you did find me. Just like you said you would," he said, forcing a smile.

He stopped. She was looking at him with cold eyes, assessing him, trying to read him. Then she smiled and said,

"Let's move away from the light, in case anybody sees us. Let's go outside. I left something there for you, as I promised."

She started walking back to the north entrance at the rear of the building.

He hesitated, skirted the wheelbarrow, and followed her, curious but cautious. He remembered her kitchen knife from earlier at the bridge.

He did not see a knife on her, but she might have left it outside. Eruya paused outside, letting his eyes adjust to the darkness, but could not see her immediately anywhere nearby.

"Pssst," he heard from the side of the building to the east, in the shadow. "Pssst! Come here," she whispered loudly.

He turned and followed the voice, slowly walking toward the sound. He could see her shadow against the building.He approached. "Come out of the shadows so I can see you," he said.

She stepped into the moonlight, holding a bag, not a knife.

She held out the bag. "See here, as I promised, for your mum."

He didn't move. "No," he said quietly. "Unless Madam gives them to me herself. I won't take them."

Her smile tightened. She looked away. "You think I'd set you up?" Silence hung between them; the answer was clear.

He eyed her warily. He did not trust her. He knew she had been stealing from the house for a long time, likely longer than he'd worked there. With proof in hand, he planned to tell the auditor tomorrow.

"No," he said firmly. "I do not want clothes from you."

He saw her jaw tighten in anger. So he would not fall easily into her trap, she thought. I will try something else.

Before she could respond, he hurriedly said, "I want money."

She stopped, a knowing smile spreading. She knew he could be bought. She set the bag down and reached into her pocket. Eruya thinking she was about to pull out a knife, stepped back quickly in panic.

"Why so jumpy?" she asked, feigning innocence. She pulled out the same wad of money and went to hand it to him.

He did not step closer. "No," he said. "I want M-Pesa. I do not want cash."

The housekeeper stopped. She was about to completely lose patience with this boy, but she knew if she wanted the evidence he was holding, she needed to play her hand carefully.

She took a deep breath and said, "No problem. Let me send it right now." Then she stopped and looked squarely at him.

"I know you have evidence about me, things you have seen me do, things I have taken. I will trade that for money. How about that?" She looked up at him with a piercing gaze. "Nothing for nothing," she said. "I will trade you money for the evidence you have on me. So, how about it?"

Eruya pretended to quiver in fear, then said quietly, "I knew you would want the evidence I was holding. I came prepared."

He reached into his right jacket pocket and pulled out a sealed envelope marked 'Housekeeper'.

He said, "I will put this envelope on the ledge over there and step away. As soon as the money hits my account, I will walk away. Our dealings are done. Fair?"

"Sawa" okay she said. "Don't you dare try to trick me. Remember... I have a way with knives."

She stepped back into the shadow, bent down, and picked up a kitchen knife from the ground. Seeing this, Eruya retreated again. She laughed softly and said, "Don't panic. I will only use this if you try to trick me. I'm sending the money now. As soon as it hits your account, we will both hear it. You check to make sure. Then walk away. I will take my packages," she said, glancing at both the envelope and placed the knife on the bag, "and go back across the river. Our dealings are done."

She reached into her pocked and pulled out her phone, as Eruya stepped away from the ledge. She sent the M-Pesa. Within moments, he heard the confirmation, checked the message, and saw she had sent him 20,000 Kenya Shillings (KShs). He was surprised. This was more than his monthly salary. She must really want that evidence.

He moved away from the ledge. She grabbed the knife with one hand and the bag with with the other. She rushed to the envelope, and using the same hand with the knife picked it off the ledge.

Just then, they both heard footsteps from inside the pigsty moving towards the north entrance. Not wanting to be seen. She rushed past him and fled into the darkness toward the river and the bridge. She did not want anyone to know she had been on the farm that evening.

Eruya looked around in panic. Then he quickly grabbed a garden hoe propped against the wall by the entrance and walked in to the lit pigsty toward the footsteps.

Chapter 18

The farm manager was walking toward him and stopped when Eruya stepped out of the darkness.

"What are you doing out here?" he asked. "Avoiding your duties? Who else is here? I heard voices."

"No, sir," Eruya said. "Good evening. I had taken out a dead rat to the garbage heap. I was returning when I heard your footsteps," he lied.

The farm manager looked at the boy sharply. Eruya returned his gaze, looking so innocent that the man believed him.

"These rats are a menace," he replied. "We don't want the dead ones smelling the place up. Good job, boy."

He started to walk back the way he had come, then stopped. Turning to face the boy again, he said, "Come. I want to show you something I noticed earlier. And can you move this wheelbarrow from the corridor?

He turned and walked away. Eruya placed the shovel on the wheelbarrow and followed. Reaching the other end of the sty, the manager stepped outside and turned away from the buildings toward the trees. It was dark; the moonlight could not penetrate through the thick canopy in that area.

"Coming?" the manager asked. "Don't worry, I'm not angry with you. I just noticed something and wanted your opinion."

Eruya, placing the wheelbarrow where it was normally stored he picked up the shovel, and followed him into the grove of trees, into the darkness.

The manager began speaking before Eruya had fully reached him. "So, my boy, have you finished your chores?"

"Yes, sir," said the boy. "Though I still need to go back and lock up."

"Hakuna Shida," *no problem* I won't keep you very long. I want to discuss your future, boy."

"I know you are ambitious," the manager said, his tone paternal. "You remind me of myself when I was your age, working hard, dreaming of more, trying to take care of everyone back home. I understand you, boy. I've been where you are. I know what it's like to want things, better clothes, a better life, to have people respect you."

He paused and smiled faintly. "And maybe, just maybe, I can help you."

Eruya was silent, still wary, eyes flicking up at him through the very dim light.

"But help," the manager continued softly, "goes both ways, right?" You have something I want, and I have something you need. That's how people like us move forward."

He took a small step closer, lowering his voice. "There's information you've been keeping, things you've seen, things you've written down. I know all about it. Give it to me, instead of the auditor tomorrow, and I'll make sure you never have to worry again. I'll see to it personally that you have a better position here, and more."

"Why are you so surprised that I know of your meeting tomorrow?" The manager chuckled in response to Eruya's visible start of surprise. "Not much gets past me on this farm, boy. I'm aware of everything that happens." He paused "No matter, you have evidence that could be detrimental to me if you pass it forward. I'm happy to make it worth your while to give it to me instead."

Eruya looked at the man and, feigning innocence, said, "And what do I tell the auditor?"

The manager laughed. "You are smart, boy, you'll figure out something. Give him information about other people, like Julius. I know you know of my dealings with him, like the sale of the tractor and the other farm equipment. I'm sure you know he sold it behind his parents' backs."

He paused, then continued. "I will be happy to back you up and tell you what I know. Between us, he doesn't stand a chance. What about the housekeeper? Surely you have something on her as well. You could give her up, too. I don't care who you implicate, as long as it's not me."

Eruya thought of Julius, loud, careless, always borrowing trouble. Yes, it was easy to believe the manager's lie.

He said nothing, looking at the farm manager as though the idea was taking root in his mind.

The manager pressed on. "If you give me your evidence against me and put the evidence of Julius and the housekeeper forward, I will surely be called as a witness. I will back you up."

For your secrecy about my affairs, I will give you a small bonus now, for you to sleep on tonight. Going forward, you will get a cut from every deal, including piglets and anything else WE see fit to sell. What do you think of that?" he beamed.

He looked at the boy and waited for his response. He had already thought that this boy could refuse…a direct threat to his livelihood. What would he not do to protect it?

Eruya watched him, pretending to weigh the options. He murmured quietly, slowly, as though to himself, "So I turn in Julius and the housekeeper. I do have evidence on them both, and then my manager, my mentor…"

He looked at the manager when he said that last part, saw him smile and nod encouragingly.

"My manager and mentor," he said louder this time, "will support me, and we will be partners." he looked at the manager.

"I like it. It will work," he added almost to himself. "I'm going to trust him."

Just then, his phone pinged. He saw the manager had sent him 30,000 Kenya Shillings via M-Pesa.

He looked up, surprised and pleased.

"See, boy?" the manager said. "I look after my own when they look after me." He raised his eyebrows

Eruya quickly reached into his left pocket and pulled out a folded envelope. It was sealed and labeled Mr. Oricha. He handed it to the manager.

The manager was about to open the envelope, on hearing footsteps, he glanced around and said hurriedly, "You'd better go and lock up. Let's speak again in the morning before ten a.m., to get our story straight."He disappeared into the dark night.

Chapter 19

She left the dining room exhilarated. Tonight, she was certain he would meet her. He would be hers. Their rooms were both downstairs. She could slip from hers into his. He might protest for a moment. Then, he smiled at the notion, she just might!

Dinner was tedious. Everyone sat stiff and proper. The food excelled, as usual, at The Manor. The staff executed their duties flawlessly. Conversation spiralled around Nairobi's freshest scandals: who wronged whom, and when. Tedious.

Naomi had other things to plan, but she did enjoy a good gossip, especially when it was particularly malicious. That was one thing she and the vulgar wife had in common. They sat across from each other at the table, adding their two cents whenever the conversation allowed.

She particularly liked the story of the man who came home from golf to find his wife in bed with the askari. When caught, the guard had shrugged and said,

"Lakini Mzee, uliniambia ni chunge nyumba."But sir you told me take care of the home.

Everyone laughed, except the master, who shifted uncomfortably, and the judge, who forced a thin, strained smile. Naomi caught both reactions. Even Madam laughed loudly.

Tonight, she would have her revenge. Tomorrow, all would be revealed. She would look each of them in the eye as she and the judge confessed their love for each other. Would they be allowed to come and stay at The Manor for weekends in time? Probably not, she thought. Still, the judge was rich and international. Maybe they could move to Lagos, Accra, or even South Africa. She did not care, as long as he was by her side.

It had started as spite toward her cousin, the cousin who had everything Naomi did not. Loving parents, money, status, class. She wanted to be Lauren, but was not. Over time, her feelings for the judge had changed. She began to truly want him. The irony was that she barely knew him. She had never been invited to his home. They always met in motels, not even in her little flat in Kilimani. In Nanyuki, it was worse: hurried trysts in the dark, away from prying eyes. She told herself it was exciting, but deep down, she knew it was squalid. Still, she didn't care. Starting tomorrow, he would be hers completely.

She helped clear the dishes, as was customary for all after dinner. Each trip, she carried as little as possible, walking slowly to stretch out the task. Eventually, she went to the kitchen and, on coming back, simply never returned to the dining room. She lingered in the area outside, appearing engrossed in nothing. Let them clear the table; nothing on that table, nor in this house, belonged to her.

She was nervous but excited about meeting the judge tonight. Hope and dread mixed in her stomach. At dinner, he seemed off. His gaze slid away whenever hers found his. He sat beside her aunt, speaking politely but seeming withdrawn. That unsettled her. He spoke exclusively with Lauren, except for a few words with Madam.

Dinner was, as always, buffet service. Wines were decanted hours ahead. Every dish was cleared in perfect order.

Such a correct family, so proper in their little rituals. She wanted to throw up. It was all too much.

It was now close to 10:30, and the house was quietening down. She overheard Madam, as they left the dining room, say to Amara and Lauren:

"I'll see you all at eleven, is that okay? Sorry it's so late, but I won't keep you long."

The exclusion burned in her chest, leaving her hurt and resentful. She clenched her jaw and smirked. All the more reason to be cruel about what I'll reveal tomorrow. Vindictiveness mingled with pain coursed through her; she even considered beginning with the sordid details of her affair. She smiled, imagining the shock in their eyes. That thought gave her a cruel satisfaction. Let them have their secret meetings tonight. Tomorrow.......?

The judge had feigned fatigue after the long drive and excused himself, leaving immediately. Madam and Master had attempted to help with the clearing, but their children shooed them out. The Vulgar wife left to bed very soon after her parents in law, typical.

Naomi went to her room and checked the time. Then, slipping into the bathroom to freshen up, she resolved to be across the bridge on the farm side by eleven to meet the judge. Only thirty minutes remained. She disliked the farm, yet it worked for secret meetings. In the past, she'd met with farmhands. Now, it was mostly the judge. Smiling, she thought, "Needs must."

Eruya had always evaded her reach. Try as she might, he would never consent to be her next conquest. She'd once suspected him of sleeping with the vulgar wife or perhaps the manager's wife. Once, she even thought she saw him and Amara emerging from the woods at dawn. But there was nothing to that. To Amara, he was like a little brother.

She'd also suspected Amara might have eyes for the judge, but her caution around him reassured her. Besides, she had known Amara's ex-fiancé intimately, before and after he proposed to her. That gave Naomi a secret sense of victory. She was glad when their engagement fell apart. To be honest, she hated both Amara and her cousin with their perfect looks and perfect lives. Any hurt they got gave her pleasure. It left her feeling vindicated, even if only for a moment.

The night was chilly but not cold. She only wanted to speak with the judge, not make love, so she dressed in black jeans, a long-sleeved black t-shirt, a dark hoodie, and black running shoes. She waited until the house was quiet, then slipped out the Veranda door and hugged the shadows.

She, too, had heard the story of the leopard, but she did not believe it. She crossed the bridge boldly and, keeping to the trees, made her way to the rendezvous. It was close to eleven; the farm was silent, most of the workers asleep. She saw a light in the pigsty above her, Eruya finishing his chores.

There was a small cluster of trees to the left of the path, between the river and the pigsty, closer to the river. An old store stood there. It was used for garden tools and seedlings once, now abandoned except by her and the judge, and occasionally whichever farmhand had caught her fancy. She made her way to it. This was their place.

She arrived first, opened the dusty door, and sat on a low ledge in the corner. She kept her phone light off so no one would know she was there. With the full moon overhead, hiding was difficult. In her all-black clothes and hood, she could have been anyone. She waited, her heart thudding.

Finally, he would be hers in more than body. Tomorrow, all of this would be a distant memory. Her new life was about to begin.

She heard it, a soft crack of a twig. She froze. Footsteps, quiet, approaching the door. Hesitation. The handle turned. A figure entered. She knew instantly it was him, her judge; she knew his familiar scent even in the dark.

"Hi, lover," she whispered, standing up.

He flinched; he hadn't seen her in the shadows. She stepped closer.

"I've been waiting for you," she murmured. "Kiss me."

He grabbed her, crushing her lips with his for a passionate kiss. She craved his kisses.

He broke off, breathless, and let her go.

"We need to stop," he said hoarsely. "This isn't why we're here. We have the whole week for this."

The moon slid from behind a cloud, illuminating the little store through its narrow window. He looked at her intently. "So, what did you want to speak to me about?"

She noticed he was still immaculately dressed, except for his shoes. He had traded his usual Italian leather for a softer, more comfortable pair, better suited to the damp, rough ground.

She smiled as she observed him, so smooth, so collected. Down to his signature cufflinks, the ones with the tiny gavels. Always so well put together.

"Us," she said. "I want us to be public. I want you, and I know you want me. I'm tired of this family, this life. I want the life we can build together. I want us, and I want it now."

Her voice trembled with longing and defiance. He looked at her, first with contempt, which softened into practised charm.

"Dearest, I want us to," he said smoothly. "We just have to wait. You know I want this as much as you do."

She stepped back, face determined. "No," she said. "I want it now. No more excuses. I'm tired of waiting, being used, and promises that never come true. I'm tired of being the woman you meet only in the dark. I want what we share to come out into the light."

She stared up at him. His expression was cold and distant. His eyes shuttered in rejection. The warmth was gone, replaced by harshness that made her feel very small and isolated.

"I decide when we can come out into the light," he said coldly. "If ever."

A wave of raw hurt washed through her. The sting of his rejection was fresh and sharp, like a physical slap. She almost faltered. Not this time, thought Naomi. She reached deep, gathering courage, rage, and pride. She looked him dead in the eye, her voice low and fierce.

"Not this time, sir," she hissed. "This time, you'll do the right thing by me, because..... I'm pregnant."

The judge staggered, leaning back heavily against the door, covering his face as he struggled to process what she had said.

"I'm pregnant" she repeated.

The two words hung between them. Heavy, impossible. yet?. For a moment, there was nothing but the sound of the night outside, the soft gurgling of the river, the swishing of leaves in the wind beyond the window. They both stood suspended in time, frozen by two words.

He stared at her, searching for any hint of a lie. She stood still, chin high, eyes glittering defiant. The silence stretched.

He let out a harsh laugh, his eyes narrowed with disbelief. "Pregnant. You?" His voice cracked on the word, betraying a raw edge of anger and shock. He took a step forward, clenching his fists. "What are you saying to me? How do I know it's my child? You're such a whore, are you sure it's not one of your many men?"

He was cruel, calculated, launching words like missiles.

She didn't flinch, didn't back down. Her smile was calm, almost pitying.

"Funny, you think I sleep with other men without protection. Yes, I like sex, and I have multiple partners, but only with you did I never protect myself. Only with you, from the first, at your insistence, did I make myself vulnerable. And now......"

She paused for effect.

"Now you must pay your dues. I am pregnant, and if you don't believe me, we can do a DNA test."

A sly smile crossed her face.

"But here's the thing," she went on, voice low and certain. "No matter the outcome, I'll make sure this family knows exactly what kind of two-timing fool you are. I have dates and times; you know, I kept records. Sometimes, after our lovemaking, I'd hit speed dial on your phone, and it would call her phone, waking her up to no one on the other end. Those logs are still there.

"I have selfies of us, you asleep beside me on my phone." As he started towards her she said hastily, "Don't bother, I don't have it with me. It's all backed up on the cloud. I have enough proof to ruin you forever. So, what will you say to that? What can you tell this 'whore' to appease her enough to keep quiet?"

He could have killed her right then, killed her and the unborn child. Rammed her head against the wall until she stopped moving. Strangled her until she no longer breathed.

The thoughts and feelings of intense hatred came unbidden. He was shocked by it, as his anger swelled, he let it stay. In this moment he wanted her dead.

He never loved her. He didn't even like her. She was only a means to an end, satisfying, pliant, disposable. He had no intention of ever being with her beyond dark rooms and broom closets or abandoned sheds. She was too common, too crass, too far beneath the Judge Olumide the world admired.

He had not been kind to her or generous. Only in bed did he grant her attention, and even that was performance, his masculine ego at play. He didn't even pay her, not even the level of a prostitute. In his eyes, she was less than that. A dirty little habit that he indulged in from time to time.

And yet, here she was, holding all the cards; all the while, he had thought he was in control. Treating her with contempt and deriving pleasure from it. All the while, she had used him just as he had used her. Now, she wanted status, revenge, and a man with power. In this moment she declared her intentions, declared her choice. Him.

A vibration in his pocket startled him. His phone. A lifeline. anything to break the unbearable tension.

He pulled it out with shaking hands. A missed call, then a message.

"Mr Olumide, this is O'Brien Onifade, remember me? From Lagos, Abuja? We were lawyers together and played golf. I need to speak with you as soon as possible. The matter of Mrs Bakari, remember her? The widow you had dealings with? You are a rich man because of her.

We need to talk. I know you are currently in Nanyuki for the week. I could come there. We must meet.

Double O."

Such politeness. Such venom beneath the words. A threat, and he knew it.

The noose was tightening, and now he could feel it. Everything was coming apart.

Somewhere outside, a night insect clicked, one hard, dry tick. loud, explosive, then silence.He drew a breath, slow and cold, and the rage within hardened into purpose.

He looked up at her again, and his entire demeanour shifted. Like a judge in court when the tide turns against his client, he realised that he must reverse it and control the narrative. He opted for calm, persuasive, and deliberate. With that, he stepped toward her. She tensed, sensing the change.

He reached for her, felt her hesitation, and pulled her closer. He kissed her gently, almost tenderly. His hands softened. His mouth found her neck, his touch light on her body. He knew her weaknesses, where to touch, how to draw out a sigh. Her anger melted into confusion, then hunger. She moaned softly, wanting him.

He held her upright, supporting her weight as he murmured between kisses:

"Tomorrow, I'll be yours."

He drew back, eyes locked on hers. He said gently

"Go back. Come to me at dawn if you dare. I'll leave the door open, and we'll finish what we started. He paused, "But now I have something I must do."

She stood dazed, unable to move or speak. He gently took her towards the door, turned her to face him, and kissed her again, softly. He brushed her cheek lightly with his hand.

"Later, darling. Remember, I'm yours. Go now."

She hesitated, then turned and slipped out into the moonlight, heading toward the river and the bridge. He watched her go until the sound of her footsteps faded.

Then he shut the door and, only then, sank onto the ledge where she had been.

That scene had taken every ounce of control he had left. He was good, he knew it, but even for him, that had been a stellar performance borne of sheer desperation.

He drew a long breath. His pulse was still hammering. He looked at his phone. 11:15 p.m.

He tried his partner's number again. And again and again. He paused and tried again. The same response each time.

"Mteja…"

He disconnected. Another message blinked on the screen:

"Tunde, one way or another, we will have that conversation. You can only run for so long. The time for reckoning has come. You must pay the piper, Double O."

The words burned through him. Hopelessness crept close, but he crushed it down. He would not be defeated. Not by her. Not by Double O or the boy, not by anyone. He would beat this, all of this.

He had survived worse storms. He had built himself from the dust of a remote village in Nigeria, then Lagos, and Abuja, each step an improvement. Now he meant to conquer Nairobi and the rest of the world. He had lied, stolen, betrayed, and won. He would win again.

He looked at his phone again: 11:25 p.m. Five minutes to the boy. He rose, straightened his clothes, checked his cufflinks, and, once satisfied, walked out of the abandoned store.

He could feel the night tightening around him, the wind picking up, the moon hiding behind clouds, the darkness and the silence adding to the night's tension. How and when would it end?

He moved with determination up toward the north entrance of the pigsty; it was more private there. He was determined to settle everything with this boy, once and for all.

As he walked, his anger simmered below the surface, ever-present. It was focused. Controlled. Useful. He needed what the boy had, and he was willing to beat it out of him if persuasion failed.

Chapter 20

Eruya walked back towards the pigsty, checking his phone as he went. It was 11:40 p.m. Those footsteps must have been the judge, he thought.

He entered through the south door, still holding the shovel, and closed the door behind him. Then he grabbed the shovel again and started walking toward the north entrance.

Suddenly, the doorway was blocked by a figure, so large it filled the entire frame. Eruya stopped abruptly at the sight. He could not move, overcome by fear.

He glanced behind him, trying to see if he could make a run for it, open the other door, and disappear into the darkness. He could make it, he thought, if he turned and sprinted as quickly as he could. He was willing to take the chance; he even had the shovel for protection.

Just as he was about to turn and bolt, the judge spoke in a calm tone.

"Good night, young man. Still at it, I see."

The judge did not venture into the pigsty but stood at the door.

Eruya heaved a sigh of relief. "Oh, it's you."

He started walking towards the judge, who stepped out of the doorway and moved to the right, east, away from the river.

Eruya walked to the end of the pigsty and followed the judge. He placed the shovel along the wall, not far from where the judge stood in the shadows.

It was dark where the judge stood waiting for him, though slivers of moonlight through the trees allowed them to see each other.

With as much charm as he could muster, the judge said, "I am here to collect whatever evidence you have on me, and I will pay you handsomely for it, and for your silence."

Eruya was shocked by the judge's directness. He didn't speak.

"So," continued the judge, "how much is the information worth? Kshs 50,000?"

Startled at such a large sum, Eruya visibly flinched.

The judge, thinking he was declining and not wanting the conversation to continue longer than necessary, said, "Okay, I'll give you Kshs 100,000. I'll send it to you right now on M-Pesa. Do you have the evidence with you?"

Eruya nodded.

"Okay, let me have it then, and you can have the money."

Eruya hesitated.

The judge smiled, though not in happiness. "Okay, I'll show good faith and give you the money first. Then you hand over the proof. I'm having a very bad night and need to get back to the house immediately. So, what's your phone number?"

Eruya called out his number. Within minutes, his phone pinged. He looked and saw he had received Kshs 100,000 from Tunde Olumide, Esq.

Wow, he thought, that's a large amount.

The judge cleared his throat impatiently. "I don't have all night, and I'm in a very, very bad mood. I want the evidence now." He reached out his hand.

Eruya quickly reached into his breast pocket, removed the folded envelope, and handed it to the judge.

The judge snatched it from him and, brushing past, strode off around the corner, towards the river.

Standing there in shock, Eruya could not believe his phone now held Kshs 150,000 from his three clandestine meetings. He smiled to himself. They thought I could be bought. Not a chance. This money is additional proof against all three of them. Proof of just how corrupt they were and what they were willing to pay for his silence. Another nail on their coffins. Eruya smiled at himself.

He would still make it to the meeting tomorrow with all the real evidence, the one that would bury all three. They were bad people and needed to be discovered and punished.

"The truth shall out," thought Eruya, more determined to go through with his initial plan

He took a deep breath, suddenly feeling the fatigue of the day and night. He noticed something glittering in the dark. He illuminated it with his phone light. It was a cufflink.

He reached down and picked it up. Another bit of proof.

He knew who it belonged to. The judge always wore them. They were shaped like the gavels judges used in court. How ironic, he thought. The most fraudulent of men wearing a symbol of justice.

Suddenly, he felt tired, bone tired. He turned the corner eastwards and crouched on the ground, leaning against the pigsty wall and the waste pipe. He needed a reprieve, a moment to decide what to do next.

Each of the three would return to their places and, on opening their envelopes, discover that they had been duped, that the evidence he'd given them was worthless. They would more than likely come back to confront him, so he needed to act fast.

He had to hide for the night. At dawn, he would slip away before anyone was up and go to Suleiman's. He would stay there until 9:45, then take a nduthi to the Manor to meet the auditor with all his real evidence.

He needed a place to sleep for the night. Then he remembered that his friend Charo had gone away for a few days, so his room was empty. No one would think of looking for him there.

Tonight, if the three came looking, they would assume he was hiding in his own room and would look there first. Eruya knew the manager had the master keys to all staff rooms. But he also knew that Charo never took his key with him for fear of losing it, and Eruya knew where he hid it.

If he could slip across the farm to Charo's room, substitute his own key in the hiding place, enter, and sleep, he would be safe. He would not even risk taking a shower in the morning. He would wake up and leave the compound. Gone by the time everyone woke up.

Just now, though, he wanted to sit and rest for a moment before putting the final part of his plan into action.

Holding the cufflink tightly in his left hand, he sat, knees up, face resting on his hands, which were resting on his knees.

He could feel the night pressing in, the same night he had enjoyed so many times, no angst, no fear, when everything still seemed ordinary. Now, all was in chaos, and he was sitting feet away from garbage and wastewater. He was so tired that he tuned out the stench of the place.

He felt the cool wall of the pigsty and the beginning of a window against his back. Ahead of him, beyond this waste area, stretched first the acacia trees gloomy and dark and beyond that, the fields, empty and silent He could feel the faint wind carrying the night smells. Somehow, in spite of his surroundings, he could just pick out the scent of Queen of the Night.

The judge's footsteps had faded into silence. All was silent. He drifted off to sleep momentarily, then, knowing he had to move, he lifted his head slightly, as though searching for the first light that would not come for hours yet. The branches of the trees stirred in the night, their shadows trembling across the ground. The farm was utterly still, holding its breath.

He felt tired… so, so tired…. And he still had so much to do.

Tired… Were those footsteps he heard…? So tired….. OUCH!

Then, oblivion.

ACT 3

Chapter 21

Morning at The Manor, how delightful! Yawning, Amara stretched and reached for her phone, 4:30 a.m. Still dark. Perfect. She leapt out of bed, completed her morning routine in ten minutes, and dressed. Satchel with journal, pen, and phone in hand, she tiptoed downstairs. Her boots waited by the kitchen door.

She flicked on the kitchen light, though she could have managed without it; she knew this house inside out. Quickly brewing coffee, she poured it into her thermos. With her satchel across her shoulder, she slipped into her boots. The door unlatched with a quiet click, and she stepped outside into the cool morning.

It was still dark. The air felt softer, quieter. The colours of nature were still half-asleep, the last chill of night clinging to her skin. The moon had waned, and its glow was softer than last night's brilliant silver. Yesterday's sky had been clear enough to tint every shadow blue. Now, it was veiled and subdued.

She smiled, remembering how she and Lauren had talked late into the night after Madam left, discussing Madam's words and considering their meaning.

Now, she walked briskly toward the river. She wanted to be there before the sun. Or before him. Or both.

The legend of the bridge leopard didn't frighten her; it thrilled her. She pulled her hoodie forward to guard her neck from the mountain air and quickened her pace. She crossed the river and started upwards, passing the cow sheds to her right, then the pigsty to her left, the smells, the soft rustle of straw, the first low grunts of waking animals.

As she passed the farm offices, a quiet voice greeted her from the shadows.

"Habari ya asubuhi, Miss Amara. Karibu." *Good morning Miss Amara welcome*

She turned, smiling. "Habari ya asubuhi, asante *thank you*. Hope you had a good night?"

"Nashukuru," I *am thankful* he replied, bringing his palms together as though in prayer and bowing slightly.

She continued along the path until the buildings were behind her. The trail curved southeast, skirting the fields until she reached a small grove of trees. The trees stood dark, swaying in time with the wind's whisper. She walked through the grove. The path rose, climbing to the small incline at the hilltop, her hill, his rock, breathless but triumphant.

She'd beaten Eruya this time. She looked back; no movement, only the stillness of predawn, the dark shapes of trees swaying under the chill. She placed her satchel and thermos beside her and sat on the familiar rock.

Waiting. Waiting for the light, waiting for him.

He was never late. He loved the dawn as much as she did, always arriving to watch the light break through on the horizon. Perhaps he was tired today; he'd had a long day yesterday, helping at the manor and tending to the farm chores. She would definitely give him a hard time about his lateness when he arrived. She smiled at the thought.

A faint gleam appeared from the east, thin and fragile as a promise. She reached for her phone and took a picture for him, so he wouldn't miss it. Then she set the phone down. Pulling off her hoodie, she watched as the sky kindled. The first blush of rose spread across the horizon. It deepened to pale yellow gold. The light came on like fire, spilling over the fields and racing toward her.

When it touched her toes, she smiled. She felt the warmth creep upward: her knees, her hands, her face, her head, her whole being. She closed her eyes and breathed deeply, letting the first sunlight wash over her. It felt like grace. She wriggled in pleasure as the glow spread and warmed her up. For a long, still moment, she simply sat there, breathing, her face lifted to the sun. The warmth was soft as a lover's touch, like silk, filling her with quiet joy.

When she opened her eyes again, she was still alone. He had not come. A faint unease brushed her, that strange, sinking feeling people described as the feeling of someone walking over your grave. For an instant, she felt a deep, inexplicable sadness. Then she shook it off. Maybe something had come up extra chores he had to do before leaving for his rest days.

She took out her journal and pen from her satchel, opened it to a fresh page, and began to write. Her hand moved easily, without plan or structure, just thoughts as they came. Sometimes she wrote what weighed most on her mind, sometimes fragments of dreams she still recalled. Other times she wrote about work, problems to untangle, ideas to test. But today she was distracted, and writing did not come so easily. Madam's disclosure last evening lingered, mixed with her excitement to see what Eruya had accomplished.

Now that Eruya was not here. The discussion about his work would have to wait until he returned from his three-night break. He deserved the rest. No one worked harder than he did, always giving 110%. She knew he'd looked forward to visiting his mother in Ngobit. Amara would still be in Nanyuki when Eruya returned. They could set their minds to his work then.

Maybe some coffee would help her focus. She reached for her thermos. In its lid were two cups; she took one, left the other nestled inside, and poured herself a measure of steaming coffee. The aroma rose around her, rich and familiar. Dawn, The Manor, and coffee, there was nothing better.

She breathed in deeply, the coffee aroma mingling with the crisp mountain air. Stillness held steady as she sipped, savouring every layer of flavour. Her special blend: dark-roasted Kenya beans, ground fresh every third day; Lamu coffee spice, blended specially; and a splash of Madagascar vanilla. Add some condensed milk and... perfection in a cup.

She closed her eyes, inhaling deeply, the aroma intoxicating. Her coffee always tasted best at this hour, in this place. The crisp air sharpened the sweetness. Sitting perfectly still, the cup warm in her hands, she watched the sun illuminate the farm and the world. Gratitude filled her, quiet, deep, complete. Regardless of what else was going on in life, moments like this, the quiet of dawn, sun shining, gentle breeze from the mountain, Amara felt blessed and utterly at peace.

Determined, she set the cup gently beside her and picked up her journal again. This time, she focused on work, the project that had brought her to Nanyuki. She was here to review tourist attractions for a client, a travel agency seeking first-hand recommendations for its itineraries. This was the kind of assignment she excelled at. Amara was a tourism consultant. She also curated private vacations and bespoke getaways for clients worldwide. These were crafted from her knowledge of hospitality, places she'd been, and people she'd met. A perfect job: well paid and interesting.

She loved this life; the travel, the discovery, the freedom to choose her own rhythm. She loved Nanyuki, especially the Manor. Its quiet mornings always gave her a sense of home between assignments.

She wrote a few notes in her day's itinerary. Closed her book and sipped her coffee, thinking again of Eruya. This was unusual; he was normally such a creature of habit. Every morning, his rhythm was the same: dawn trek to the hill, then chickens, pigs, and the farm briefing. He had said he would meet her here today. Where was he? Time to find him.

She slipped her journal into her satchel, nested the empty cup in the thermos lid, and decided to check the chicken coop, then the pigsty, just in case he'd started late. She could still share her coffee with him; she knew how much he liked it. Behind her, farm sounds began: footsteps, soft voices, the metallic clanging of buckets. The milkers headed to the cow sheds. It must be close to six. The farm day had began.

She stood, stretched, and took one last loving glance at the fields ahead. The sun's warmth lingered on her face. She let it sink in before turning and slinging the satchel across her shoulder. She took one last deep breath and, picking up her thermos, made her way down the hill, his rock, as they called it.

She walked back through the trees and fields, and on the way, met a few staff who nodded as they passed.

"Habari ya asubuhi!" they greeted.

She smiled. "Mzuri, asante, na yenu?" Good, thank you and yours. "Twashukuru!" We are thankful, they cheerfully replied and went on their way.

At the chicken coop, she looked around but saw no sign of Eruya. She called out softly, but there was no answer. She glanced inside and noticed the eggs hadn't been collected. Clearly, he had not been there this morning.

Walking past the closed farm offices, she reached the south entrance of the pigsty. The door was latched; she unlatched it and stepped inside, expecting to see Eruya feeding the pigs. She entered and closed the door behind her. The pigs moved eagerly toward the troughs, expecting breakfast. Still no sign of him.

"Sorry, pigs," she said lightly. "You'll have to wait for breakfast. Someone will come along shortly, I'm sure." She could not fail to notice the little piglets running around. They were really cute.

She walked down the long corridor to the other end. The north entrance door was pulled shut but unlatched. She opened it and stepped into the full light of morning, still no sign of Eruya.

As she turned to leave, something caught her eye, a shovel on the floor near the east corner of the building. Its blade was wet and glinting. She paused but didn't approach. She knew it was used to clean up pig manure and worse. She did not go closer; that was the pigsty garbage area, where runoff from the pens collected. The smell there was, to say the least, very "tropical."

She closed the door, walked past and turned left, walking along the wall of the pigsty, and joined the main farm track leading west. The cow sheds were to her left as she continued toward the river, she continued to the river, crossed the bridge and followed the gentle rise on the other side until she reached the Manor House.

Amara entered through the side gate, slipped off her boots, and left them neatly outside to be cleaned. She set her thermos on the kitchen table, then climbed the stairs to her room in the suite she shared with Lauren.

Her phone showed 6:10 a.m., just enough time to take a quick shower, change, and be ready for her 8:30 a.m. breakfast meeting with the General Manager of Sweet-Waters Serena Tented Camp at Ol Pejeta Game Reserve. But she had a slight detour first, and Ol Pejeta was a good 30-minute drive, and the Sweet Waters lodge was an additional 15 minutes from the gate.

In her room, she set down her satchel, took out her personal journal and put it out of reach of prying eyes. She packed instead, her laptop, phone, a map of Nanyuki, a new notebook, a few pens, her iPad, and her reading glasses.

She showered quickly and dressed. By 6:30 a.m. Amara was ready. She picked up her handbag, the satchel, and her shoes, then walked barefoot down the stairs. Sitting on the last step, she slipped on her shoes, went into the kitchen to collect her thermos, and returned to the front entrance.

She unlocked the main door, took her car keys from the hook, and stepped outside, closing the door behind her. Her car gleamed in the soft morning light, freshly washed. The night guard, bless his heart, must have cleaned it for her. She made a mental note to give him a small thank-you later.

She got into the car, started the engine, and slowly drove down the gravel driveway towards the gate. Destination: Ol Pejeta. Just outside the gate, she noticed the morning staff arriving and waved happily at them as she drove by. She really liked this team. She looked forward to seeing them all this evening.

Chapter 22

It was 6:45 a.m., and the Manor was quiet. The kitchen staff had just started walking into the kitchen to get the day's cooking started. They all gathered, greeting one another, waiting for the housekeeper to arrive and begin issuing instructions. She was very obviously absent.

The senior staff member, Felicity, looked at her watch. It was 6:50, no sign of the housekeeper. If they did not get on with it, 8:00 a.m. would find them with nothing to give the family for breakfast. Where was the housekeeper? This was not like her at all, she thought. Taking a deep breath, she made an executive decision.

"Morning everyone" they all responded. "Ochi 2 a morning prayer please?"

Ochi 2 obliged and said a a prayer to bless the day ahead. After everyones "Amen" Felicity continued.

"Okay, this is how we are dividing the duties," she said calling out names. "Wairimu and Ochieng, you're on house cleaning duties. Please start with the lounge and dining room."

They nodded and started off, first going back to the store outside to gather their tools for cleaning, dusting, and light mopping, then heading back inside to begin their work.

"Frida, begin with the eggs. Akinyi, the master's and Madam's breakfast is your responsibility. Who's left? Ochi 2 (because there were two Ochiengs) and Sara, *matunda na juice ni yenu* fruit and juice is yours. Imma, stand free and help where you can. The master's and Madam's breakfast trays should be upstairs by their door by 8:00 a.m., and the buffet breakfast for the rest of the household should be in the dining room by 8:30 a.m. at the latest. Let's go, people, this breakfast will not cook itself." Everyone started moving to their stations.

Felicity often filled in for the housekeeper when she was away. Today would be no different. What the heck is happening with the housekeeper? I hope she's not sick, she thought.

"Imma, can you please go to the housekeeper's room and knock on the door? See if she's okay, awake? She might be sick and need help. Go as quickly as possible and then come back to help."

With that, Felicity turned, started the grill, and began her day. She had pulled out the bacon and sausages, and Frida, after starting the scrambled eggs, would make the pancake batter for Akinyi or Felicity to cook. At the kitchen table, Ochi was preparing the fruit while Akinyi was busy prepping what she knew the bosses always ate for breakfast, mostly kienyeji *traditional* porridge, smoothies, and a small bowl of fruit salad each. Tea for the master and coffee for Madam. They would then come later, if still hungry, and eat some of what was in the dining room.

Felicity surveyed the kitchen, satisfied. The staff were dependable and understood their routines. She valued their teamwork. Most of them, except herself, Imma, and Akinyi, were day labourers brought in whenever the family was in residence. Every morning, they arrived at 6:30 a.m., and left once the dinner dishes were cleared and the kitchen was spotless.

The family had even arranged a minibus to collect the staff from their homes, ensuring they arrived at the Manor in time to report for duty by 6:45. On quiet days, they left around 9 pm; sometimes after midnight if the family was entertaining.

It was good, honest work, and they all knew it. The pay was good, the hours long, but compensated with time-and-a-half after 8 hours of continuous work. Every meal during their shift was included. They knew each other well and worked together smoothly.

Felicity was grateful for this team, loyal, cheerful, and proud of their place in the Manor's rhythm. The housekeeper was always calling them lazy, untrue, she might have been describing herself, as she did little to no work herself. She always said she had a headache or was concentrating on management duties. Which management duties? The inventory counts, ordering, and such operational functions were handled by Felicity. But the housekeeper was the boss, so they all kept their mouths shut and their heads down.

Just then, Imma came back into the kitchen. Speaking softly so only Felicity could hear, she said, "Madam is just waking up, I think, a long night. I left her going into the bathroom to get ready and come to the kitchen."

As she spoke, a sudden gasp came from the kitchen door leading to the staff quarters. All eyes turned.

The housekeeper stood there, looking like death warmed over. She was disheveled, her head cloth crooked, her face ashen and drawn, as if she hadn't slept a wink all night.

"Good morning," she said, and everyone responded.

"I hope you were not all waiting for me to do what you know how to do?"

"No, madam," came a response from one of the girls.

She glared at Felicity, her eyes full of accusation. "So what are you doing? Having all the others do all the work?"

Felicity pursed her lips and turned to respond, but Imma stepped gently on her toe. Felicity turned back and busied herself turning over sausages and bacon as though she hadn't heard.

The housekeeper walked out of the kitchen and staggered to her room. The other staff started to giggle.

Felicity looked sternly back at all of them. "Back to work, all of you. This food needs to be ready on time." Then she looked directly at Imma and mouthed, "Thank you."

Just then, there was a knock at the outer kitchen door from the garden, and Imma went to see who it was. She opened it and found one of the farmhands standing there with eggs and milk. She ushered him in and, at his bidding, went to get the housekeeper.

Chapter 23

At 7 a.m., all the staff gathered for the morning briefing. The air was tense; no one knew why. Were the chickens clucking louder than usual? Had a mongoose entered the chicken coop? No, because then there would have been very loud squawking. Still, something was wrong and they all felt it.

The Supervisor, Okelo, looked at all the farm staff staring expectantly at him.

One farmhand asked, "Ako wapi Mzee?" *Where is the boss, referring to the Farm Manager*

Another cheekily replied, "Amelemewa Leo," *he is unable today,* and they all broke into giggles.

This was not the first time the farm manager had gone on a bender with his beloved Richot and been unable to make it for his farm duties. But it was the first time he had done that with the family here. Such a risk to take! What if the Master, or worse, Madam, decided to wander over to the farm early? How could they possibly explain away the manager's absence?

Okelo smiled at the unruly farmhands, wagged a finger, and said, "Wacheni tabia mbaya, labda Mzee hajiskii..." *Stop your bad behaviour, maybe the manager is not feeling well.* He couldn't hide his amusement when they all burst out laughing.

"Sawa, sawa," *okay, okay* he said. "Tuendelee." *Let's get on with it*

Okelo had anticipated the managers absence, not seeing him in the office before briefing. He had adjusted the duty roster to account for absences.

"Okay, so who can lead us with a prayer? Mr Maende?"

Maende began, "Let us all bow our heads." Everyone bowed their heads.

"Our Father, thank you so much for seeing us through the night…" He continued until "Amen!"

Everyone repeated "Amen."

They then looked to Mr Okelo, who was now looking curiously at the man. "Mr Maende," he said, "you prayed very well and even wished those who are not with us God's grace. That was beautiful. Thank you."

Maende bowed slightly at the praise, and they all waited.

Okelo reached into his pocket and read out the staff members' names and their duties. Towards the end, he said,

"Kipkorir, you will take over Eruya's duties in his absence. See me after this briefing."

"Okay, everyone, the family is here, so no funny business. Breakfast at 10, lunch at 2, dinner at 7. Grab tea and bread now, then get to your tasks. You'll take turns for breakfast and lunch per the roster. You know the drill. Have a good day, and let's work hard. Dismissed."

Everyone dispersed except Kipkorir, who remained behind to speak with Mr Okelo as instructed.

"Kipkorir," Okelo said, "please, take the eggs and milk to the Manor. They should have enough for breakfast. I don't think Eruya collected the eggs this morning. When you return, your tea will be waiting, and then you can go finish that little section of the fence you were working on yesterday, you know, the one by the river?"

Kipkorir nodded.

"Once that's done, you'll feed the pigs and clean out the pigsty, then you'll be assigned to the kitchen garden at the Manor House for the rest of the day. You've worked there before with Eruya, right?"

"Yes, sir," Korir, as he was fondly known, replied. "He has been teaching me everything, sir."

"Good. Those will be your tasks until Eruya returns. Remember to help out at the house if the housekeeper needs assistance, okay? When you take the milk, introduce yourself to her and let her know you'll be handling Eruya's tasks while he's away. Give her your phone number."

"Yes, sir," he responded.

"Okay, off you go. Get the milk from the barn and the eggs to the Manor as quickly as possible."

"Okay, sir, and thank you for the opportunity."

It was a special opportunity to work at the Manor's kitchen garden, an honour given only to those who were honest and trusted. Usually, Eruya handled that work exclusively, but now Kipkorir had been given the chance, and he was not going to let Okelo down.

Okelo called after Korir as he left. The boy turned as Okelo approached.

"When Eruya's back, you'll work with him full-time. He picked you. The job's too big for one person. He'll train you."

Korir broke into a grin. "Thank you, sir," he said happily. "I'll not let you or Eruya down. I'll make you both proud of me."

Korir walked swiftly to the chicken coop. Eruya hadn't been there this morning. He had replenished the feed last night, so the chickens weren't fully out of food or water.

Korir quickly cleaned the coop, refilled food and water, and collected all the eggs into a big basket.

He left the coop knowing he'd have to return at lunchtime to check on water and again at night for the final replenishment.

He'd start each day like Eruya, beginning his chicken and pig duties at 6:30 a.m., so after briefing, he could take the eggs and milk to the Manor to start at the garden. He would get his early tea with bread on his return and his breakfast later from the Manor kitchen.

He walked to the shed and taking the milk for the Manor. He crossed the bridge, to the Manor House, approached the staff entrance, knocking gently.

It was opened by one of the house staff. On seeing him, she smiled, waved him in, and called for the housekeeper.

The housekeeper, upon seeing him, seemed surprised. Her face was ashen, with dark circles shadowing her eyes; she looked like she hadn't slept all night.

He smiled tentatively. "Good morning, madam. I'm Kipkorir. I'll be taking over Eruya's duties until he returns from Likizo."holiday

She stood there, staring at the boy. She swayed a little and steadied herself on the table.

"Madam, are you okay?"

She steadied herself. "I'm fine. Your name again?"

"Kipkorir, madam. But everyone calls me Korir."

"Okay, Korir. Thank you for the eggs and milk. Are you headed to the kitchen garden?"

"Yes, madam. Later. I have to complete a few chores at the farm first, I will return, probably around 10 a.m.?"

She stared at him again, her gaze distant and hollow. It was as if she looked through him, not seeing him at all. Korir was confused.

"Madam? Is there something you needed me to do?"

She blinked, coming out of her reverie. "What? No, I don't need anything. Thank you. Give me your phone number in case I need you."

"Okay, madam. My number is 07—"

"No, no," she interrupted, calling out, "Imma! Come here with a pen!"

Imma came running. The housekeeper said, "Take his number and give it to me later. I must check something I forgot." Saying that, she walked off toward her room, leaving Korir and Imma staring after her.

"Alaa," said Imma to the young man, "what did you say to her?"

"Nothing," Korir said confused. "I was just giving her my number in case you all needed anything. I'm taking over Eruya's duties while he's away."

"Oh," said Imma. "She's behaving very strangely today. I'm not sure what's going on with her. Labda boifee amemuacha." *maybe her boyfriend left her*

They both giggled at the housekeeper's expense.

"Anyway," continued Imma, "what's that number? And what time are you coming back this way?"

"The number is 072— and I'll be back around 10 a.m. Also, count me for lunch; I'm in the kitchen garden today, and the rest of the week."

Imma wrote down the number, said thanks, took up the eggs which the housekeeper had ignored, and said, "Nisaidie *help me* with that milk, please?"

He grabbed the milk and followed. She pointed to a table. He set it down.

He turned and left. "Baadaye," *later* he said.

"Baadaye," said Imma.

Chapter 24

Inside the main house, the staff were already at work preparing for the day. Ochieng and Wairimu moved briskly from room to room, opening curtains and windows, dusting, mopping, and sweeping away the quiet of the night.

In the dining room, Sara completed breakfast setup. She arranged chafing dishes for the hot food from the kitchen. Next, she set out plates, bowls, and cutlery. Finally, she laid out the fruits, muesli, and cereals, each with its own serving spoon. All was ready. She moved to the dining table, added a vase of fresh flowers, table mats, and trays on the sideboard for anyone wanting breakfast on the Veranda.

Every detail mattered. The staff prided themselves on anticipating the family's needs and preparing for every possibility. Breakfast and lunch were always informal here. Family members wandered in as they pleased, unless guests were expected. On another credenza, juices, coffee, tea, milk, and condiments were arranged and labelled.

Sounds upstairs meant the family was rising, so Sara went quickly back to the kitchen to let them know. It was almost 8:00 a.m. Felicity organised the team. Akinyi, with Imma's help, carried two breakfast trays upstairs to the master and Madam. After setting them on a table outside, Akinyi knocked. "Breakfast."

From inside, she heard, "Thank you. Akinyi?"

The question was not lost on the two women. It was usually the housekeeper who brought the morning breakfast trays. Akinyi smiled, first surprised and then pleased, saying,

"You're welcome," marvelling that Madam knew it was her from just one word.

As they reached the bottom stair, the vulgar wife, still in her robe, called out, "Imma! Imma!"

Imma stopped, and Akinyi continued to the kitchen.

"Yes, miss?" Imma started up the stairs.

"You don't need to come up," the vulgar wife said. "Breakfast iko tayari? *Is breakfast ready* I'm so hungry I could eat a horse."

Imma smiled. "It will be by 8:30 a.m., miss."

"Okay," and she walked back to her room.

"You're welcome," Imma said to the bannister, smiling as she continued down.

As she was just about to turn to the kitchen, she heard a whisper.

"Imma, Imma."

It was Naomi calling from her room. She was whispering. "Come here, please."

She didn't sound well, and when Imma walked to her door, she looked quite ill.

"Imma, please get me some fruit salad and some pancakes with syrup, and coffee, black, with sugar. And…" She hesitated. "What juice do you have today?"

"We have passion mango and watermelon, miss."

"Sorry to trouble you," Naomi said.

Imma almost fell over in shock. Her eyebrows shot up. This girl never said 'please' or 'thank you' for anything. Hearing both, she nearly dropped the serving cloth she held.

"Ni nini?" *what's up*, Imma wondered.

"Please add one glass of watermelon juice and two bottles of cold water. Okay?"

Again, Imma almost gaped in surprise. Was she actually being nice?

"Yes, miss. Just to be clear, you'd like fruit salad plain, a few pancakes with syrup, a glass of watermelon juice, two bottles of cold water, and black coffee, right?"

Naomi nodded. "Also, some vanilla or strawberry yoghurt? Thanks, Imma, and sorry again."

Imma said it was no trouble and left shaking her head, still reeling. The world was going mad today, for sure. People were behaving completely out of character. At least the vulgar wife was predictable. That con

Imma went back into the kitchen and walked over to where Felicity stood watching them fill the chafing dishes. She pulled her aside gently and told her what had transpired. Felicity smiled, gave her a knowing look, and set to the task. When Imma told her that Naomi had said thank you and please numerous times and even apologised, Felicity almost dropped the pancakes she was plating in surprise. They burst out laughing.

Imma left with the tray. Akinyi came over to Felicity to find out why they'd been laughing. When she heard, Akinyi laughed so hard that tears rolled down her cheeks.

She said, "Imma had better watch her back. That kindness is coming before something not so nice."

Felicity admonished, "Stop it, Akinyi. Can't someone turn over a new leaf without you being so suspicious?"

Akinyi snorted. "That one? I'll believe it when she turns over a whole tree, not just a leaf. And not just any tree, a Mugumo *fig* tree."

They laughed and returned to work. The housekeeper still hadn't appeared; she must have gone back to sleep.

The family came down one by one. First, the vulgar wife stuck her head in the kitchen to say the sausages were not enough, could they do their jobs and add more, not keep them in the kitchen to eat later. They all rolled their eyes as soon as the kitchen door closed.

Next was Julius, a while later. He put his head in to wish them all a good morning, then returned a bit later. Looking at Akinyi, he said, "Sorry, Akinyi, but the coffee has gotten cold. Could you refresh it for me?" He'd even brought the jug.

"Thanks." Then to everyone: "The breakfast looks lovely. Thank you all." He left the kitchen again.

The staff sympathised with Julius for having married such a woman.

Sara grinned. "I look much better than her! Wacha, I seduce him and convince him to divorce that horrible thing and marry me instead." Her eyes twinkled with mischief as she spoke. "Then you'd all have to serve me, and I'd be queen sumbua." *annoyance*, laughter erupted in response to Sara's boldness.

Felicity said, "Quiet! You know the sound carries." She wagged her finger at the cheeky girl with mock seriousness. "Wewe, chunga, *you take care*, she doesn't hear you, or you'll be out of a job. Also, chunga, I don't tell your boyfriend you've got thoughts of another man." Felicity's tone mixed warning and teasing, eyes dancing with amusement.

Their laughter was quieter as they returned to their work, the camaraderie restoring the morning's rhythm. A little later, Lauren came to the door. Unlike the others, she walked in, hugged Akinyi, Felicity, and Imma before turning to Sara, Ochi 2, and Frida, hugging them as well.

"I'm so happy to be here," she announced, smiling. "And so happy to see you all again!" Where is everyone else? Felicity responded, "Ochieng and Wairimu are outside starting laundry."

"And the housekeeper?" Lauren asked. Felicity said quickly, "Just missed her, she has just gone back to her room." Lauren shrugged; she did not like the housekeeper anyway, she was just being polite. She stepped outside, waved at Ochieng and Wairimu, who waved back, then stepped back inside.

As she passed, she reached over the grill and grabbed a sausage, dodging Felicity's mock swipe.

"Wewe, if you burn yourself, what do I tell your mother?" Felicity said, laughing.

Lauren laughed and was walking out of the kitchen when she saw Akinyi pick up the hot coffee to follow her. She stopped her and said, "I'll take that, save you the trouble." Taking it from her, she balanced the coffee in one hand and munched her sausage with the other.

Lauren and Amara were everyone's favourites in this team. They were always kind to the staff. Always willing to help. Not once or twice had they both stepped into the kitchen when their parents were entertaining, putting on extra aprons, cutting, cooking, cleaning. Anything they could do to help.

Amara was a particularly good baker. She would always be in the kitchen early, baking desserts for the family. She always made something special for the staff as well.

Then Felicity said, "Amara ako? *where is Amara*? She's usually the first one down."

Imma responded, "Amara? She left the house at 6:30. I saw her leaving as I was going to the bathroom."

"That's true," agreed the others. "As we arrived, we saw her car drive off, and she was waving at us and smiling."

"I think," Imma continued, "this is a working holiday for her."

"I look forward to her return this evening," said Felicity.

Then she remembered hearing Madam's instructions last night and ran to get her phone. She needed to call the Indian cuisine chef, Nduati, to come and make dinner tonight.

Morning had begun at The Manor House.

Chapter 25

It was a beautiful morning, the kind that promises a bright, sunny day. Yet, inside her, something felt off. A sudden shudder ran through her. More foreboding, more apprehension.

"Get it together," she muttered. What was wrong with her today?

Apparently, Eruya had promised to provide concrete evidence of the wrongdoing that Madam suspected. Maybe that explained her unease. Confrontations with staff rarely ended well, and it was always difficult to see trusted people as thieves. Yet, according to Madam, the housekeeper was more than likely a thief and would have to be dismissed. Amara had never trusted her, meek with the family, cruel with staff. A leader ruling through fear, not respect.

She sighed and turned the car toward the petrol station. She hadn't refuelled last night. The last thing she wanted was to run out of petrol on the way to Ol Pejeta.

She had time. Her breakfast meeting with the Sweet Waters Lodge GM wasn't until 8:30 a.m.

At the station, she opened the bonnet and petrol tank. An attendant approached.

"Jaza asante. *Fill it up thanks* Na habari ya asubuhi?"

"Mzuri, madam, na yako?" *Good, madam and yours*

She smiled, palm to her heart. "Nashukuru."

Another young attendant joined in. "Sasa, Auntie?" *what's up, Auntie* he said cheekily.

She made a face, smiling. "Fiti." *Am fit- slang for am well*

"Can I check something? Oil, water?"

"I'm checking the oil, thanks, but you can give me a cloth and add water."

He nodded and helped her close the bonnet once she was done. After paying via M-Pesa and collecting her receipt, she drove slowly to the air pump.

"Thirty-five all around," she said.

He finished quickly, and she tipped him fifty shillings. "Asante, Auntie!" He called out as she drove off.

The tarmac gave way to smooth Murram, winding through farmland and ranches. As she drove, cool morning air drifted in, crisp and gentle. Behind her, Mount Kenya hid behind a veil of clouds. She liked driving without music, just the hum of the car and the rush of wind. Perfect for thinking. She mentally outlined her project as she sipped the last of her coffee.

Eventually, she reached the Ol Pejeta main gate, showed her ID, and received a visitor tag. "Do you know the way to the lodge?" the guard asked.

"I don't remember it very well", and listened to his directions. Within fifteen minutes, she pulled into Sweet Waters Tented Camp.

8:00 a.m. perfect timing. Amara greeted the receptionist, used the restroom, then returned to announce herself for her 8:30 appointment with the General Manager. She sat briefly, then wandered around, admiring the décor; a blend of old-world charm and rustic African luxury. Serena Hotels was renowned for this modern Afrocentric aesthetic.

Her last stay here had been with her ex-fiancé. Though it was a while ago, the memory of that visit still made her chest tighten. She recalled the scent of fresh jasmine in the air during their last evening walk from dinner, a smell that now suddenly felt overwhelming. This was the last holiday they took together before she found out about his infidelity and broke off the engagement. She shook off the feeling. In time, she was sure it'd stop hurting.

"Amara!"

She turned smiling. Felix was striding toward her.

"Look at you, fabulous as always," he said.

"Felix, you charmer," she smiled. "Come here and give me a hug."

He lifted her clean off the ground, spun her once, and set her down. "The one that got away," he whispered.

She laughed. "Well!"

"That's all I get? You break my heart and give me 'well'?"

"Stop it, you melodramatic man. You didn't really want me."

He sighed dramatically. "So you don't want me, but you want my food?"

"Yes and I'm hungry," she said. "Now take me to breakfast."

They laughed and headed to the dining room. It was quiet, with only a few early guests. The supervisor hurried over, and Felix ordered tea.

"Could I have coffee, please?" Amara said. "A cappuccino, dark roast, freshly ground…."

Felix cut in. "Musyoka, ask the barista to take this order personally. I don't want trouble for bad coffee."

She scowled at him. "You're impossible."

"Sparkling water with lemon or lime?" Felix asked her.

"Sparkling, with lime, and cold," She added, sticking out her tongue at him.

At the buffet, she chose her breakfast items and settled at a table by a window overlooking the watering hole. A young barista approached, a young man who looked so much like Eruya that she almost did a double-take.

"Good morning miss, I understand you have a complicated coffee order?" he said shyly.

She scowled again at Felix, who was silently laughing.

"Good morning, its not a complicated order, I just take my coffee seriously. You'll grind the beans fresh?"

"Yes, madam."

"Double espresso, single cappuccino, hazelnut syrup on the side."

He repeated the order correctly, and she grinned.

When he left, Felix said, "See? You're not a sumbua troublesome, just a woman who knows what she wants."

She tossed a napkin at him. "Oh, stop."

They ate and talked easily. She scribbled notes as Felix shared insights into the Nanyuki hospitality industry, which properties were worth visiting and which were poorly run. She respected his knowledge and appreciated his candour. Her cappuccino arrived, and taking a sip, she gave the boy a thumbs-up. He beamed.

Chapter 26

Korir returned to the farm and entered the staff mess.

"Korir, you're back," said the cook. "I was just about to eat your bread!"

"Wewe!" Korir admonished, smiling. "Wacha mchezo." *stop playing* "I'm starving."

He sat, and the cook brought him tea, sugar, and bread with jam.

"You don't like Blue Band right?" the cook confirmed, grabbing his tea and sitting. "I just made this fresh," he said in a hush. "The greedy workers drank all I'd made earlier, and the bread, wee! You'd think they were vultures." He smiled. "I always set mine aside, or I'd get skinny like…"

They ate and drank in comfortable silence. Before long, Korir rose to take his plate to the wash-up area, but the cook said,

"Just leave it there, I'll take care of it. Siku njema, kijana." *have a good day, young man*

"Asante," Korir responded, "na wewe pia," *you too*

"Not having lunch here?"

"No," Korir said. "I'll be in the kitchen garden, so I'll eat lunch there. Tuonane jioni," see you in the evening

"Sawa," said the cook as Korir left.

He walked to the shed and collected some tools, then headed past the cow sheds to a fence near the river. It had a hole. He needed to mend it so the cows couldn't get out, or strangers in. He worked diligently and neatly. He had started yesterday, and soon it was done. It was now close to 9:30

a.m. He rose, took his tools back to the shed, washed his hands at the sink outside, and headed to the pigsty.

He grabbed the wheelbarrow, loaded it with feed, and set the measuring can on top. He unlatched the south entrance door and entered, leaving it open.He filled troughs with feed, first the right, then the left, refilling as needed until done. Next he turned on the water, filled each trough, then turned the taps off in sequence. Once the first troughs were ready to be turned off he had finished with turning on the first. Once all were full, he turned off al the taps.

Now the pigs were happy, they had food and fresh water. He smiled to himself, thinking how proud Eruya would be to see him working this way. Then he noticed water pooling around an empty sty near the north wall, on the east side. This usually happened when something large, such as food or pig waste, blocked the drain.

He knew what to do. He looked for the shovel, which normally rested by the north entrance door. It wasn't there. He walked back to the south entrance, no. Then outside, to the store, still no. Where was it? It was always there. Then he remembered: sometimes they used it outside to clear debris or toss out dead rodents and such. Because of that, they'd sometimes rinse it off and leave it outside against the wall to dry.

He walked back toward the north entrance and stepped outside. He looked left, no shovel. Then right there it was, at the far end.

"There it is," he thought. Who left it lying there like that? Not even cleaned.

As he approached, he saw something shiny and sticky on it. What was that, blood? Yuck! he thought. Eruya would never leave it like that. He walked past it, picked it up by the handle, and took it to the outside tap to clean it. But as he bent to pick it up, standing at the corner, something caught his eye. He stopped, rubbed his eyes in disbelief, and looked again. He walked closer. Saw it clearly.... and screamed.

He screamed as never before, wild, hysterical, his voice probably carrying all the way to the Manor House. People raced toward the sound, fearing injury. Korir stood there, pointing, trembling, howling.

The first on the scene were farmhands working nearby. Then Okelo came bounding through the pigsty; they arrived together.

"Korir!" Okelo shouted. "Ni nini?"*what is it*

Korir was just shaking and pointing.

Okelo advanced carefully, thinking maybe it was a snake poised to strike. He turned the corner and saw what Korir had seen. He stopped dead.

For a moment, his mind simply refused to understand. Then the reality crashed in.

A sound escaped him, not quite a word, more like a choked, broken gasp. His hand flew to his chest. The breath that tore out of him was sharp and ragged, as though the air itself had turned solid in his lungs. His knees threatened to buckle. His throat tightened.

"Dear God," he whispered.

Okelo staggered back a half-step, eyes wide, throat working. His stomach lurched. He pressed a shaking hand against the wall, fighting the urge to retch. For several heartbeats, he could do nothing but stare. Horror rooted him to the spot. He forced himself to breathe. Once. Twice. Again. He steadied himself.

Then instinct, the part of him that had worked as a farm supervisor for decades, the leader in him, shoved its way to the surface. He turned sharply to the older farmhand.

"Nyarandi, take Korir away. Strong tea, a lot of sugar, now. Don't leave him alone, not even a minute."

He barely recognised his own voice; it came out harsh, raspy and raw.

"Nani, Mwambi, run! Fetch the Master and Madam. Go!" He shouted.

Okelo's hands were trembling, his heart hammering. Still, he pushed everyone back, away from the corner. Away from the horror.

"Stand back, all of you! Nobody crosses this point!"

Then he saw the day guard and called to him. "Koiye! Kuja! Simama hapa! *come stand here* Do not let anybody past you."

He looked at his team. He didn't even ask them to return to work. Very little work would be done that day. He needed to preserve the scene. It was a miracle that Korir hadn't picked the shovel up. He needed to find his boss, the farm manager, and let him take control of the situation. "Nyambok, run to the boss's house and ask him to come here immediately."

Another askari guard came soon after, the supervisor, Mr. Nderitu,

"I'm glad you're here," Okelo said to him. "Can you please take charge of this? I need to meet the Master and Madam before they see this tragic scene."

Nderitu nodded, walked past his guard, carefully stepped over the shovel on the ground, and, seeing what the others had seen, gasped.

"Heavenly Jesus, have mercy," he whispered, crossing himself.

He returned, shocked to the core, and stood alongside the other askari, barring the way and keeping the staff at a distance.

Chapter 27

Lauren walked out of the kitchen smiling, a pot of hot, fresh coffee in one hand and a sausage in the other. She was munching the sausage with relish. She loved being at The Manor. She loved the mornings, even though it was 9:30 when she ventured from her room. Late-night speaking with Amara was her excuse.

She thought of Amara now and shook her head. How does that girl do it? No matter what time she slept, Amara was always up at the crack of dawn. Lauren hadn't heard her at 4 a.m., but knew Amara had gone across to the farm. She had mentioned last night her intention to meet Eruya on her "hill." Lauren knew that the hill at dawn was therapy for Amara.

She walked happily into the dining room, happier still when she realised she would be alone for breakfast. She could tell others had been before her; there were dirty plates piled on the trolley. She placed the coffee on the warmer and looked at what was on offer.

She didn't have much of an appetite, but she knew lunch would be a light fare; the main meals here were always breakfast and dinner. She decided to eat a heavier breakfast to take her through the day.

Just as she was about to sit down, Imma walked in.

"Don't mind me," Imma said, checking dishes. "Just topping things up."

"Go ahead," Lauren smiled. "Seen my brother or his..." She paused.

Imma looked at her, feigning innocence but failing to hide her smile. "They finished," Imma said. "He's out on the Veranda. Her, no idea."

"What about the rest?" Lauren asked. "The judge?

"Not seen the judge," Imma said. "Ochieng cleaned his shoes; he must still be asleep. Everyone sleeps so well here."

"And my cousin?"

"She's fine. I took her breakfast to her room," Imma said.

Lauren scowled. "Is she unwell, or her nightly farm shenanigans?"

Imma hesitated, then said quickly: "She didn't look well, miss. But she was apologetic and polite."

Lauren looked up in disbelief. "She what?"

Imma almost laughed. "Yes, miss. She was very polite. I didn't mind at all."

Lauren rolled her eyes. "Sick or guilty," she muttered.

They exchanged knowing looks and laughed.

"Your parents ate early in their room," Imma continued, " and Amara left for work."

"Thanks for the morning report, Zazu," Lauren teased.

Imma gave a mock bow, grinning, and was about to leave when Madam entered.

"Good morning, madam," Imma said.

"Good morning, Imma," Madam replied.

Imma took the trolley of dirty dishes and left the room. Lauren stood and went to hug her mother.

"Good morning, Mum," she said. "I hope you had a good night?"

"Good morning, darling," her mother replied, hugging her back. "Yes, we slept well. I just came to check everything I ordered was served. Sometimes that housekeeper has a mind of her own."

She walked around, lifting chafing-dish lids and nodding in approval. When she reached the sausages, she picked one with her hand, poured a cup of coffee, and came to sit next to her daughter.

This was nice, the quiet before the storm. She knew today would be a reckoning for at least two of her senior staff, unlikely they'd be in the clear after the audit.

Her daughter interrupted her thoughts. "Where's Dad?"

Just as she spoke, her father walked in.

"Is that my favourite daughter asking after her dear old dad?"

Lauren laughed, got up, and went to hug him.

"I'm your only daughter, Dad."

"Are you?" he said with mock indignation. "I wonder what Amara would say about that?" They laughed.

He hugged her tightly and sat down with them.

"Still eating, my dear?" he asked his wife fondly.

"And if I'm too thin," she retorted, "the neighbours will say you drive a big car instead of feeding your wife. You see, dear, I'm doing this for you." She popped the last piece of sausage in her mouth.

He laughed. "Well, thank you for protecting my reputation with your waistline."

"Did that man, that your father just mention my waistline?" she demanded, looking at her daughter. "Did he?"

Lauren laughed. "You two leave me out of your marital squabbles. I won't be the grass trampled when elephants fight. Siko hapo!" *I'm not there*

"I get no support in my own home, huh?" Madam said dramatically.

They all burst out laughing.

Just then, the door burst open, abruptly shattering the family's quiet laughter. Imma stumbled in, her face grey, shaking, tears running down her face.

"So sorry, madam, sir, here's someone from the farm to see you."

Before anyone could respond, she turned and hurried out.

Just then, Julius entered.

"What's going on? Why is Imma crying?, did you fire her?" His tone was accusing, and he looked directly at his stepmother.

Before Madam could answer, Imma returned, dragging one of the farmhands with her.

Trying to control her tears, she said, "Sir, madam, this is Mwambi from the farm. He has something to say to you."

She burst into fresh tears, apologised, and ran out again.

Mwambi stepped into the room, cap in hand, eyes fixed on the floor. Then he looked up.

"Sir, madam," he said solemnly, "I'm sorry to tell you that Eruya is dead."

The world seemed to stop.

Lauren's breath hitched sharply, her hand flying to her mouth as her vision blurred. Julius dropped into the nearest chair as if struck by a physical blow. Madam's coffee cup slipped from her fingers and clattered onto its saucer, the sound slicing through the suddenly airless room. The master blinked once, twice, his eyes wide and lost, as if the world had tilted under him.

Mwambi went on quietly, "Mr. Okelo sent me. He asked that you come."

No one moved. Even the air seemed frozen in place.

Then the master pushed back his chair and rose slowly. His shoulders, always so square, seemed to fold inward, and in that moment he looked twenty years older. He turned to his wife.

"Dear… let's go."

Madam tried to stand, but her legs wobbled beneath her. She gripped the table, breathing unevenly. Lauren reached for her mother, but her father gently steadied his wife, slipping an arm around her back.

"Dearest," he murmured again, firmer now, "let's go."

He turned to his son. "Call the OCS (Officer Commanding Station) and ask him to meet us at the farm. Introduce yourself, he'll know who you are."

Julius swallowed hard and nodded, though he remained seated for a moment longer, staring at the floor as if forcing his mind to catch up.

To Lauren, the master said softly, "I'm leaving you in charge of the house. No one goes to the farm. Check on Imma, make sure she is okay."

Lauren wiped her cheeks, breath shaky, and nodded.

"Son," the master added, "when the OCS arrives, bring him to the farm."

He helped his wife to her feet. She leaned into him heavily, her fingers trembling as she reached for her shawl. At the doorway, she paused, turning back as though remembering a forgotten piece of herself.

"Call Amara," she whispered. "Ask her to come home. We need her. But don't tell her why… not until she's here."

Then the two of them stepped out, walking with Mwambi through house, out of the Veranda toward the farm, Madam clutching her husband's arm, the master guiding her gently, both moving as though the ground itself had shifted beneath them.

Lauren shakily reached for her phone to dial Amara, her hands trembling so much the phone nearly fell, tears streaming as she tried to steady herself. Her brother came to her, pulled her into a hug, and let her cry.

After a moment, he whispered "Let me call Amara. You call the OCS. She'll worry if she hears your voice. We don't want her having an accident rushing back." She nodded through her tears, sat back down, and dialled the OCS. He left the room for the Veranda.

Lauren tried to collect herself when Naomi appeared in the doorway. She looked terribly tired, red-eyed, like she hadn't slept.

"Where have you been?" Lauren asked accusingly. "We needed you, and you weren't there. Have you not heard? Eruya is dead!"

Naomi froze, then burst into tears. She sat down heavily, and Lauren hurried to her side. They held each other and wept because sometimes there are no words at all.

Chapter 28

The master and Madam clasped hands in a show of solidarity and walked purposefully toward the farm. Mwambi, the farm hand, followed slightly behind them, quietly observing but remaining silent. As they walked down the slope towards the river, they saw someone pacing on the bridge. He looked up, saw them, and hurried over. It was Okelo, the supervisor. He looked terrible.

"Habari ya asubuhi," he said out of habit, stretching out his hand to greet first the master, then Madam. Neither replied, though they both shook hands. He fell into step beside the master, while Madam lagged slightly behind with Mwambi.

"Sir," Okelo began as they crossed the bridge, "you heard the tragedy that has come upon us?"

The master nodded. "Mwambi informed us, but he gave us no details."

"No, sir. He had none. May I explain?"

The master nodded again.

"We all noticed Eruya hadn't done his chores this morning, no chickens fed, no eggs collected, no pigs fed. Those are his daily duties, sir."

The master, noticing a crowd by the north entrance of the pigsty, placed a hand on Okelo's arm by the cowsheds and stalled him.

"I think you had better explain everything to us before we go on."

Okelo nodded, his agitation clear, his hands trembled as he forced a breath, bracing himself.

"At the briefing, I assigned Kipkorir, one of the young farmhands, to handle all Eruya's duties in his absence."

He stopped again. The master touched his arm, urging him to continue.

"You see, sir, I assumed Eruya had left early to avoid chores," Okelo said, shaking his head. "It seemed out of character, but it was the only possible explanation."

A shiver ran visibly through him as his eyes pressed tightly shut, trying to block out the scene.

"Continue," the master said quietly.

"So, sir," Okelo managed, "Korir had other work to do. He didn't get to the pigsty until after 9:30 a.m. He did his work and, while doing it, found Eruya."

Okelo stopped, unable to continue. The memory was too fresh. The master gave him a moment to gather himself.

Okelo steadied himself. "I sent Mwambi to fetch you."

The master nodded. "Thank you. Mwambi. Okelo, is Mr. Nderitu already there?"

Okelo nodded.

"Good. Please ask the farm manager to come too."

Madam moved closer. "I assume from your reaction, Okelo, that no one has seen the farm manager this morning?" she asked knowingly.

"No, madam. He has not been sighted."

The master looked up sharply. "Is he on the compound?"

Madam touched her husband's hand lightly. "Dear, I'm sure he is, in his house, sleeping off the effects of his favourite drink, Richot," she added bitterly.

"Unacceptable," the master said sharply, stopping as Mr. Nderitu approached.

"Good morning, sir, madam," Nderitu said solemnly. They both nodded. "Calamity has struck us today." He hesitated. "May I take you to see?"

The master shook his head. "Not until the OCS comes, Mr. Nderitu. Mr. Okelo, disperse that crowd. No one is to leave the compound, is that understood? Let them all go back to work or something. I'll address them in the mess hall after the OCS arrives. Please send someone to the Manor kitchen," he turned to Madam. "Dearest?"

She took over smoothly. "Mr. Mwambi, ask them to speak to Lauren; she'll arrange for one or two of the staff to assist in the mess kitchen. I have a feeling today is going to be a very long day."

Okelo turned and began walking quickly toward the crowd to carry out the instructions.

The master turned to Nderitu. "Please alert your teams at the gates. No one is to enter or exit the compound. Except, of course, for OCS and his team, and Amara."

Madam then remembered, "Oh, the auditor was supposed to be here at 10 a.m. I wonder why he hasn't arrived. Could he come and begin his work in the study, dear? Or should we wait until after the police?"

She shuddered; he was to meet Eruya. Tears rolled down her cheeks.

Her husband looked at her gently. "I know the audit is important, but I think having more people on the compound is not a good idea."

She nodded, wiped her tears and stopped Mwambi.

"Mwambi," she called to him as he walked towards the Manor, "could you ask Lauren to get our phones from our bedroom? Bring them to us after you've delivered the message."

He nodded and ran towards the Manor.

She turned back and saw that Nderitu was already radioing his teams.

Addressing her husband, Madam said softly, "I know you want to wait for the OCS, and neither of us wants to face this. But that boy, Eruya, we owe him this last respect. Let us go and see where he fell. I don't want to, but I think we must."

He thought for a moment, then said, "Then let me go. You don't have to. It definitely will not be pleasant."

She shook her head. "Life is unpleasant; that should not stop us from doing the right thing. I will be okay. I need, no, I must see him one last time."

He nodded. Holding her hand again, they moved toward Nderitu. At a nod from the master, Nderitu turned and led them toward the pigsty's north entrance.

The crowds had been dispersed. Only two security men remained by the entrance to ensure no one disturbed the scene. As they approached, both guards took off their caps and bowed slightly.

"Sir, madam," they said, moving aside to allow them through.

Nderitu led the way in silence. When he reached the shovel, he stopped, stepped aside, and pointed.

Again, the master held his wife's hand, and they proceeded forward.

She gasped at the sight of the bloodied shovel, halting abruptly. Her breath caught in her throat as she clamped her eyes shut, pain radiating through her.

He said gently, "You don't have to come further."

She shook her head. "I'll be okay. It's just the blood." She shuddered.

"I know," he said quietly.

Reaching the corner, they turned and saw him. He crouched against the waste pipe. The air was heavy with the smell of manure, but the couple, lost in grief, did not notice. Except for the blood, one might think he was merely asleep.

Madam began to cry silently, looking at the boy. He was so young, so innocent, struck down in the prime of his life. Tears rolled freely down her cheeks. She was not ashamed to mourn him openly.

They stood in silence. The master put his arm around his wife. They just stood and looked at him helplessly.

They were interrupted by Mr. Nderitu, who cleared his throat quietly.

"Sir, madam? The police are here. Shall I bring them to you?"

The master and Madam took one more look at Eruya quietly saying their final goodbye. Then they nodded and walked back towards Mr. Nderitu. Madam was still crying, the master supporting her by the shoulder. They made sure not to touch the shovel.

As they walked, they saw their son, sombre and dull, standing beside the OCS and a few other policemen.

The OCS stepped forward and said quietly, "Sir, madam, so sorry." He shook hands with both. "Let us take it from here."

They nodded and let him and his team pass.

"Mr. Nderitu," the master said, "please stay with the police and assist them in any way you can."

Then, taking his wife's hand, he said, "Son, go to the mess and get your mum and me a cup of hot tea. Bring it to the manager's office."

He turned again. "Mr. Okelo?"

"Yes, sir."

"Please lead the way."

They walked through the pigsty and out the other side to the farm office. Mr. Okelo fetched a few chairs and let them sit down. He stood waiting for instructions.

"Mr. Okelo," the master said, "send someone to see if they can wake that manager up. This is ridiculous." Just before Okelo left, Madam stopped him and said,

"Please check on the staff and make sure everyone is okay." Okelo nodded and left.

Julius walked in with a tray of tea. He placed it on the table and, after giving one to each of his parents, sat down.

After sipping her tea quietly, Madam spoke. "Did your sister call Amara? Is she on her way?" Tears were streaming down her face. He looked at her, reached into his pocket, and handed her a handkerchief. She took it gratefully, wiping her tears, her face a mess.

Then he said, "I called Amara. She did not pick up, but I left her a message telling her you needed her. I alluded to the audit." He confessed. "I am sure she will come as soon as she gets my message. I left Lauren and Naomi consoling each other."

Madam raised her head in surprise.

"Yes," he continued, "Naomi has been amazing this morning. It's completely out of character, but exactly what we need in a time like this. We're all surprised."

All the while, the master sat staring out the window. He sipped his tea in a daze, barely hearing them.

"Oh," Julius added, "I also brought your phones, as you'd asked." He reached into his pocket, took them out, and handed them over.

The master placed his phone in his coat pocket. He stared out the window. Saddened by the demise of a young boy in his prime, he looked into the distance and mourned, a father mourning a son.

Madam excused herself and stepped out of the office to call the auditor. When she reached him, he explained there had been a delay on the road from Nairobi. That was why he wasn't there yet.

She listened and said it was not a problem. Then she told him not to come to the house. She would call to explain later. She paused in anguish. "Let's speak after the weekend, and I will explain." Again, she paused. "Do you have enough money to get back to Nairobi?" He answered that he did. "I will compensate you for your trouble, but the audit may not be necessary after all."

He said in surprise, "Oh, okay, Madam. I will head back to Nairobi. We can speak next week. I hope all will be well."

"Thank you," she responded. She offered no further explanation and rang off. She returned to the office.

Sitting down, she quietly resumed her tea, and they all sat in silence.

Chapter 29

By the time Amara and Felix left the dining room, it was 10:30 a.m. They headed straight to reception. At reception, she saw missed calls from Naomi but ignored them. Focused on work, she silenced her phone, left her satchel at the desk, and joined Felix on the property tour. The visit was fruitful. Felix promised to send high-quality photos for her report. She wrote her email address on the paper, winked, and handed it to the assistant.

Felix scowled playfully. "You don't trust me?"

She shook her head, and they both laughed. He took her arm and walked her to the car. At the door of the car, she turned, reached up, kissed his cheek, and whispered, "You're the best. Thank you."

"Anytime," he said, hugging her warmly. He stepped back as she pulled out of the parking and drove off.

The drive back was calm. As the landscape slid past, she mulled over the productive morning and everything she'd learned. Reaching the Ol Pejeta gate, she returned her visitor tag. Her phone buzzed again, but she kept her focus on the road.

Once on the main road, she finally pulled over. Seven missed calls, mostly from Naomi and Julius. Both had messaged, but she hadn't read them. Now she listened to Julius's voice note.

His voice was strained. "Amara, Mum needs you to come back as soon as possible. It's… It's about the audit."

Julius's tone made her heart race. Something was wrong. She hung up, started the car, and sped to the Manor. The askari opened the gate with a grave look; his eyes carried bad news. Her stomach turned to ice. She sped up the gravel drive, hands clenching the wheel, urgency clawing at her chest. The car jerked to a stop, and she jumped out, heart pounding wildly as she ran for the entrance. Lauren opened the door, her face puffy, her eyes full of tears.

Amara froze just inside the doorway, pulse screaming in her ears. "Mum? Dad?" Her voice splintered, small and sharp with fear.

Lauren shook her head, then broke down, sobbing as she threw her arms around Amara.

"It's Eruya," she cried. "He's dead."

Amara's knees buckled, nearly sending her and Lauren to the floor. Felicity, having seen the car pull up and sensing what might happen, rushed from the kitchen. Her hands trembled as she caught them, her face filled with concern, and she gently guided them to the lounge.

Lauren sobbed, her shoulders shaking. Next to her, Amara sat stiffly, fidgeting with her handbag strap. She stared into nothing. At last, silent, unrelenting tears fell. That foreboding she'd felt all morning, she understood it now.

She whispered through tears, numbness masking her pain: "He was already dead… Already…dead."

ACT 4

Chapter 30

After sitting in the office for what seemed like forever, Julius heard a knock on the door. The OCS walked in. Julius immediately stood up and offered him his chair. Then, Julius gathered all the cups and placed them on the tray.

"Would you like some tea or coffee, sir?" he asked.

The OCS nodded. "Coffee, black, with sugar."

Julius nodded and departed, closing the door behind him.

The OCS looked at the two owners of the Manor. Pity welled in his chest; they seemed so beaten, so broken, so hopeless. He remembered how strong they both once were. Now, they looked like hollow, fading shadows.

He hesitated to speak. When they both looked up at him, he said gently,

"The police doctor has confirmed that the boy, Eruya? Died sometime last night, around midnight. He did not suffer; it appears he died instantly."

"Thank God," Madam murmured, her voice trembling, a tear slipping down her cheek.

The OCS continued. "I'm sorry, madam, I have to be graphic here. It appears that his death was caused by the shovel you found on the ground. That will have to be confirmed with an autopsy." he paused, "Who killed him, we do not know. For that, we'll have to conduct a full investigation.

The couple nodded, and he continued, "My team, through early interviews with your staff, already have a few possible leads. Sadly, it appears that whoever did this was on the compound. Perhaps one of your own staff."

Madam's hand flew to her mouth, her eyes wide with shock at the horror of that insinuation.

"So," the OCS went on carefully, "what we'd like to do is set up an interview room here on the farm for my team to use as a base for a day or two while we interview and hopefully clear as many of your staff as possible. Do all your staff reside on the premises?"

Madam answered, her voice trembling slightly.

"No, some live in Nanyuki town and the surrounding areas. But we do have at least eight staff who stay here. Some aren't on duty today. Mr. Okelo can give you a list of who was here yesterday and who's away."

The OCS nodded. "Thank you, madam."

He turned to the master.

"Sir, I'd like permission to work closely with Mr. Nderitu during the interviews. I understand he's a former policeman?"

"Yes. Whatever you need," the master said, taking his wife's hand.

The OCS continued, "I think it would be more comfortable if we interviewed the staff here, rather than summoning them to the station. One of your senior team members, either Mr. Nderitu or Mr. Okelo, can assist us. Perhaps even your farm manager…"

The master interrupted sharply. "No, not the manager."

The OCS exhaled in relief. "I'm glad to hear that, sir, because, between us, he's one of the people implicated."

At that moment, Julius reentered the room carrying a cup of coffee and a bowl of sugar. He handed them to the OCS.

"Mum? Dad?" he asked softly. "Anything else for you?"

They both shook their heads.

He took the tray and was about to leave. Then he added, "I'm sitting in the mess with Kipkorir, if you need me. He's in a bad way."

The OCS looked up. "Wait, is he the one who found Eruya?"

"Yes, sir."

The OCS nodded gravely. "He must be in shock. If you step outside, you'll find a police officer nearby. Ask him to direct you to the police doctor and have that young man, checked. Tell the doctor I sent you."

"Yes, sir. Thank you."

As Julius turned to leave, his mother called him back. She stood and hugged him tightly, whispering, "Thank you for being so strong for us."

He hugged her back, then left the room.

The OCS cleared his throat.

"As for your supervisory team and the Manor staff, is there somewhere at the Manor where we could interview them, if it's not too much trouble?"

The master and Madam looked at each other.

"Whatever it takes to get to the bottom of this," the master said quietly. "We'll find you the space you need."

The OCS nodded, relieved. At least this family was committed to seeing justice done for the young man. That wasn't always the case.

Finishing his coffee, he stood up.

I think it might be best if you head back to the Manor now. We'll begin our work here: interviews, and evidence collection. I will stop by before I leave to brief you on our progress.

A moment of silence filled the room, heavy with shared grief.

He turned to leave, then paused.

"Also, we'll need to take custody of the body. Do you have contact information for his next of kin?"

Madam gasped, her shoulders shaking with fresh sobs. "Oh no," she choked out. "His mother… she'll be devastated."

Her husband stood, moved to her side, and put a comforting hand on her shoulder. She took a shaky breath, wiped her tears, and said,

"I'll give you his mother's number. But please, could someone go to her in person? She's not well, and it would be best if she had family around when she's told."

The OCS nodded. "I understand she's from the Ngobit area? I'll contact my counterpart there and ask him to handle it personally. He's a good man and knows most families in that area; he'll know how best to approach it. Leave it with me."

She smiled gratefully, scrolled through her phone, found the number, and handed it to him. He copied it down and thanked her again before leaving the room.

Husband and wife looked at each other, embraced, and the master said softly,

"All right, dear. We've hidden away long enough. Let's go give the rest of the family the strength they need right now."

"Let's see Kipkorir first, and you promised to address the staff."

He agreed. Then, looking at her thoughtfully, he asked,

"Why didn't you tell me the manager had a drinking problem? Where is he today, of all days? Maybe he's ill or worse."

Madam sighed.

"I wouldn't call him an alcoholic. It only happens when he's under pressure, especially when his wife's away, which she is this weekend. I didn't hide it from you. It just doesn't happen often. It's almost a standing joke on the farm," she added bitterly.

He nodded. "And now?"

"Mr. Okelo peeked through his window," she said. "He was passed out on the sitting room floor with an empty Richot bottle beside him, definitely alive. There's nothing wrong with him that sleep and painkillers won't fix. I learned that, when I went outside to call the auditor,"she added.

After listening, the master said, "I'd still feel better if the doctor could check him, just to be sure."

She nodded in agreement. They walked out of the office and met Okelo.

"Mr. Okelo," said the master, "please clear out the office by the gate, the one you share with Mr. Nderitu, and let the police use it for their interviews. Also, I'm putting you in charge of the farm until further notice."

"Yes, sir," Okelo replied. "But what about the manager?"

The master looked him squarely in the eye.

"Where is he now? No, I need someone in charge who's here. That's you. You'll take over, please, immediately."

"Yes, sir," Okelo said quietly.

"Good. And gather the team in the mess. I'd like to address them all. Don't bother calling the Manor staff, we'll speak to them later."

They proceeded to the mess and found Julius and the doctor there.

After greeting them, the master said to his son, "Please find Okelo and have him open the manager's house. Daktari doctor could you check on that man for me, and assure me he's only drunk and not… worse?"

"No problem, sir," the doctor replied, and they both left.

The cook was in the mess with additional help from Wairimu and Ochieng from the Manor. They all greeted the master and Madam soberly.

When the staff had gathered, the master asked Mr. Nderitu to lead them in a prayer, after which he asked them all to observe a minute of silence for their fallen colleague He began to speak. He spoke about what had happened then outlined how things would work for the next few days. He asked them all to be strong and continue with their duties, explaining that there would be a police presence on the farm until the matter was resolved and justice served. Finally, he thanked them for their hard work and loyalty.

"We'll get through this together, as a family," he said firmly.

Before leaving, he called Okelo forward. "Until further notice, Mr. Okelo is in charge, seconded by Mr. Nderitu, head of security. Any issue or concern can be brought to them. But remember, my wife and I are just across the river. You can always come to us."

With that, he took his wife's hand, and they left the mess, walking slowly back toward the Manor.

Crossing the bridge, they stopped in the middle and leaned on the railing, looking down at the river below. For the first time that day, they were alone, able to breathe, to grieve, and to speak without fear of being overheard. They stood there, between two worlds. The quiet Manor and the farm, now marked by tragedy. Then, bracing themselves, they held hands and walked on across the river, toward home.

Chapter 31

The master and Madam returned from the farm and found their children on the Veranda, subdued and quiet. When the couple appeared, everyone stood.

The master waved them back into their chairs. "I need to go upstairs first," he said softly. "I'll be right back."

He turned to his wife. She shook her head. "I'm going to the kitchen; I have things to sort out."

As Lauren and Amara rose to accompany her, Madam looked at them and shook her head, signalling them to stay.

As she passed, she touched Amara's arm. "Thank you for coming home," she said quietly. "We need you."

Amara nodded and sat down beside Lauren. The master went upstairs while Madam made her way to the kitchen. As soon as she entered, she could tell people had been crying. She looked at Felicity.

'Any sign of the housekeeper yet?"

Felicity shook her head.

Madam took a deep breath. "You all know what has happened." She paused "Life must continue. We all need to support one another and be strong through this tragedy. I hope I can count on your support to carry on?"

She looked around the room. The staff nodded, some murmuring, "Yes, madam. Count on us."

"Good," she said, managing a small smile. "I'm glad to hear that. You're a wonderful team. I thank God for you all."

Then, after a pause, she shifted tone. "Is there any lunch?"

The staff laughed, and the tension eased.

"Jokes aside," she continued, "I know it might be a lot to ask under the circumstances..."

Felicity interrupted gently. "Madam, I hope you don't mind. I made some executive decisions in your absence. We've organised a meal for the family. We just need to know whether to serve it in the dining room or on the Veranda. Everyone could use something to eat."

Madam hugged Felicity warmly. "I knew I was right about you! Thank you, Felicity. Please arrange the food on the Veranda. Once it's ready, let Imma know to call everyone together. The master will want to speak to the whole team before we eat."

She turned to Akinyi. "Please, I don't care what you have to do, go with Imma, get that housekeeper out of bed, and bring her to the Veranda for that meeting."

Then to Felicity again: "I assume you've sorted out your food as well?"

Felicity nodded.

Madam suddenly put a hand to her mouth. "Oh no, I'd asked the Indian cuisine chef to cook dinner tonight."

Felicity touched her hand lightly. "I called him earlier, but when we got the news, I cancelled. I hope that's all right?"

"Yes, thank you," said Madam. "We'll have him come back in a day or two. You've organised what we'll have for dinner instead?"

Felicity started to reply, but Madam waved it off. "No need to tell me, I'm sure whatever you've picked will be perfect."

"Okay, everyone," she said, straightening, reassured. "Thank you again. Once the food is set, please call me upstairs."

With that, she left the kitchen to join her husband upstairs. She saw Naomi walking from her room. Madam stopped and hugged her. Naomi did not pull back as she was wont to do. The embrace was warm and genuine.

Then, stepping back, she said, "Please call Julius from the farm. Tell him we're about to eat lunch and we want him to join us."

Naomi nodded.

"And when the food is served," Madam added, "no one should eat until we're all together. I've asked the staff to join us. Your uncle wants to address everyone first. Can you take charge of that for me, please?"

"Of course, Auntie."

Madam smiled as she headed upstairs. "Don't forget to call Julius. Thanks."

"Of course," said Naomi, pulling out her phone.

In what seemed like no time, there was a knock on their bedroom door.

"We're all waiting for you on the Veranda," Naomi said.

"Thank you," replied Madam. She turned to her husband. "Dearest, we'd better go."

A few minutes later, they followed Naomi downstairs.

When they stepped out onto the Veranda, it was to a sea of anxious faces, family and staff together. Everyone fell silent and looked expectantly toward them.

Madam spoke first. "Thank you all for being here, in spite of the sad circumstances. Would someone volunteer to say a prayer?"

Naomi stepped forward. "I'll say a prayer for Eruya, and for all of us."

Madam blinked back tears, and a hush fell. Imma pinched Felicity, surprised by Naomi's courage.

"Thank you," Madam said softly.

Naomi began to pray, a simple, beautiful, and heartfelt prayer. It honoured Eruya, comforted everyone, and, in its honesty, touched everyone listening. When she finished with a quiet Amen, the echo of her words lingered. There wasn't a dry eye on the Veranda. Even the master turned away, to "remove"something from his eye.

Naomi went to sit beside Lauren and Amara. Both women took her hands and whispered, "Beautiful."

The master cleared his throat, drawing everyone's attention.

He spoke briefly about what had occurred and what had been done so far. He laid out the next steps of the police process, the interviews, and how things would proceed.

The master reassured them all: "You'll each be interviewed by the police, but don't be alarmed. It's procedural. If anyone knows anything, please come forward at any time, either to the officers or to us."

He informed them that the police would be using the study as their base of operations. Someone gasped.

The master looked up, paused, then continued, "No one will be allowed to leave the compound without police permission. Interviews will begin in about an hour and a half.

Staff who normally live out will be interviewed first. Everyone leaving will be subjected to police inspection and bag search at the gate."

He paused, then added gently, "Don't be afraid. Just tell them what you know. Tell the truth."

With that, he thanked everyone and dismissed the group. As people began to move,

Naomi called out, "Lunch is served." She and Imma started opening the chafing dishes.

Felicity caught Madam's eye and nodded toward the garden. Madam followed Felicity's gaze and noticed the housekeeper sitting on a chair at the edge of the Veranda.

When Madam approached, the housekeeper stood quickly. "Madam, I must go to the hospital," she said. "I'm afraid I'm not well."

Madam looked concerned. "I'm so sorry. No problem, there's a doctor on the premises. I'll have him come to you immediately."

She turned to find someone to send, just as Julius appeared. She asked him to fetch the doctor.

He smiled. "No problem," he said. "He is still across on the farm. I'll call him now. Maybe he and the OCS can join us for lunch?"

"Great idea, son," she said. "Yes, call them both."

The housekeeper's face turned ashen, her features frozen in alarm.

"No, no, madam," she stammered, scrambling out of her chair. "I feel suddenly much better."

Madam shook her head. "I insist you see the doctor. You've been sleeping all morning, completely out of character. I'll feel much better knowing you have not come down with something." She paused, "It is no trouble, since the doctor is already on the compound. Seeing the housekeeper start to shake her head, Madam said again, "I insist."

With that, she turned to Felicity with a subtle knowing wink and walked away.

As she crossed the Veranda, she saw the judge approaching. He looked unwell, drawn, but composed, his usual confidence subdued.

"Judge," she greeted him, "we missed you this morning. Everything all right, or did you succumb to the mountain air and oversleep?"

He smiled thinly. "I have a slight headache, madam. This home is so quiet, I decided to rest a bit longer."

"Ah," she said lightly, "if you're not well, I'm sure the doctor would be happy to give you a once-over."

Someone nearby stifled a laugh.

The judge shook his head. "Nothing a good meal won't cure, I'm sure. And madam, I'm sorry for your loss."

"Thank you," she said softly, then moved across the Veranda toward her husband, who was speaking with the three young women.

When she joined them, all three ran to hug her.

The master, left mid-sentence, said in mock indignation, "What am I, chopped liver? My wife walks up, and suddenly I'm invisible? I'm going to get some food, and I shall not speak to you three again… until I've eaten, maybe."

He turned and walked toward the buffet. Laughter burst out from Madam and the girls, light and uncontrollable. After all the sorrow of the morning, that bright sound seemed almost miraculous, releasing the pressure they'd all been holding inside. They clung to it, even as they moved to get their food.

Chapter 32

The OCS and the doctor both came for lunch. Afterward, the OCS and his officers were shown to the study, to begin their inquiries. Felicity, anticipating their needs, had prepared a list of all the Manor staff. She separated those who left at night from those who resided on the estate.

At Madam's insistence, the doctor examined the housekeeper. His findings were revealing.

Afterward, the OCS requested a private meeting with the master and Madam to brief them on developments at the farm. His report was as follows:

The young man's body had been taken away by the police. A cursory post-mortem would be done unless the gashes on his head proved insufficient to explain his death.

The shovel, believed to be the weapon, had been taken into custody. It had been fingerprinted at the crime scene. The prints would be compared with those collected on the farm and at the Manor. Many people had used that shovel, so it would likely carry numerous innocent prints. Still, if a print appeared belonging to someone with no reason to have handled it, that would help narrow the search.

The police set up their base in the larger office, which Mr. Okelo and Nderitu had previously used. The doctor examined the farm manager and confirmed Madam's suspicions. The only issue was excessive drinking. The manager would not be fit to work for at least another day. His wife, expected in a couple of days, would be allowed onto the farm to take care of him.

The key safe was removed from the manager's house and placed in the office, while Mr. Okelo changed the lock on Eruya's room, ensuring that no one could use an old key or tamper with any evidence within. He handed the keys to the police. The doctor treated young Korir for shock, saying he could resume duties the following day if he wished. His questioning was postponed until he was stronger, as the doctor recommended.

The manager would also be interviewed once he recovered. Officers suspected he might have more information than he had disclosed. Once all staff interviews were complete, the OCS would personally interview the family. All sessions were to be recorded and transcribed. The master and Madam could attend if they wished.

The doctor reported that the housekeeper was not physically ill but was clearly under severe nervous strain. It was suggested that she might be withholding information relevant to the case. Witnesses had seen her near the pigsty the previous evening after dark.

A security guard, Mr. Githenji, would also be interviewed, preferably at the Manor House. He was the one on duty on the farm, on the fateful night. Mr. Nderitu would assign at the Manor there for the night and send another guard to the farm.

Once all staff interviews were complete, the OCS would personally interview the family. All sessions were to be recorded and transcribed, and the master and Madam could attend if they wished.

Madam provided a list of all family members and guests in residence. When the OCS reviewed it, his eyebrows rose at the name of the judge. He asked the master and Madam for their consent to his interview. They agreed. The OCS let out an audible exhale. The judge, too, had been sighted near the farm the previous evening. The OCS did not divulge that fact.

After interviews, staff and guests could move freely within the compound, but they were not permitted to discuss the interview or investigation details with anyone outside the compound, nor could they leave Nanyuki until the investigation concluded.

The meeting ended quickly, as the OCS wanted his team to begin questioning staff immediately. He asked if Madam wished to sit in. She declined, suggesting Amara or one of her daughters could take turns in her place.

Naomi surprised everyone with her transformation. She was suddenly kind, generous, and eager to help. She spent part of the afternoon assisting in the kitchen and planning dinner. Her change was both astonishing and welcome. It came at the perfect time.

It was clear that her interactions with the judge were markedly strained. In the past, she sought his attention, but now she avoided him. When she could not ignore him, she spoke briefly before finding an excuse to leave.

The vulgar wife, however, remained consistent. She seemed unmoved by the day's events. Subdued, yes, because everyone else was, but not especially shaken by Eruya's death.

Julius, on the other hand, stood taller. Since morning, he had taken charge and acted as liaison between the Manor and the farm. He was thoughtful, checking on everyone's well-being and ensuring things ran smoothly. He checked on the judge before the OCS's arrival. He also arranged for the police officers to be served tea and biscuits. Another welcome surprise, and the timing was excellent. With all that had happened, his previous behaviour would have been a hindrance. The whole family was thankful for the change and hoped it would last.

The judge spoke little. Though he tried to maintain his usual charm, his explanation for his absence that morning did not ring true. The strain between him and Lauren was clear. Lauren, still very distraught over Eruya's death, seemed oblivious to his discomfort, but he felt it keenly.

After the meeting, Madam sought out the girls in their suite and summoned Naomi to join them. Once gathered, she explained what the OCS had shared and asked if any of them had information that might help. Then she asked them to take turns sitting in on the interviews.

Naomi declined, explaining that she needed to assist in the kitchen, especially that evening, when half the staff would be released early, and replacements might not arrive the next day.

Lauren also declined but nominated Amara, as she felt Amara would be the most objective of the three. Amara agreed. Madam thanked them and left. Their tea meeting dissolved soon after.

Chapter 33

Lauren rose from the window seat where she and Amara had been consoling each other, remembering Eruya. It was bittersweet. They had both loved him like a little brother, though he'd been closer to Amara. Losing him felt unreal. He'd been so full of promise, loyal, hardworking, endlessly curious. His death hung over the house like a heavy fog.

Perhaps that was why everyone was taking stock of their own lives. Eruya's death reminded them of what truly mattered and forced them to face the cracks in their own foundations. Beneath the sadness was anger, too. Whoever had done this had decided to play God; someone would have to be brought to justice and pay the price. In their own ways, each family member made silent vows: to uncover the truth, to help the police, to protect the family, to live better, and to restore what they could of what had been lost. Tears could come later. For now, there was work to do.

For Lauren, that resolve began with the Judge. He'd been acting strangely, distant, irritable, jumpy. Usually the charming centre of attention, he'd become withdrawn, even rude. When the OCS joined them for lunch, he had nearly jumped out of his skin.

She needed answers. By the time she returned to Nairobi, she intended to know exactly where they stood, together or not. To her surprise, the second option was not unthinkable.

After a quick refresh, she checked her watch. 3:30 p.m., The interviews should begin soon, so fewer eyes and ears.

She called the judge to meet her on the Veranda. When he arrived, he suggested they stay there, but spotting the OCS nearby, he abruptly took her hand and led her out onto the lawn. He asked a passing staff member for two chairs. When she suggested the river, he declined, commenting lightly that it might damage his Italian shoes. Once seated on the lawn further from the house, she studied him.

"What's going on with you?" she asked quietly. "Aren't you happy to be here with me, with my family?"

"Sweetie," he said, taking her hand, "I am happy. But there's a deal in Nairobi that might fall through. I may need to leave early."

She pulled her hand back. "Eruya was just killed, and you're thinking about business? How can you be so cold?"

"I care," he replied. "But this deal matters." He added softly, looking into her eyes, "for our future."

Her anger softened slightly. "You know the police won't let anyone leave."

He shrugged. "I'm a judge. I expect a little professional courtesy. If need be, I'll call Nairobi; someone can put pressure on the OCS." When he saw her set face, he added hastily, "Still, I'll volunteer for questioning. It wouldn't look right otherwise."

She nodded, half reassured, half unconvinced.

I won't be going with you. My family needs me here," she said flatly.

He seemed initially annoyed but recovered quickly. "Of course, darling. Stay and be with your family. We'll meet in Nairobi." Then, added quietly, "And please, don't repeat this conversation. Not yet."

She nodded silently, though her unease deepened.

Amara had remained by the window when Lauren left the room. She sat there until a knock sounded at her door. Imma entered to say the police were ready.

From her suitcase, she drew out a new journal. She tucked it into her satchel, beside her phone, a small recoding device and a pen. She'd made her own vow: to find out who had taken her friend's life, and why. She didn't yet know how, but she was determined.

Her role would be to observe quietly, notice what others missed, and ensure the police didn't bully anyone into false confessions. She'd heard of too many investigations where the innocent suffered just to close a case.

The study was tucked behind the main living room, large enough to double as a library. One door led to the house, the other to a small Veranda and a secluded walled reading garden, one of Amara's favourite retreats.

The staff had already rearranged the room for interviews. A table stood in the centre with two chairs behind and one before it. The Veranda door was closed, shades drawn. On the side table sat flasks of hot water, tea, coffee, and sugar. A platter of scones and biscuits lay under a mesh cover beside it were a pitcher of juice and another of water with respective glasses for both. They had thought of everything.

A sound behind her made her turn. Naomi stood in the doorway, smiling.

"Hi, Amara," she said lightly. "Did I miss anything? You're the hotelier, you'd know if we forgot something."

Amara smiled back. "It's perfect. You've outdone yourself."

Naomi shrugged modestly. "We all have to do our little bit," she smiled and left.

Amara stared after her, stunned. The same woman who'd been openly hostile the day before was now polite, helpful, even charming. Miracles, it seemed, did happen.

Chapter 34

Moments later, two policemen entered.

"Good afternoon, Miss Amara," said the first policeman, extending his hand.

"Good afternoon, and please, just Amara."

"I'm Senior Detective Lewa. This is Sergeant Kipsang. We'll conduct the interviews today. The OCS may join tomorrow, perhaps for the family."

She nodded and gestured to a chair set slightly aside from the two behind the desk. "I thought I could sit here, slightly aside. Is that all right?"

"Perfect."

Naomi peeked in again. "Ready for your first culprit? I mean, interviewee?" she teased.

Lewa smiled. "Give us two minutes for tea please."

Sara from the kitchen entered, nervous but composed. The sergeant greeted her warmly, offering tea or water. He then guided her to a chair. Amara smiled reassuringly. Sara relaxed.

The questioning flowed like a conversation, gentle, friendly, deceptively casual. Amara admired the detectives' technique; key questions were buried within easy conversation. She watched their rhythm, ever alert for inconsistencies. Quietly, she wrote in her journal.

Fifteen minutes later, it was over. Lewa thanked Sara, walked her to the door, and reminded her not to discuss the interview. Returning, he poured some water and addressed Amara and Kipsang: "Any thoughts?"

The sergeant spoke first. Amara added her observations. Lewa nodded, clearly impressed by her insight. The process continued. A staff member entered, answered questions, received thanks, and then left. The rhythm was methodical and humane. Amara found herself admiring the precision with which each step unfolded.

By six o'clock, nine staff had been interviewed, some of the house team and a few guards. They agreed to pause and resume the next morning with Mr. Githenji, who, Lewa said, "might know more than the rest." The housekeeper, too, would wait until tomorrow.

Then Lewa's phone rang. After a short exchange, he hung up, his expression grim.

"That was the OCS. Orders from Nairobi, the Judge is to be interviewed immediately. The OCS will handle it personally. We're not to record the interview. Six-thirty sharp."

Lewa glanced at his watch, jaw tightening. He said to Amara and Kipsang, "Let's take a short break, then reconvene. It's going to be an interesting evening."

With that, they left the room.

Chapter 35

Amara returned to the study library at 6:15 p.m., well before the others. Rearranging the chairs for the next interview, she asked Imma to clear all the tea things. When she finished, only a vase of flowers, several bottles of water, and a few glasses remained on the table.

The OCS and senior detective would conduct the interview, while Amara and the sergeant observed. She believed the judge would probably respond only to the OCS, far too arrogant, she thought, smiling faintly. Her hope was that Lauren would see through his façade before making any commitments. Though Amara lacked evidence, she did not trust him.

Moving her chair farther back, Amara became just a quiet backdrop, not part of their conversation. Once she finished setting up and was sure she was alone, she slipped a small voice activated recording device among the books on the shelf nearest the interviewee's seat. Despite the OCS's remarks about the ban on recording, she felt strongly that this conversation needed to be preserved. By capturing every question, pause, and reaction, she could later focus entirely on the judge, his tone, posture, and even his smallest flinch.

At 6:25, the OCS, detective Lewa, and the sergeant entered the room and found Amara waiting. They greeted her warmly, thanking her for being on time. The OCS once again explained that, though the judge had requested the interview not be recorded, a request that broke protocol, he had to defer to his superiors.

Just then, the door opened, and the judge sauntered in. Immediately, the OCS stepped around the table and greeted him, saying, "Thank you for your time, Your Lordship. We hope to finish this quickly."

The judge smiled thinly and replied, "Always a pleasure to cooperate with the law," though his eyes stayed cold.

The OCS led him to a chair, offered water, which he declined, and then sat. Detective Lewa noticed Amara had switched the interviewee's chair to a stately one, what an important man might expect. Sharp young woman, he thought, hiding a smile.

The OCS resumed his seat. "Your Lordship, may I introduce Senior Detective Lewa?" he said. The detective stood, nodded politely, and sat again. "Sergeant Kipsang," the policeman, stood and nodded politely. "And of course," the OCS continued, "you know Miss Amara? She'll also be observing the interview this evening."

The judge's head snapped toward her.

"This is highly irregular," he snapped. "A civilian at a police interview? This can't be the proper procedure. And what does she," he jabbed a finger, "have to do with this? She's not family. Absolutely not. She must leave."

The OCS's voice remained calm as he said, "Your Lordship, I understand your concern. While this isn't typical protocol, the Master and Madam requested that Miss Amara be present for all interviews, including this one. She's merely an observer and will not speak."

The judge stayed firm. "I'll call Nairobi and speak with the Chief Justice about this breach".

"Of course, Your Lordship," the OCS replied, still calm. "Though I should mention that I spoke with the Chief Justice not five minutes ago. I explained the request, and he agreed Miss Amara may attend as long as she remains silent."

The judge froze, then sighed heavily. He slid his phone back into his pocket and glared at Amara, remembering her teasing comment the day before about 'Double O'. He didn't like this woman or trust her.

"Proceed," he said curtly. "I don't have all day."

Amara hid her smile. The interview began. Even with the most basic questions, the judge was curt and combative; answering only after being asked more than once. As the questioning continued his confidence returned. With that came his usual arrogance.

When asked what he had done after dinner, he replied smoothly that he had gone straight to bed, exhausted from the long drive from Nairobi and a busy week prior.

The OCS nodded and replied, "Of course. A few of the night staff mentioned movements near the grounds, but people do misremember things in the dark."

The judge stiffened. "I never left my room after dinner. Anyone who says otherwise is deluded, or needs their eyes checked," he insisted.

The OCS simply nodded again, jotting something down. "Noted, Your Lordship," he said. He asked a few other mild questions. Finally, he asked, "Did you see or speak to the young man, Eruya, at any point yesterday evening?"

The judge replied, "I saw him only when we arrived, around lunchtime. I greeted him. That was all."

The OCS nodded once more, thanked him, and wrapped up the interview.

Before leaving, the judge announced, "I have an urgent matter in Nairobi and intend to leave tomorrow morning."

The OCS replied with a courteous smile, "I'm afraid that won't be possible, Your Lordship. Until we've completed all interviews, no one is permitted to leave the compound, for those staying within, let alone Nanyuki."

The judge rose sharply. "I am a Judge, therefore beyond reproach! How dare you detain me here?" he demanded.

The OCS's tone didn't change as he said, "My apologies, Your Lordship. You know better than most that we must appear fair to all. If the Master himself is not permitted to leave his own home, it would be inappropriate to allow a guest to do so. A young man was killed here, and we must be thorough."

He paused, eyes mild but steady. "I'm sure you appreciate my position."

The judge glared, then muttered, "Just get on with it. I must leave as soon as possible." He straightened his jacket and added sourly, "Still, I always cooperate with the law."

The OCS stood quickly and opened the door for him. The judge swept out without another word.

When the door closed, the OCS turned back toward the others and said dryly, "Well."

Amara and the sergeant burst out laughing, covering their mouths so they wouldn't be heard.

Just as they began discussing the session, the OCS's phone rang. He stepped aside, answered, and after a moment returned, expression grave. "That was the doctor," he said quietly. "The postmortem is complete."

They gathered near the desk. "The cause of death," the OCS continued, "was indeed the blows to the head, three to be exact. Consistent with what we suspected."

Amara closed her eyes, letting the grief wash over her. She sat heavily in the nearest chair and breathed deeply until she could look up again, tears in her eyes. No one spoke, understanding her pain.

The OCS went on. "Eruya was holding something tightly in his hand, a cufflink." He unlocked his phone and showed them the photograph the doctor had sent. The image glinted under the light.

The OCS watched Amara's face. “You know who that belongs to, don't you?”

Amara nodded slowly. “Yes.”

Before she could speak, Detective Lewa murmured, "The judge. Of course, a gavel."

They exchanged grim looks. The cufflink spoke louder than any confession. It placed the judge at the farm, at the pigsty, the very night he swore he'd been in bed. Amara was sure she'd seen those cufflinks on his shirt at dinner. She shared that with the team. They would have to do a DNA test to be certain, but they all knew now that, the judge was definitely lying.

The OCS leaned forward. "Miss Amara," he said, surprising her, "Though I can't ask this officially, will you help us quietly gather what information you can… Catching this killer may depend on your assistance. We may have some suspects who were on or near the scene, but that does not bring us any closer to the actual perpetrator." He continued, "You have an eye for detail and the trust of these people. Will you help us quietly gather, what we are not able to get through official channels? The staff may open up to you in ways they never would with us."

Amara nodded. "I'll help any way I can. I also spoke briefly with Eruya when I arrived. He found evidence of wrongdoing at the Manor and farm. He planned to meet Madam and an auditor today and said it would change everything." She paused, feeling the weight. "He never got the chance."

The OCS softened. "I understand your pain. Thank you for agreeing to help us. Also, please, don't wander alone at dawn as I hear you are prone to do. The killer is still probably on this estate. For now, what we've discussed stays between the four of us, agreed?" They all nodded.

"Good. Let's regroup tomorrow at ten a.m. That gives you time for your morning walkabout," the OCS said.

Amara agreed.

The OCS smiled faintly. "We'll see you then. And don't worry about dinner for our team; the station will feed the officers we've posted here."

He rose, and the three men left quietly. Amara remained seated, letting the silence settle around her.

She whispered, "I'll make your sacrifice count, Eruya. I'll fight for you in death as I couldn't in life."

After a long moment, she straightened, retrieved the recorder with a swift motion, and tucked it into her satchel. She walked to the washroom, washed her hands thoroughly, gathered herself, and went to join the family for dinner.

Chapter 36

At 4:30 a.m., Amara woke as usual, her body clock reliable, even with the alarm off. She lay still, listening to the night beyond the curtains. She didn't dare wander outside so early. Not after what happened. Would she ever feel safe before dawn? Maybe, but not yet. Facing that hill, his rock alone was unthinkable. Grief hit her hard. She paused, letting it wash over her.

After freshening up, still in pyjamas and a robe, she put on her slippers and quietly went downstairs to the kitchen. The room was empty, but someone had set out everything for coffee. She brewed it and sat in silence, waiting for the aroma to fill the room.

She recalled last night's subdued dinner: little laughter. Even less talk. Shared grief united the family. By the time Amara entered, dinner was already underway. The sounds of cutlery echoed in the quiet, anchoring everyone.

When she entered, both Julius and the judge abruptly stood to pull out her chair, catching her off guard. The judge seized the moment with a performative gesture. His smile was sharp and insincere, concealing a flash of resentment in his eyes.

"Miss Amara," he said smoothly, the words dripping with false charm. She sat, returning a polite nod. His smile hardened, more grimace than grace.

Everyone smiled at her, though it was clear to see strain of the death etched into every face. The master and Madam seemed to have aged years overnight, weary and broken yet still holding their composure. Julius had grown into himself, quietly watching over his parents, anticipating their needs, steering conversation to keep minds from sinking too deep into sorrow.

Lauren was subdued; the judge attempted to engage her in conversation, but received only monosyllables. He didn't give up. He spoke to the mother, then Lauren, pretending to be his usual charming self, but the charm had cracks.

Naomi, calm but distant, avoided the judge with precision. When he spoke directly to her, she quickly got up to check the chafing dishes or speak with someone in the kitchen. She was polite but clearly unavailable. Though he felt rebuffed, nothing was overt. Amara noticed: something had definitely shifted. Normally, Naomi welcomed his attention.

Only the vulgar wife seemed untouched by the tension. She ate noisily, talking about trivialities, until her husband silenced her with a gentle hand. Even that gesture felt strained. Their marriage looked dangerously frayed. Amara ate little, her head full of thoughts. She needed solitude to process grief, observations, and suspicions.

At the end of the meal, the master turned to her. "Amara, we thank you as a family for stepping in so seamlessly to assist us with this police business."

The others murmured their agreement.

She inclined her head. "Of course."

The master continued, "We won't ask about the details, as we know that must remain confidential. But is everything going well? Do the police have all they need?"

Amara nodded. "Yes, it's going smoothly. They have everything." She glanced at Naomi. "Thanks for the tea and refreshments, and for coordinating the staff interviews." Naomi smiled.

Amara turned to the master. "Tomorrow we'll continue interviews and may begin speaking with the family in the afternoon."

At that, the vulgar wife spoke up, her mouth full. "What, me too? I don't know anything. I didn't do anything. I hardly knew the boy! Why would they want to interview me?"

Her husband laid a calming hand on her arm. "No one's accusing you of anything. It's just routine, right, Amara?"

Amara nodded. "Exactly. Routine."

The vulgar wife pulled her hand away. "I'm not even family, so what does it have to do with me?"

Gasps circled the table. Julius pursed his lips. He stood abruptly and walked to the buffet, struggling to contain himself.

Amara replied calmly, "Everyone here will be interviewed, family or not. You were present last night, and that's what matters." Her voice was mild but pointed. "Even the judge was interviewed."

The judge's eyes flashed. His lips tightened in resentment. He remembered all too well the sting of humiliation, being questioned in her presence. He shifted in his seat. His jaw set with lingering annoyance.

The vulgar wife turned to Amara accusingly. "And you? Have you been interviewed?"

Amara smiled. “Of course. I’ve already told the police everything I know. No special treatment for me.”

The master raised a hand, ending the discussion. "That’s settled. We’ll all make ourselves available to the police at their convenience. Including you," he said firmly to the vulgar wife. He offered a weary smile. "Now, let’s call it a night. This has been a long and heavy day."

His wife nodded. “Naomi, please arrange a tray with tea and desserts for us to be brought upstairs.”

“Of course,” said Naomi, standing at once.

“Thank you, dear.” Noticing the positive changes in Naomi and Julius. Madam thought, sometimes it takes tragedy to bring out the best in people. She was grateful and hoped the change would last.

The couple rose, wished everyone goodnight, and left the room together.

Naomi walked up to Julius at the buffet and gave him a quick hug. “Can you help me get the desserts? I’ll fetch fresh tea. Meet me at the bottom of the stairs in three minutes?”

He smiled and nodded, busying himself with the desserts.

The judge watched, his sneer growing. Seeing cracks in the "perfect family" pleased him. He turned to his own trouble: the forgery and nearly finished documents. Soon, he would leave for Nairobi. With police now in the study, he considered hiding the originals under a mattress or perhaps in Naomi’s room instead. Let her family find them, let her explain. The idea made him smile as he stood.

“I’m heading to bed,” he said. “It’s been a long day.”

He circled the table, kissed Lauren on the cheek, and left, pausing briefly outside the dining room door, hoping to catch sight of Naomi. When he didn't, and heard Julius coming with the dessert tray, he walked quickly toward his room.

Naomi, having seen him lurking, lingered in the kitchen until she was sure the coast was clear. When Julius called out softly, she emerged, carrying the tea. Together, they went upstairs to their parents' suite.

The vulgar wife continued eating as though nothing had happened. Amara, still finishing her food, sat with Lauren, who shared light, funny anecdotes from a recent golf tournament. They were meant to lift the gloom. Julius and Naomi returned soon after, got dessert, and took their seats again.

Conversation gradually loosened. Quiet laughter softened the tension. Only the vulgar wife seemed immune, scrolling through her phone while eating dessert. Something she'd never dare in her parents-in-law's presence. She finished, left her plate on the table, and announced, "I am going to bed, goodnight," before leaving.

They all got up. After clearing dishes and tidying the room, they were leaving when Julius stopped them. "I'm going to divorce that woman," he said flatly. "I've never loved her. I knew from the beginning, but I tolerated her. Now…" he shook his head, shrugged." It has become unbearable even being in the same room as her." He ended angrily.

The three women stopped in their tracks, then sat back down.

Lauren said gently, "Maybe it's the shock of everything that's happened. Give it time."

Amara added, "Have you tried counselling? Maybe start there."

He shook his head. "We tried everything, counselling, patience, pretending. This weekend was our final attempt. We've been in separate rooms for over a year and a half." The girls watched him in silent surprise. "I've already spoken to a lawyer. The papers are ready."

He looked at them earnestly. "Please don't tell Mum and Dad yet," he smiled, then said gravely, "I would like to be the one to tell them myself."

Naomi whispered, "Of course." Looking at the other two, she continued, "You can count on us." The other two nodded in agreement.

He smiled, emotion softening his face. "I know I don't deserve it, but thank you."

Naomi grinned suddenly. "Brother sandwich!"

All three women stood up and surrounded him in a warm group hug. He laughed, mock-protesting that he couldn't breathe, and for the first time that night, they all laughed genuinely.

When they broke apart, he kissed each of them on the cheek. "Goodnight, my sisters," he said, and left the room. None of the women had any special feelings for Julius's wife, but it was never nice for a marriage to end. They were sad for him.

As they prepared to follow, Naomi stopped them. "I need a favour," she said quietly. "Would you mind if I slept upstairs with you guys?"

They understood instantly that she didn't want to be alone.

"Of course," said Amara. "Slumber party it is."

Naomi smiled. "I hoped you'd say that. I already had my things moved up."

They laughed softly and headed towards the stairs together.

Amara lingered at the bottom of the stairs.

"I'll grab some water from the kitchen," she said.

"Bring us some too, please," the two women called back.

Amara returned to the kitchen, collected three bottles of water, and switched off the lights. As she stepped into the corridor, she caught a movement ahead, a shadow. The judge.

Hearing her approach, he flattened against the wall, waiting. Amara's steps slowed. Thinking she'd gone, he continued down the passage. She watched him disappear up the hallway, then pause by Naomi's room. He knocked softly. When there was no answer, he tried the handle. A muffled sound of frustration escaped him, and then he turned sharply, striding away toward his own room.

Amara stood still for a moment, the house silent around her, then smiled faintly. Things were changing, and others, unravelling.

After a while, Amara broke out of her reverie, stood up from the kitchen table, and prepared the now-brewed coffee onto a tray along with milk, three cups, and a plate of shortbread in case her sisters might want some when they woke. She carried it quietly upstairs.

The corridor was hushed. Everyone was still asleep behind closed doors. She moved softly, careful not to let the tray rattle or the stairs creak beneath her feet.

In the suite, she set the tray into the small kitchenette, poured herself a cup of coffee, and took a few biscuits. The silence wrapped around her, complete and heavy with the lingering sorrow of the night before. Coffee in hand, she crossed to the window seat and settled there. She slowly inhaled the aroma of her special brew and remembered Eruya. Outside, the world was beginning to breathe again. The first pale light touched the edge of the sky. She sipped slowly, nibbling on her shortbread, waiting for the dawn to herald a new day.

Chapter 37

Amara must have sat there for a few hours; at some point, she drifted into a light sleep, the warm sun on her face. When she opened her eyes, two faces were peering at her. Recognising them, she smiled and sat up as both Lauren and Naomi grinned down at her.

"Any more coffee left?" Lauren asked, tapping Amara's empty cup.

Amara nodded. "I left some for you at the kitchenette."

"And biscuits?" Naomi asked, with a hopeful look at the crumbs.

Amara laughed. "Yes to both!" she called as they dashed off. "You're welcome. Good morning!"

"Thanks! Good morning!" they chimed together.

The girls soon returned with coffee and shortbread. They joined Amara at the window seat. Together, they sipped and ate in companionable silence.

"This is great coffee, Amara," Naomi said. "Why can't I ever get mine to taste like this? You've given me the recipe so many times."

Lauren laughed. "It's because she leaves something out of the recipe. She's done the same with me, wicked girl!" She winked at Amara, and the three burst out laughing. It was good to laugh again. Things were, returning to normal, or perhaps becoming better?

Just then, the door opened, and Madam stepped in, smiling at the sight of the three girls at the window. "Is there any for me?" she asked.

Amara stood and hugged her. “Let me see if these greedy girls left any.”

The four sat together, chatting idly about this and that. It was an ordinary, lovely moment that felt precious in a world that had recently turned upside down. At 7:30, Amara stood. "Got to check something," she said. Before Naomi could offer to tag along, Amara grinned, "Police business," already moving toward her room.

Naomi feigned offence. “I didn’t want to come anyway,” she lied, following Amara into her room. She dropped herself dramatically onto the bed. She said through muffled laughter, “Since you won’t need this, I’ll take full advantage.” A moment later, she had snuggled inside the duvet and was “asleep,” complete with exaggerated snores. Amara chuckled, shook her head, and headed for the bathroom.

After a quick wash and change, Amara stepped outside into a bright, clear day. Walking toward the river and across to the farm, she tried to steady her nerves. Her satchel over her shoulder; journal, pen, and recorder inside. When she got across to the farm, she was unsure where to begin. Amara was relieved to find the staff eager to talk.

Her first stop was the mess, where the farm cook, Ochieng, and Wairimu were preparing breakfast. They took a moment to condole with one another before the cook told her about Eruya’s last meal.

Leaving the mess, Amara met Okelo, who drew her into the office. Speaking in hushed tones and glancing around for privacy, he revealed that he had seen the manager coming out of the store that night and had caught the shaken look on Eruya’s face. Okelo also mentioned that since being stripped of his position, the manager had barely left the house.

As Amara and Okelo spoke privately, Mr Nderitu entered and joined their conversation. Sensing an opportunity to clear the air, both men began openly sharing their observations about the night of the incident. Amara listened carefully, knowing that if she accused the wrong person, the real killer could walk free. The two men, drawing from their own experiences and what they'd heard from other workers, identified three likely suspects: the farm manager, the housekeeper, and the judge. They understood the first two; each had something to hide. But the judge? That was murkier. Still, both men swore he had been seen near the pigsty at 11:30 p.m. that fateful night.

Means were easy: the shovel was right there by the north wall. Motives, too, were whispered. The manager was rumoured to be stealing pigs and equipment, something Amara was shocked to hear might also implicate Julius, although he had not been on the farm that night.

The housekeeper was suspected of theft within the house, possibly working with the manager. The same buyer who took the pigs was, apparently, her former employer. Amara remembered that brass figurine: missing one moment, mysteriously reappearing the next day after Amara asked about it.

Mr Nderitu suggested Amara speak with the security guard, Mr Githenji, who had been on duty that night and might be more open with her than the police, this had already been suggested. Amara made another note for her growing list.

As for the judge, well, the rumours were salacious. He was having an affair with Naomi, and they were said to have met secretly that night in the abandoned shack by the river. Amara didn't believe Naomi was capable of murder though the rest of the accusation?. Amara wondered if Naomi might be forced to admit to their rendezvous that fateful night, since the judge currently denied leaving the Manor. Her notebook was filling quickly.

Amara asked if someone could take her to the site of Eruya's death. She felt she owed it to him to "pay her respects." Mr Nderitu volunteered. As they set off, Okelo was called away by the manager's shouts. Amara stopped him briefly.

"Don't repeat our conversation. You haven't seen me, especially with the manager. He hasn't been interviewed yet. We don't want evidence destroyed." Okelo nodded and hurried off.

At the pigsty, they found Kipkorir working. Amara condoled with him apologising gently for him having been the one to discover the body. She asked him if he shouldn't take some time off.

He shook his head. 'I'd rather work, it keeps my mind off it. Eruya would want me to carry on. I want to make him proud.'

She understood he wanted to be useful and busy whilst he processed his grief. Tears welled in both their eyes, and Amara placed a comforting hand on his shoulder before walking to join Nderitu at the north entrance. As she moved away, Kipkorir called softly, asking if she could speak to him later. She nodded.

The scene was still marked: chalk outlines, numbered tags, the shovel's location on the ground encircled in white. Amara skirted around it. Tears spilt freely as she stood in silence looking at the scene where Eruya fell. When she finally turned away, a policeman and a security guard appeared quietly nearby, taking up positions. She hadn't noticed them before. They were there to guard the scene until the case was completed and a culprit brought to justice.

Amara thanked Mr. Nderitu and he departed. Standing at the north entrance, Amara called to Kipkorir to walk her to the abandoned shed. Leaving his broom, Kipkorir quietly led the way. They walked mostly in silence. He led her to the right of the pigsty, down a the narrow path parallel to the main farm path. It was half-hidden by overgrowth, visible only to those who already knew it existed. Inside the shed, Amara scanned the small space, unsure what evidence she was seeking. A moment later, she stepped outside again, circling the structure and noting directions. She sketched a rough plan in her journal.

Korir was waiting for her outside the shed and when she finished sketching, he let her south on another path which ran parallel to the river, back towards the main path. As they walked Kipkorir told her that Eruya had handed a parcel to a friend the night he died, a friend who lived in Nanyuki. Korir hadn't told the police because he didn't want to get anyone in trouble.

He continued to say that the manager had gone into Eruya's room while Eruya was still at the pigsty. Kipkorir, coming from the toilet, had seen him enter the room and heard him rummaging frantically, searching for something.

Korir said that when he saw the manager leaving, he looked furious.

Kipkorir's face tightened. "If I'd followed him, maybe I could have stopped it," he said bitterly.

Amara touched his shoulder gently. "You're not to blame. We are not even sure the manager did it."

He nodded, struggling for composure. "Eruya's friend is Mwangi," he added softly. "His uncle is Mr Githenji, the guard who was on duty that night."

"Thank you," said Amara.

He nodded, then he turned and walked back up the main path past the cowsheds and towards the pigsty. What a breakthrough she thought to herself as she walked down towards the bridge. The OCS was right in sending her to the farm that morning. This information would never have made it to the police.

On the bridge, she paused, leaned against the rail, and called Nderitu and Okelo to meet her there. As she waited, she listened. The river gurgled; leaves rustled. The cool wind from Mount Kenya brushed her cheek. For a moment, life felt as it had in better days, peaceful, dignified, alive. But sadly, she remembered Eruya would never cross this bridge again.

When the two men arrived, she spoke quietly. "I need a favour. Move Kipkorir to another room, quietly, and place a guard with him at all times, day and night. He may know something that puts him at risk, and we can't let the killer know what we know."

Though surprised at what she said, they both nodded gravely. Okelo said he'd move the boy into his own quarters, and Nderitu promised to coordinate protection with the police.

Amara thanked them both, shook hands with them and crossed the bridge toward the manor. As she walked, she caught movement, a figure half-hidden among the trees. She realised then that the OCS had kept his word. She was being watched over, though she would never have known it. The knowledge steadied her. She checked her phone for the time: 9:15 a.m. Excellent, just enough time to grab breakfast before the interviews began.

Chapter 39

Ten minutes before the first interview, Amara arrived at the library. She scanned the room, gathering her thoughts as she waited for the days interviews to begin. Detective Lewa and Sergeant Kipsang were already setting up their files. The OCS soon entered, closed the door, and after brief greetings, they all gathered at the table.

The OCS summarised what they had established the day before, including the discovery of the cufflink. Then he turned to Amara and asked about her walk to the farm. She told them she needed to speak privately with Mr Githenji before his next interview, convinced he knew more but would not share under formal questioning.

The policemen agreed. Githenji's earlier statement had been guarded and cautious. Amara approaching him privately might help. The team planned to interview the housekeeper and farm manager that morning, then let Amara seek out Githenji during the break.

At 10:30 a.m., Naomi knocked, wishing them all good morning. She checked that refreshments were okay, asked if they were ready, and left. The OCS excused himself as well, leaving Lewa, Kipsang, and Amara to proceed.

Amara took her usual observer's chair. They were using the same setup as they had for the judge's interview, though the interviewee's seat was back to an ordinary one. The housekeeper entered, looking better than the day before but still strained and nervous. Her hands trembled as she sat.

Detective Lewa was at his best, calm, charming, patient. As soon as she sat, he rose, poured her a cup of tea, and handed it to her. She smiled shyly, murmuring thanks. He poured one for himself, pulled his chair closer, and sat beside her, as though two old friends were simply sharing tea.

From her seat, Amara watched the transformation. Lewa spoke gently, asking about the woman's family, her home, her years at the Manor. He shared a few personal stories of his own. Slowly, the tension drained from the housekeeper's shoulders, she visibly relaxed. Amara thought of the nursery rhyme, "Come into my parlour, said the spider to the fly." She couldn't remember how it ended, but she knew the fly had not fared well.

Once the housekeeper relaxed, Lewa took their empty cups to the trolley and sat behind the desk again, now official. The shift was subtle but effective. She was already disarmed and ready to cooperate. By the end of the interview, the housekeeper had confessed to far more than expected. She admitted being on the farm the night of the murder.

She told them Eruya had caught her stealing from the house and that she'd paid him twenty thousand shillings via mpesa for his silence, first meeting him on the bridge, then later at the pigsty. "I didn't hurt him," she whispered tearfully. "I just wanted him to keep quiet."

She confessed to introducing the farm manager to her former employer, who wanted to set up a pig farm and buy piglets cheaply. For each pig sold, she took a small commission. She explained how she stole from the Manor, how often it happened, and the types of items she stole. She kept a record of all her transactions in a notebook which she had now in her possession. She offered it to the policemen and Lewa accepted.

As the housekeeper handed over the notebook, Amara watched her movements closely, noting the hesitation in her hands. Despite the confession, Amara sensed from the woman's guarded expression and averted gaze that something remained unsaid.

Amara remembered the brass figurine and smiled bitterly; her instinct had been spot on. Though the housekeeper seemed remorseful, ashamed to have betrayed the family's trust, she still insisted she had needs and that the family had vast wealth; they could afford the loss.

Detective Lewa thanked the woman for her candour and reminded her not to discuss the interview with anyone. He helped her to her feet and escorted her out. Without a word, Sergeant Kipsang donned gloves, sealed the notebook in an evidence bag and handed them to an officer outside the study for immediate analysis.

Lewa, Kipsang, and Amara gathered again. Progress at last: motive, the boy's trickery, and money sent via Mpesa, evidence enough. She could well have killed the boy.

"She's still holding back," Amara said quietly.

Lewa met her gaze. "Agreed. We'll speak to her again when the prints come back, and we've checked her story."

They refreshed their drinks, reset the room, and called for the next interview.

Chapter 40

The Farm Manager entered the study. He looked like a ghost of his former self. The last two days had stripped him of bluster. His shoulders slumped. His voice was dull. When offered tea, he declined, eyes downcast.

Detective Lewa was gentle but more formal this time. He asked the preliminary questions for the record, then began in earnest. The manager answered most of them plainly, admitting to confronting Eruya at the storeroom that night. He said he'd wanted to speak to the boy before he could pass information to the auditor the next day. Amara raised her eyebrow in surprise. How had the news about the auditor reached the farm? She didn't speak.

He confessed: he'd pulled the boy from the pigsty, offered a bribe to keep him silent about the farm thefts. He'd sent thirty thousand shillings via M-Pesa and promised a future share of the profits.

"He accepted. Joked we could blame everything on the housekeeper and Julius," the farm manager said bitterly.

Amara, listening quietly, recognised details matching what she'd learned that morning. Yet something in his version didn't align. She made a note in her notebook as Lewa continue.

The manager also admitted to ransacking the boy's room. He used a master key while Eruya was still at the pigsty. The boy had tricked him and given him fake evidence. He found nothing in the search. He returned home to drink in frustration. He claimed he never left his house again.

Amara noticed a discrepancy and again noted it, remaining silent.

When asked about the evidence Eruya had given him that night, the manager claimed he had burned it, along with the envelope. He offered nothing further. Lewa thanked him and dismissed him.

The three regrouped. Again, they all felt the manager was withholding information and decided to interview him again later. Both suspects admitted to bribing the boy. Both had motive, opportunity, and means. Neither was cleared by this interview, on the contrary they were obviously embroiled with what happened that night. The pieces were falling into place.

Amara reminded the team that Julius also needed to be questioned. She suggested the two men interview him privately. "He will be hesitant to open up if I'm in the room," she said.

She could use the time to speak with Mr. Githenji. They agreed and would reconvene after. Amara gathered her things and headed toward the gate.

She found the old guard at the gatehouse. Greeting everyone, she asked Mr. Githenji to walk with her. He agreed, and they strolled toward the river, detouring into a copse of young trees. It was quiet, open enough to see anyone approaching, yet private enough to talk freely. They sat on a wooden bench. At first, neither spoke. Amara studied his lined face, deciding to be honest.

"I know you saw more that night than you told the police," she said softly.

He looked startled, but her calm voice reassured him. She explained that she understood his reluctance, his wish to keep his job. Then, her voice broke as she spoke of Eruya's senseless death. Tears filled her eyes. She made no attempt to hide them. "He deserves justice, Mzee Githenji," she whispered. "Please help me find it."

Defeated by her sincerity, the old man's shoulders sagged. He let out a long sigh, then began to speak. He confirmed seeing a lot on the farm that night including the housekeeper several times once by the bridge speaking with Eruya, earlier in the evening and later by the pigsty. He told her he saw judge and Naomi together near the abandoned store by the river, and later, the judge heading toward the pigsty.

"The judge left with something in his hand. After that, I didn't see him again."

Mr. Githenji explained he spent most of his time at the gate and patrolling the upper farm by the fields. He had not been there to protect Eruya or seen who had killed him. He said how badly he felt about that, and he wished he could have done more. Amara touched his hand gently and reassured him. He was not at fault. He nodded, but did not seem convinced.

Amara asked about Mwangi, his nephew. Mr. Githenji was surprised she knew their relationship. His response hadn't heard of any package or seen one with Mwangi, but confirmed the boys were close.

"If you want to speak to him, I'll call," he offered.

She accepted gratefully.

He placed the call, spoke briefly to his nephew, before handing her the phone.

Amara greeted Mwangi, offered condolences, and asked about that night. Mwangi remembered her from before and from what Eruya had told him, then surprised her.

"Shall I come and tell you all about it? I can take a boda *motorbike* right now."

She agreed and asked him to come to the Manor. They ended the call.

Before leaving, Amara thanked Mr. Githenji. She asked him to call her when Mwangi arrived, explaining that she did not want him to speak to the police first. Githenji looked relieved. They exchanged phone numbers. Finally, she promised to protect them both from wakubwa, the bosses, in case anyone might want to punish them for speaking. They walked back together and parted near the gate.

From his window, the judge saw Amara emerge from the trees and walk towards the gate, then detour to the house. She had been meeting someone, but he couldn't tell who. A muscle in his jaw twitched. He watched her, warily. The woman was learning too much. That could be dangerous.

Chapter 41

Amara returned to the house after meeting Mr. Githenji and found Julius stepping out of the study. He paused, then crossed to her quickly and wrapped her in a hug.

"I'm so sorry for my past behaviour," his voice low and unsteady. "I feel ashamed, Amara. I pray I wasn't the reason that Eruya had to die."

Amara held him a moment. He let her go, still holding her hands, and she studied his face. He continued,

"I'm going to see Mum and Dad now, to come clean about everything. They'll be hurt, but they need to hear it from me. I know I have a lot of years and wrongs to make up for. I am going to do everything in my power to earn back everybody's trust. I'm really sorry, Amara. You know that, right?"

"I know," she said gently. "You've made mistakes, but you're ready to make them right. It will take time, but with determination, you can do it, and I'll support you however you need."

She hesitated, then said to him, "After lunch, could we take a short walk? I have a proposition for you."

He nodded, grateful. "Thank you." He kissed her cheek, started for the stairs, then looked back. "Wish me luck."

"Good luck. Be blessed," she said with a small smile.

When he disappeared up the stairs, Amara walked into the study. Detective Lewa and Sergeant Kipsang were deep in conversation. She joined them, grabbing a glass of water from the side table. They reviewed the morning's progress.

Julius's statement matched the manager's about the sale of farm equipment, one dishonest act. They'd found no evidence of ill feeling toward Eruya. Staff confirmed that the boy and Julius had been friendly. He hadn't gone to the farm that day or night; his alibi held. They agreed to strike him off the suspect list.

Julius's interview had disclosed that the manager had grossly understated the value of the equipment they'd sold. That discovery reinforced motive; the manager had far more to lose if Eruya had talked.

Then Amara shared what she'd learned from Mr. Githenji. He'd seen all three suspects at the farm that night, and he placed them all at the pigsty. The policemen exchanged a glance. They both understood why Githenji was afraid; they hoped he'd never need to testify.

Amara then mentioned she was expecting Githenji's nephew, Mwangi, Eruya's close friend, who had something important to share. She asked to speak with him privately first, to gain his trust. Lewa agreed; he'd seen how much more she could draw out in informal conversation.

Just then, her phone buzzed: a call from Githenji. Mwangi had arrived.

Amara excused herself. "Give me fifteen minutes," she said, already heading for the door. She found Mwangi by the gate and recognised him from earlier visits.

He grinned shyly. "Sasa, Miss Amara? Vipi." what's up

She smiled back. "Poa, cool, let's take a walk."

They returned to the same little grove where she'd spoken to his uncle and sat on the bench. For a moment, he said nothing. Then, with a deep sigh, he began.

He told her how he and Eruya had worked together that evening, offloading a truck. How during the evening, he'd brought tea to his friend and almost collided with the manager coming from speaking with Eruya, "he scared the life out of me and almost spilled the tea I was carrying" Mwangi said. "And Eruya, looked frightened. Whatever that man told him… it really shook him."

Mwangi explained that over tea, Eruya had asked him to take a package off the farm and deliver it quietly to their common friend Suleiman. "He didn't say what was inside," Mwangi said, "just that no one must see it leave the farm."

They agreed to meet at 9:30 p.m. Right before Mwangi left the compound for the night. Eruya handed him a small rucksack. Mwangi never opened it; he took it straight to Suleiman, who seemed to be expecting it. After securing the package at his home, Suleiman had joined Mwangi, and they had gone clubbing.

Mwangi didn't learn of his friend's death until the following afternoon.

"He told me not to let Uncle see the package," Mwangi said softly. "He was desperate to make sure it left the farm." He paused, "I think…" he paused again, "I think what is in that bag is what got him killed."

Amara gasped and asked, "And your uncle never noticed you had it?"

Mwangi smiled faintly shaking his head. "He knows I'm honest, number one. And number two, I started telling him a story about Mum, his sister, and he got so caught up he didn't even notice the bag."

Mwangi explained how, after leaving the farm, he'd texted Eruya from his Boda to confirm the departure. "I told him, 'Package clear.' That was the last message I ever sent him." Mwangi ended sadly.

He fell silent, staring into the trees. "I had tried to get him to join us after his chores. He said he was tired but he might. At first, I thought he might come, but he never did. Maybe if he had come with us that night, he might still be alive today." Mwangi lowered his head sorrowfully.

Amara placed a hand on his arm. "You did the right thing, Mwangi, reaching out. Now, with this information, we might be able to get the answers that help us get justice for Eruya."

Mwangi nodded. Internally, her mind was racing. The puzzle pieces were aligning. She needed to speak with Suleiman.

She turned to Mwangi. "Can you take me to Suleiman? I have to see what's in that package."

Mwangi hesitated, then nodded. "Let me call him first."

A quick call later, he said, "He's home. Let's go."

With Mwangi's consent, Amara phoned the OCS, updating him briefly without really divulging any information. She just said she needed to leave the compound to speak to someone, and the OCS consented.

Amara suggested that Mwangi leave on foot from the Manor, and she would pick him up on the way, to avoid undue attention to him. He headed for the gate and left, walking away slowly.

Back at the house, Amara slipped in quietly, grabbed her car keys from the rack, and left. Detective Lewa and Sergeant Kipsang had been briefed by the OCS. They then contacted the police at the gate to allow her to leave. At the gate, she spoke to a police officer and asked for a few pairs of gloves. She also offered Mr. Githenji a lift home on her way. He climbed in gratefully.

A few minutes later, she collected Mwangi from the roadside and continued toward Nanyuki town. She dropped the old man at his home and drove on, following Mwangi's directions to a small apartment block near the market.

Suleiman met them outside, polite and soft-spoken. He shook her hand. "Karibu, Miss Amara. Pole sana" *very sorry* she acknowledged the pole, and then he said softly. "I was expecting you. She looked up in surprise but didn't say anything, following him and Mwangi inside.

Inside, the small flat smelled of spiced tea. Through the window, Amara noticed a car parked beneath the trees a ways away, a quiet guardian she hoped. She smiled to herself

They sat. Suleiman offered her tea or soda; she opted for tea, and Mwangi and he opened sodas. After a short prayer for Eruya, Suleiman began.

He described receiving a text from Eruya around 9:20 p.m. that Friday night. When he tried to call back, Eruya disconnected the call and sent a text. "The walls have ears, kaka brother," Suleiman said of the text. "He sent another text telling me that Mwangi would bring me a package, and that I must keep it safe until morning." Suleiman paused and shook his head sadly. "He also told me to expect him early the next morning. He said he would not join us clubbing; he was too tired."

Eruya never arrived the next day as planned, and when Suleiman tried to call him, his phone was off. Amara texted the OCS to ask if they had recovered Eruya's phone. The reply came quickly: found during the post-mortem, in evidence. She exhaled in relief.

Suleiman disappeared briefly into his back room and returned with a rucksack.

"I'm giving this to you," he said quietly. "Yesterday, when I learned from Mwangi that Eruya was dead, I opened it and found a letter addressed to me. I read it." He handed it to Amara. She pulled on gloves, opened it carefully, and read.

"Wee Kaka, things are kidogo thick around here, and I don't know if I can get out of this hot soup, Nimejiwekelea. In case… kuna bestie yangu, Miss Amara, amekuja kutoka Nairobi. Mtafute and give her this entire package from me. Tell her nilijaribu, but… life… and sometimes death… happens… but the truth will out!

Sawa kijana? Baadaye.

— Eruya."

You, brother, things are a little thick around here, and I don't know if I can get out of this hot soup I have put on myself. In case…. There is my friend Miss Amara, who has come from Nairobi. Find her and give her this entire package for me. Tell her I tried, but… Life, and sometimes death... happens, but the truth will out!

Okay, young man? Later, Eruya

Amara's hands trembled. Tears slipped down her cheeks. Eruya had known the danger, and still he'd pressed on. Suleiman handed her tissues; Mwangi bowed his head.

Wiping her tears, Amara opened the rucksack. Inside, she found folded clothes, the old laptop she'd given him, journals, a flash drive in the pocket of the jacket, and another envelope, this one still sealed and addressed to her. She opened it and read aloud.

"Miss Amara,

If you're reading this, my gamble failed, and I'm no longer with you. I'm sorry. I thought I could handle this alone. I wanted to prove to you that I learned something from you.

I found evidence that is very damaging to the people involved, against my beloved family. I had to protect them.

You'll find journals with names, dates, and amounts, enough to prove everything. If I die, it will be at the hands of one of three people: the farm manager, the housekeeper, or the judge.

The housekeeper is a thief and once stabbed a woman in the market. The manager is ruthless and greedy, and will stop at nothing to protect his interests.

Finally, there is the Judge. But Miss Amara, the judge, isn't even a judge. He's a con artist. I heard him brag about it. I've recorded proof and photos. He's been forging documents, title deeds. I saw him take papers from the Master and Madam's safe and photograph them. The next time he came, I followed him and found him hiding things in the study. I copied what I could onto a flash drive; it's in the bag.

He's also been having a relationship with Naomi. Everyone on the farm knows. Please, don't let Lauren marry that man. He's not to be trusted, and I believe he is dangerous. Finally, I have included a note with all my passwords, phone number, and computer details, just in case…! The truth will out!

Thank you for believing in me, Miss Amara. You saw something in a farmhand when no one else did. If you're reading this, finish what I started. Protect this family, and avenge my death.

Your little brother,

Eruya."

Amara folded the letter and pressed it to her chest. Tears flowed freely. The two young men sat quietly, eyes glistening, tears rolling down both their cheeks.

At last, she wiped her face and stood. "All right," she said softly. "We have to finish what he started." They both nodded, wiped their eyes, and stood up. "I have a plan," she explained, and they divided responsibilities.

They worked together,, photographing every page of every document, in every notebook. Amara copied the data from the laptop using the password Eruya had left for her; she also copied everything off the flash drive he had left onto the computer. She copied that as well onto her flash drive. She decided she'd keep her own letter and Suleiman's private for now. She told the young men to keep that just between them. She promised she would hand the letters over to the police later. They both agreed. The rest would go to the police. She slipped the two letters into her satchel along with her flash drive..

When they were done, she called the OCS. Within minutes, he arrived, greeted everyone, and listened as Mwangi and Suleiman told their stories. Suleiman handed over the rucksack and all it contained. The OCS placed it carefully into an evidence bag without looking inside.

"Will you come to the station to make formal statements?" he asked.

Both young men agreed.

Amara said she'd return to the manor. She hugged them each in turn, whispering thanks. She was now feeling more hopeful.

After the OCS drove off with the young men, Amara hesitated, then reached for her phone. She was seated in her car outside Suleiman's apartment. It was time to find out more about this judge. Based on what she'd learned, he, too, had been given a fake notebook in an envelope; had that also been destroyed?

Who was Mr. O'Brien Onifade - Double O? When Amara had mentioned him during the interview, the judge's reaction had been unmistakable. Beneath his bravado, he'd been afraid. There was a story there, and she intended to uncover it. Double O might hold some crucial pieces of this puzzle.

She called him, he picked up immediately. Their conversation was long and revealing, the kind of details that could never have surfaced in any official report. By the time they hung up, Amara understood what Eruya had meant about the judge being a con. His instincts had been right, and Double O had just confirmed it.

Here, finally, was the judge's motive. He had every reason to protect his fraudulent past, and the evidence of how much he had to lose. She queried just how far he'd go to silence anyone who threatened him. With all she knew, she still had to accept that motive was not proof of murder. Eruya's death remained unavenged. There was more work to do to get to the truth.

She had made a plan with Double O. Without revealing the situation at the manor, she suggested he speak with Detective Lewa, who might assist him. With his permission, she agreed to give Detective Lewa his number.

Amara started the car and turned toward the manor. In her rear-view mirror, she saw the vehicle on the hill reverse from the clump of trees and pull onto the road, following her at a distance. The OCS was still taking no chances with her safety.

ACT 5

Chapter 42

Amara drove back into the compound and parked. Leaving her satchel hidden beneath the seat, she locked the car and slipped the keys into her pocket. She had too much evidence to risk carelessness. After washing her hands, she hurried to the Veranda where lunch was underway. Conversation paused as she stepped out of the house. She smiled, said hello, and walked to the buffet.

The master rose and followed her. She turned to meet him. He took her hand gently. "Thank you, Amara. We truly appreciate it. I hope it's not too much."

She hugged him lightly. "I'm up for the task and happy to do it."

He smiled and touched her cheek. "You're a good girl, Amara. Thank you."

From the table, Madam called out, half-teasing, "Dearest, let the poor girl get some food! Yours is getting cold." He chuckled and went back.

Naomi approached. "There's enough for you; most people have eaten. Dessert's next."

"Please don't wait for me," Amara said. Naomi nodded and smiled.

Seeing the judge approaching, Naomi slipped quickly back inside.

Amara stepped into his path, smiling. "Hi, Judge. Have you left me a place to sit?"

He felt a flash of irritation, glancing after the retreating girl, but charm won. Looking at Amara, he smiled. and said smoothly, "Of course. Let me help you with your food."

"Thank you. Could you take these?" Amara handed him her drink and salad.

He hesitated, then shrugged took the items and walked off, seething. Did she know who he was?

Amara joined the group and sat between the siblings. "Where did you disappear to?" someone asked.

After swallowing, she said lightly, "Had to check something for a client. It's a working holiday for me, and he's flying out tonight."

Dessert arrived, and everyone stood to get some, except Amara, who was finishing her main meal and the judge, who did not seem interested in dessert.

As Amara stood to clear her plate, he leaned in. "Something for your client? On a Sunday?"

Amara smiled sweetly. "In the hospitality industry, Judge, there are no weekends or holidays, just 24/7, 365 service." That shut him up

She stacked her plates and added them to the other dirty dishes on the trolley. She wheeled the trolley toward the kitchen. On her way back to the Veranda, Naomi intercepted her near the bar.

"I'd like to speak privately, Amara," she said quietly. "It's important. And I think I have information that could help the investigation. Amara took her hand and smiled, "later tonight. Is that okay?" Naomi nodded. She grinned suddenly. "Come taste the steamed pudding, I used your recipe!"

Amara tasted. She pretended to grimace. Naomi's face fell. Amara burst out laughing. "Kidding, it's delicious! Where's the custard?"

"You're wicked," Naomi laughed in relief.

Their laughter drew smiles from the others. For a moment, the house felt normal again, shared jokes, simple joy, and a fragile hope. Later, as people drifted away, Amara noticed the vulgar wife was missing but thought little of it. She and Julius walked toward the lawn, hand in hand. When Lauren tried to follow, Julius shooed her away, grinning.

"Go away, private chat. You always have Amara. Find someone else to play with. Oh, look, your boyfriend!" Julius pointed at the judge's retreating figure.

Lauren scowled and linked arms with Naomi. "Just trying to save Amara from dying of boredom," she tossed back and walked away.

Down by the river, Amara and Julius sat on a bench in companionable silence, listening to the water.

"This place," he said, finally looking around, "I never appreciated it before. Even after everything, it's still" he paused "peaceful." He sighed. "I promise never to take life for granted again, it's too fragile."

Amara nodded. She looked keenly at Julius, another person who had transformed in the face of tragedy. She was very happy to see his change; she had always liked Julius because, even though he had been a wastrel and very irresponsible, he had always been lovable. She was glad he was now changing and taking his rightful place as the eldest son. He seemed ready to embrace his new responsibilities, and she was determined to help him at every turn.

He glanced at her. "So, what's this proposition? Want to marry me?" He grinned.

She laughed. "Absolutely not! I'm not into incest."

"Then what?"

"I'm going abroad for a month or so for work," she said. "I need someone to house-sit. You'll need a place once the divorce is filed. Just promise not to kill my plants, and please drive my car from time to time?"

He looked at her, speechless, then swept her into a hug that nearly lifted her off the bench.

"Are you serious?"

"Yes," she gasped, laughing, "if you let me breathe long enough to give you the keys."

They planned until her phone alarm chimed: 4:30 p.m., time for her meeting. Standing up, they hugged. Then, sitting back down, Julius said, "I'm going to sit here awhile and take it in, if you don't mind." She nodded, kissed his cheek, and walked away.

Sitting back down alone, Julius looked at the river. Amara's steps faded behind him. He could hear voices from the Manor in the distance, but mostly he focused on the sound of the river gurgling past from the Mountain, on its long journey to the sea.

Julius was filled with sadness for Eruya and disappointment in himself. He sat quietly listening to the wind whistling through the leaves above him and the sounds of the farm across the bridge. He took stock of himself and how he had lived his life thus far. Shame burned in him. He could barely face the mess his choices had made. He was ashamed of not being a better son or a better sibling to Lauren, Naomi, and Amara. He was ashamed of his behaviour toward his father, knowing how disappointed the old man must be, and how he had eventually given up and stopped expecting anything from him.

Finally, he was ashamed of how he shunned and hated his stepmother, the one who had never given up on him, always pushing him to do better. Yet she was the one he had resented most.

When she married his father, Julius was 10. She became the mother he had known the longest. Unlike the rumoured wicked stepmothers, she was wonderful, loving to their father and his children, and later Naomi, when she joined the family and of course Amara. His Stepmother tried to get close. Lauren allowed her in; Julius resisted with every fibre of his being.

Julius, still resentful that his mother had passed away and that his father had, within 3 years, married again, trying to replace her, at least that is how the ten-year-old boy saw it, could not cope. He had loved his mother with all his heart. She was truly his favourite person in the world, and when she was taken away by sudden illness and then death, Julius missed her terribly.

His 10 year olds grief for his mother, had turned into rage. He was angry at God, the world, and mostly his father. He needed to focus that anger, and his new stepmother was the softest target. Every effort she made, he thwarted. He loathed her with all his little being and decided to do and become the opposite of what she and his father asked or wanted.

He would not yield to their love and understanding. He would not become the son they wanted. He wanted to punish them, make them pay for the anger he felt inside and the grief he was unable to reconcile.

As he sat on the bench by the river, remembering his mother, tears ran down his face. He remembered her smile. It had been so many years since she had died, but he felt it in his gut like it had happened yesterday. The pain of losing a beloved person, feelings and thoughts he thought were quashed forever, were now at the forefront again. The death of Eruya had done that.

Though Julius and Eruya had never really been close, and Julius resented the fact that Eruya had found out a lot about what he and the farm manager were up to, Julius held no real animosity towards him. Eruya had been a kind, hardworking, and dedicated young man whose life was cut short in its prime. He deserved justice.

Eruya's death was sudden and unexpected, as had his mother's. That terrible and swift illness that had taken her from him all those years ago. Julius sat and wept, for her and for himself. The anger and resentment from wasted years poured out in his tears, leaving him empty yet feeling cleansed at last.

Eventually, he reached into his pocket and pulled out a handkerchief. Wiping his tears, he took a deep breath, and sitting on that bench, under that tree by the river, Julius made some decisions.

The very first: he chose to forgive himself. He had felt wrong and wronged for years. He was now determined to atone for his past behaviour. He marvelled at the fact that no matter how badly he had behaved in the past, he was still loved by his parents and his siblings. Amara's recent gesture proved that beyond a doubt.

Julius now saw the possibility of redemption. It would take time. It would take a lot of effort on his part. It would not be easy to make the change, but it was necessary. The biggest hurdle had been fessing up to the police. Then coming clean to his parents about his role in the farm thefts. He had been embarrassed to admit to the two police officers just how much of a wastrel he had always been. The officers were professional. They did not make him feel like the vermin he felt himself to be.

Julius also realised that the changes had begun before this trip, with his decision to end his sham of a marriage. He had made an effort with her, even going to couples counselling to try and salvage what they had. There had been no children, and for that he was grateful. He could make a clean break.

When he finally got a lawyer, he knew there would be no turning back. He knew his family had never bonded with his wife, who had never made any real effort to become a part of them; he barely knew her family. This ending was inevitable.

He was more fortunate than most, and now, in the face of Eruya's death, was he truly able to take stock and be grateful for what he had? He was determined not to waste any more time. He was going to live. He was going to make his family proud. He was going to earn the love they had always given him, though he had not deserved it. Finally, he would do everything he could to make Eruya's life count and give back tenfold.

Julius had one final, happy thought in all his musings at the bench. He would finally become the man his birth mother would be proud of. He imagined her looking down at him, smiling her gentle smile. He also knew, deep down, that his mother would have approved of and respected his stepmother and been grateful for the way she had loved the children and their father.

Julius was ready to take his place. Kuteleza si kuanguka *to slip is not to fall*, he said to himself, and with determination coursing through him, he stood up, and for the first time in days, maybe years, Julius felt good about who he was and excited about who he knew he could become. He now believed that, with time, everything would be all right. Turning, he started slowly back toward the Manor House.

Chapter 43

Amara walked into the study and closed the door behind her. She found Detective Lewa and Sergeant Kipsang deep in discussion. When she entered, they both stood up and greeted her. She walked over to the desk and pulled up a chair.

"An exciting afternoon you've had," the detective said with a wink.

Amara nodded and smiled.

"You never know where an investigation will lead," he said. "You've got sharp instincts, Miss Amara. Ever consider joining the force? I...we...would vouch for you in a heartbeat."

The sergeant agreed and smiled. Amara laughed and gave a little mock bow.

"You've found very valuable evidence. Good thinking, and thank you for calling us in," he continued. "We took statements from the young men and reviewed all the documents. Thanks also for the passwords for Eruya's phone and computer. At least Eruya had loyal friends," he paused. "At this rate, we should wrap up the investigation in a couple of days. There's enough information to incriminate the three persons of interest. Finally, evidence the judge can't just high-handedly walk away from." He smiled a little at that.

Detective Lewa paused deep in thought. Then he spoke again, "The problem, of course, is that none of this tells us which of these three people actually committed the act. And it's clear they weren't working together. There's some overlap between the manager and the housekeeper on a few things, but generally, they all operated independently. On the night in question, they were all acting purely for their own self-preservation." He looked down at his note. "What if we were missing something? What if there was another motive none of them have admitted to?"

The question hung in the air, unresolved. The three looked at each other. Sergeant Kipsang nodded in agreement.

"What if, " Amara said, knowing the detective was right.

The evidence of fraud and theft was heavy, yes. But it was not enough to prove who took Eruya's life. They needed to dig deeper. She owed Eruya that.

"What if..." began Sergeant Kipsang, smiling at the repetition, "we call the three back, and confront them with the new evidence?" See if anyone breaks and confesses? Should we start with the judge?"

They all smiled at the thought. The judge and his high-handed behaviour were not well-liked in this room. They agreed. Call the judge in "just to confirm a few things." Detective Lewa offered to fetch him himself. The judge was on the Veranda.

Both policemen left the room; one to the washroom and the other to call the judge. Amara moved quickly. She took out her recording device and placed it in the same hidden spot as before. Then she switched the judge's chair. She had just finished when Sergeant Kipsang, Detective Lewa, and the judge walked in. Lewa saw the grander chair, winked at Amara, and took his place behind the desk.

"Let it be known I am sacrificing my relaxation with my future family to help the police," the judge said, voice icy. He sneered at Amara. "A judge's duty never ends." He sat imperiously and set down his cocktail.

"Where is the OCS? Is he not the one conducting this interview?"

Detective Lewa, deferential, replied, "Apologies, your lordship. The OCS is called into a closed-door meeting with some Wakubwa from Nairobi. He asked me to stand in. He wanted me to explain, apologise and hopes you'll understand." He looked down at the table, suitably apologetic.

"Continue, then," the judge said. "I don't have all day. I must go and get ready for dinner soon."

Amara watched, impressed, as Lewa shifted from lowly, respectful officer to sharp detective in seconds. She was learning a lot from this man.

"Your lordship, after dinner that night, did you leave your room?"

"I remained in my room."

"Several witnesses are ready, under oath, to swear they saw you outside after dinner."

There was a long silence. Then the judge sighed.

"I took a turn in the garden that night. I had indigestion. The food was very rich, and I had trouble sleeping."

"In the garden of the Manor House, I assume?"

The judge nodded quickly.

"Thank you, sir," Lewa noted. "Did you, at any point, cross the river to the farm that night?"

The judge started to shake his head.

"We recovered a missing cufflink," Lewa interjected softly, forcing the judge to lean in. "Is it yours?"

Lewa did not say where it had been found.

The judge started visibly. He had not expected that. It took everything he had to regain his composure. He mumbled, blustered, and dodged. He couldn't meet Lewa's eyes.

"Again, your lordship," Lewa pressed, "witnesses saw you on the farm that night, near the pigsty. Is that true?"

The judge shot to his feet, nearly toppling the side table. His cocktail glass hit the floor and shattered into tiny pieces.

"This interview is over!" he snapped, storming out.

Detective Lewa smiled to himself. "Think on that, Judge. You'll be back here tomorrow for another round of questions."

All three allowed themselves a small smile. Amara went to the kitchen to get cleaning supplies, cleared the glass off the floor and switched the chairs back.

As soon as Amara finished tidying up, Sergeant Kipsang headed out to fetch the farm manager, who was waiting for a second interview.

This time, Sergeant Kipsang led while Lewa and Amara observed. The sergeant quickly had the manager on the defensive. He put the evidence of the manager's wrongdoing in front of him. They all expected the man to give in and finally admit what he'd been holding back.

But the manager was more afraid of whatever he was hiding, than he was of the police. He refused to speak further, even under threat of jail time. He would not say another word.

Next, the housekeeper was brought in and shown the evidence. She repeated, sneeringly, that she had already admitted her misconduct, refusing to say more. It was clear she still withheld something as well.

Amara eyed the two suspects thoughtfully, searching their faces for any sign of a crack. She realised they would need to dig up something specific, some trigger, to push them past their wall of silence.

After they left, it was clear that, except for rattling the judge, little headway had been made. The other two were still holding back. There was still a missing piece of the puzzle, either one of the three could have killed the boy. That much was clear. But which one? To break the case, they must eliminate two people and get concrete evidence of who committed the crime. With that in mind, they agreed to convene again at 10 a.m. the next morning.

Amara remembered a promise. She explained it to Detective Lewa and shared O'Brien Onifade's number. None of them knew how this man fit in yet. Still, he seemed a good source of background information on the Judge. Lewa promised to contact him before the next session. They all said goodnight, departed the room, and left Amara to close up. She got her recording device, locked the room, and went upstairs. Two people were visibly not at dinner that night.

The judge had sent Lauren a message apologising that he was unwell and would skip the meal. When she asked if she should fetch the doctor, he declined. He said he sometimes got these "attacks," and he had his own medication, and that he only needed to rest.

Amara also did not go to dinner, asking for some soup, a slice of bread, and cheese to be brought to the suite upstairs. She'd said she had too much work to do. Everyone assumed it was her hospitality work, and she let them believe that. In truth, she needed to sit in her room and go through her notes, access the cloud account, and understand what Eruya had collected.

They had to find a way to make one of the three crack and accept responsibility for the boy's death. She felt that the proof, that final, proverbial straw, was somewhere in what Eruya had left behind. Amara gathered her notes, spreading them before her, jaw set with determination. She would find the proof... soon.

Chapter 44

Amara took a long, hot shower, slipped into her pyjamas, and settled at the desk in her room to begin work. Lauren and Madam stopped by before going down to dinner, checking on her to make sure she wasn't unwell. Lauren mentioned that the judge would also not be joining them; he was feeling unwell. Amara smiled to herself. She knew the reason for his ailment.

After a while, Naomi came up, carrying a tray of soup, bread, and cheese. Amara was grateful; she was hungry. Naomi said she'd return later to collect the dishes.

Amara sat and began her work. She went through her notes. She reopened Eruya's letters and studied them again. Using the passwords he'd given her, she accessed the cloud platform and began combing through the files, opening folders, reading documents, and uploading the photos she and the young men had taken earlier that day. Still nothing. No closer to the truth.

Then she opened a folder marked Miscellaneous, and froze. There it was: concrete evidence of the judge's wrongdoing. Images of title deeds. Recordings of the judge's conversations with an accomplice, boasting about how easily he could strip the family of everything they owned. His voice was full of pride and contempt. Amara's stomach turned. What a vile man. This family had opened their lives, their home, and their hearts to him, ready to welcome him as one of them, and all the while, his plan had been to destroy them.

She stood, pacing to contain her anger. Now she understood Eruya's courage. He must have felt the same outrage, that same burning need to stop this man. Were she more impulsive, she would have marched straight downstairs to confront the judge. But…

Amara knew there was a far greater crime at hand than fraud or deceit. Someone had taken the life of an innocent boy who'd tried to protect what he loved. Greed had driven all three suspects, but one of them had gone further, ruthless enough to kill.

Her instincts told her it had to be either the judge or the housekeeper. The manager, she felt, was too much of a coward. Greedy and bullying, yes, but not murderous? But then again, it would not be the first time greed and desperation had driven someone to kill; she could not rule him out. Amara shook her head in frustration. She thought out carefully what she had learned so far. She had to accept the possibility that the manager could have been desperate enough to commit the heinous crime.

The housekeeper had once stabbed a woman in the market to keep her silent; the act proved she was capable of violence. In her interview, she had tried to justify her actions. Yes, that woman could have picked up a shovel and bludgeoned Eruya to death.

What about the judge? Double O had told her the man had been implicated in a suspicious death in Nigeria, among other things. A scammer, a narcissist, and ruthless to boot. But would he have dirtied his own hands, or paid someone else to do the job, as he was said to have done before?

Cons rarely touched anything directly; they preferred to manipulate others into doing their dirty work. According to Double O, the judge had done exactly that in Nigeria when someone he'd been dealing with had an unfortunate accident. He'd escaped justice then, but Double O now had new evidence.

Even so, none of that proved anything in this case.

No, right now, the housekeeper was the most likely culprit. She had a clear motive and the temperament. Yet Amara knew that woman would never confess, none of them would. Not to the police, not under threat of prison. The truth would only come out with new evidence or an eyewitness who'd actually seen the crime. What was the chance of that?

Amara went over the witness statements again and again, then back through the recordings, her journal, and the cloud information. Still nothing. She felt she was going crazy, certain she was missing something obvious. She decided to stretch her body and ran some water on her face, hoping this might help clear her mind.

When she returned, Naomi was there, standing over her desk, looking through the notes. At Amara's entrance, Naomi turned, startled.

"I… I was coming to check whether you'd finished your food," she stammered. "And I brought you some dessert. It's on the counter."

Amara's anger rose at herself, not the girl. She'd been careless, leaving everything so out in the open.

"You've seen what I've been working on?" she asked quietly.

Naomi nodded, eyes downcast.

Amara sighed. "Can I ask that you don't share what you've seen, or what I'm doing?"

Naomi nodded again, then suddenly burst into tears. She ran past Amara into the bathroom and slammed the door. Amara blinked, confused. Guilt over snooping? No, this was something deeper.

She remembered Naomi's earlier request for a private conversation and the change in her demeanour since that first night. Whatever was weighing on her, it was time to find out.

Amara locked her bedroom door, then knocked gently on the bathroom door.

"May I come in?"

After a long pause came a muffled, tearful, "Yes."

Amara stepped inside. Naomi sat on the floor, knees drawn up, face buried in her hands, sobbing with raw, wrenching grief, as if her world had ended. In many ways, maybe it had.

Amara sat beside her, slipped an arm around her shoulders, and let her cry. Then she reached for a hand towel from the shelf and handed it to her. Naomi wiped her face, blew her nose, and sat quietly for a moment, gathering herself. Then she began to speak.

She confessed everything, her hatred for the family, born of envy and a sense of inferiority. Her behaviour with the farmhands meant to shame the family. Her deliberate seduction of the judge, first as revenge, later as escape from this world where she felt second best. She told it all, not boastfully, but with shame and bitter remorse.

When she spoke of the night in question, she admitted she had met the judge on the farm and had threatened him. She admitted lying to him that she was pregnant.

"He still believes it," she said with a watery smile.

Amara laughed mirthlessly. "Serves him right. Let him stew."

Naomi went on. "He promised that by the end of the week, he would confess his love for me in front of the whole family, humiliate them all, and take my unborn child and me away. I believed him." She smiled bitterly. "What a fool I was."

She said she had left the judge at 11:30 p.m., and he told her he was going to a meeting. She didn't know with whom or why, but later…She hesitated, and Amara sensed there was more she wasn't yet ready to share.

"When I came back to the house," Naomi continued, "wanting to still feel close to him, I snuck into his room. I started looking around and found evidence of his corruption, papers, photos, things that proved what he was doing to this family. I didn't take them, but I photographed everything. I can show you the pictures, I'll give them to you. Feel free to give them to the police."

She paused. "Only then did I see what he really was. We were all just pawns, Lauren and I alike. He was never going to love me. I was just a means to an end."

Her voice broke. "I'm sorry for what I did to Lauren and to my family."

She went on to explain that she had returned to the abandoned store to confront him about what she had found, but once there, she had been afraid of what he could do to her and had hidden outside instead. She described finding a torn envelope and a notebook later that night inside the old store, items she'd hidden away and still had. She believed the judge's and Eruya's fingerprints would both be on them. She offered to give those too to the police via Amara.

"That's all," she said quietly. "I came back to the manor and went to bed. That's why I was so unwell the next morning. It's guilt. Shame. I've been trying to make amends, to change."

She looked up at Amara, took her hands, and looked her in the eyes.

"I am so sorry for the way I treated you all these years. I was horrible to you. I hated you," she said quietly. "I was jealous of you. You have every reason to hate me."

Amara was silent.

Naomi continued, "I know I have no right to ask," she gulped, "but I could really use a friend right now. Please forgive me." Tears filled her eyes as she added quickly, "I will understand if you don't forgive me. But..." Her voice tapered off.

Amara let go of Naomi's hands and pulled her into a hug.

"Thank you for your honesty," she said softly. "It is not an easy path back, but... You can count on my friendship and support. I am here for you, and I'll do what I can to help you."

Naomi nodded, wiping her eyes.

"That man is dangerous, Amara. We can't let him get away with what he's planning. And I swear, until that night, I had no idea what he was doing."

Amara nodded and smiled reassuringly at her. "I believe you. Wash your face and come join me for that dessert you promised."

Naomi managed a shaky laugh, washed her face, and joined Amara in the little lounge. She lacked pallor and looked exhausted, a shadow of her former self. They both served some dessert and, sitting down at the little table, began to eat.

Amara appreciated her honesty; it confirmed a few things that Amara already knew. It also answered a few questions, like the location of the judges' package given by Eruya. It also further confirmed timelines. Still, she could tell the girl was holding something back. What was it?

"Naomi," she said, "thank you for the information you have given me.

Naomi nodded.

Amara continued, It is important, I think, that you make a formal statement with the police."

Naomi visibly balked and began shaking her head.

Amara put her spoon down, reached for Naomi's hands, and held them gently.

"I can be there with you, but it is important that your statement is official and comes from you directly."

Naomi shook her head again. "Why can't you tell them what I have told you? Why do I have to be the one? What if they...? She stopped looking frantically at Amara, who smiled reassuringly.

"Naomi, you have nothing to be afraid of. No one is going to blame you for what you have done in the past. Remember, none of it is criminal; it does not even have to come up in your statement with the police."

Naomi did not look convinced, but Amara continued.

"All the police need to know is what happened on that..." she hesitated, "that night."

Naomi did not look like she was going to budge.

"Naomi, please," Amara pleaded. "I really need you to help me get justice. I think with what you know and everything the police have been able to discover, we can find the person who took Eruya's life. Please help me." Now, Amara was begging.

Naomi seemed hesitant, but finally nodded.

"But can we please do it all at the police station? I don't really want to do it here. My life could also be in danger if the murderer found out that I know as much as I do. That I was there that night, a witness," She paused. "I am afraid, Amara."

Amara felt Naomi tremble. She wrapped her arms around her and said, "This will be our secret. I will speak to Detective Lewa, and we will arrange when you go to the station to make your statement."

Naomi still looked sceptical.

Amara continued. "You know, since you are running the daily operations of the house, food shopping is one of your responsibilities. " You will plan a shopping trip, and I will simply volunteer to take you," Amara explained, then winked. "Since my car is bigger than yours." She smiled. "Trust me. No one will be the wiser."

Naomi nodded, finally convinced, and hugged Amara to seal her commitment. Then, after a moment, she added,

"Please, let me be the one to tell Lauren about the affair. She has to hear it from me, okay?"

Amara agreed. They sat together in silence, eating dessert, both women emotionally drained. That was how Lauren found them.

"You've already eaten dessert!" she laughed. "And here I was, trying to surprise you both."

The two women looked up guiltily.

"I couldn't stay another minute in that dining room," Lauren continued. "It was so depressing. I followed after you left and thought I'd bring dessert and coffee up to you, Amara. I'm not going back down there."

Amara smiled. "Good! I'll have another helping then. Its yummy! Join us?"

She got up, dished herself more dessert, and coffee, and. The three of them sat together, eating, laughing a little, the weight of the day lifting just enough. It was a gentle, quiet end to an otherwise exhausting, emotional day.

Chapter 45

The day dawned bright. Amara had not set her alarm, but still she awoke after 5:30 a.m. Mentally and emotionally, she was exhausted. She got out of bed, rinsed her face, and slipped on her slippers. Then she headed downstairs for her early coffee. She was truly a creature of habit.

Again she made enough coffee for three. Adding ginger biscuits this time. She carried everything upstairs on a tray. In the kitchenette, she poured herself a cup and settled into the lounge window seat.

The darkness had lifted. Dawn came clear and bright, full of promise. Through the open window drifted the crisp morning air. Amara shivered slightly and pulled her robe close. She loved the contrast, the cold air, her warm robe, and the steaming coffee. The rich aroma filled the air, mingling with the fresh morning breeze.

Amara smiled, trusting her instincts that today the truth would emerge. Sitting quietly with hope, she enjoyed her coffee and the solitude of morning.

After a while, she heard the door open softly. Naomi appeared, holding her own cup and biscuits, and joined Amara on the window seat.

"Morning." Amara greeted Naomi with a warm smile.

They sat side by side, sipping coffee and nibbling biscuits in the lovely warmth of the rising sun.

Naomi said quietly, "I wasn't fully honest with you yesterday."

Amara looked at her, and waited.

"After I went back to the abandoned store," Naomi continued, "I saw two others, the manager and housekeeper, both running from the pigsty. I may have seen someone else, but I'm not sure."

Her voice trailed off, and she looked away.

Amara nodded gently, her voice low, "Thank you for telling me. Remember, you have to tell them everything." She did not need to say who they were.

Amara still sensed Naomi was withholding something, maybe about being pregnant. Still, she decided to let Naomi speak in her own time. With this new information, Amara was convinced one of the two, the housekeeper or the manager, must be guilty. Perhaps even a coward could kill. Either way, they needed to speak to both immediately.

She set down her cup and took Naomi's hand.

"All will be well. I can't promise smooth sailing, but I'll be right beside you, as your friend. Whatever happens today, you won't face it alone."

Naomi looked at her with tears of gratitude in her eyes. In that moment, Naomi understood why Lauren loved Amara so much. She felt grateful for Amara's kindness and knew she could trust her.

A while later, Lauren joined them, and they sat quietly, sipping their coffee, in companionship and quiet.

Amara sent a message to Detective Lewa and went to the study before breakfast. The first interview was with the manager. It ended quickly. Once confronted with the evidence, his fingerprints on the shovel handle and the fact that he'd been seen fleeing the scene around the time the boy was killed, the man broke down.

He confessed to being there that night and bribing the boy. That was all they could get from him. Detective Lewa tried to get him to implicated someone else. He refused to speak further and was asked to wait at the gate.

Next came the housekeeper. She entered, brazen and belligerent, sure they had nothing solid against her. When confronted with the news that she had been seen fleeing the scene and that someone had witnessed her committing the act, she completely lost control. She lunged at the detective, screaming, clawing, spitting, and hurling insults.

The policemen subdued her quickly and handcuffed her to the chair. She writhed and hissed, snarling accusations. They waited. Eventually, she tired herself out. When Lewa lied and told her she had been seen committing the murder, she stopped struggling, then began to laugh, a hollow, bitter laugh.

"Go on." Lewa's tone remained cool.

Finally, she admitted that she had gone back to confront the boy for tricking her. She had taken a kitchen knife, intending to threaten him into returning her money and giving her the real evidence. With instructions via text, it was found. That was all she was willing to say.

Both the manager and housekeeper were obviously withholding some information to protect themselves. Then there was the judge. So nothing was yet conclusive, still, three suspects.

Amara, Detective Lewa, and Sergeant Kipsang moved to the far corner of the study, whispering. Then Lewa nodded, and they put their plan into motion. Amara opened the study door. At the same time, Sergeant Kipsang removed the handcuffs from the housekeeper and helped her to her feet.

"We're arresting you for the murder of the boy," the sergeant announced.

She started shrieking again, wild and defiant. Seeing the master and Madam descending the stairs for breakfast, she shouted to them,

"I've been framed! I didn't kill him. Si mimi" *its not me*

Hearing the commotion, everyone converged outside the study to witness the spectacle. The housekeeper was led out firmly, still yelling, and placed in the back of a waiting police car.

From the doorway, Amara noticed the judge standing apart, watching, and smiling faintly. He believed he was in the clear. Good, she thought. Our plan might just work.

Moments later, the manager was also escorted to a second car. Both vehicles rolled slowly down the drive and out through the gates.

Detective Lewa returned and asked to speak briefly with the family. They all gathered on the Veranda. Amara noticed that Naomi was missing, and that the judge's satisfied smirk had only deepened.

The detective cleared his throat. He began formally, "I apologise for the disturbance. The housekeeper has been arrested for the murder of the young man. She was assisted by the manager. They'll be charged accordingly. Thank you for your cooperation and patience during this investigation."

Turning directly to the judge. He said, "And, your lordship, I especially apologise to you for any inconvenience. I hope you understand this was never personal."

The judge inclined his head. "Of course." His tone was smooth.

Detective Lewa thanked him for his grace, then added,

"All interviews and curfews are lifted. You're free to move about as you wish."

A cheer of relief rippled around the group. The ordeal, they thought, was over.

Lewa excused himself to collect his things inside.

Amara turned to the master.

"Well," she said lightly, "since that's over, maybe a game of golf is long overdue? It's only nine-thirty."

The master smiled back at her.

"You're right on the money. Judge, what do you say? A round of golf to cleanse ourselves of this dreadful business?"

The judge returned the master's smile.

"Excellent idea, sir. I'll meet you at the course. Eleven o'clock tee-off?"

"Perfect," said the master, rising to get ready.

The judge turned and walked onto the lawn, phone in hand.

Madam groaned in mock dismay.

"Amara, what have you done? Now I've lost my husband to the golf course again."

Amara laughed. "I'll take the blame and keep you company," she said, smiling to herself. She had noted the judge's departure. She excused herself to fetch her satchel.

Inside, she found Detective Lewa. Quietly, she said, "He just made a phone call."

Lewa looked up but said nothing, only nodded and shook Amara's hand in farewell before leaving.

Amara returned for breakfast. The judge was back, helping himself to food. Naomi had joined, her face ashen and strained, her mood in stark contrast to the newfound lightness in the air.

Amara looked at her and said across the table, "Naomi, remember we need to go and do the shopping?"

Naomi nodded.

"What time?" Amara asked, waiting for her cue.

Naomi looked at her phone. "I'm waiting for Felicity to finish the list."

"With lunch and all, why don't we go around three p.m.?" Amara asked.

Naomi agreed, then addressed the rest of the table.

"Is there anything anyone would like us to pick up at the shops for them?"

Everybody shook their heads, except Lauren.

"Naomi, could you get some of those mini Mars Bar packets, please? AND", she emphasised, "don't let Amara open the packet."

Amara looked up in surprise as Lauren continued, shaking a finger at her.

"That one will eat them all."

Amara held her hand to her heart seeming shocked by Lauren's words

"You wound me with your accusations, Lauren. Why would you say that?"

Lauren laughed.

"Last time we bought some Amara, you ate almost all of them. I got two! Greedy girl."

Amara folded her arms, turning away in mock sulk. Everybody laughed.

Madam spoke to Naomi."I will give you a credit card to use for shopping." Naomi nodded.

"Buy a pack for Amara too, and for yourself," Madam added.

Julius protested, "What about me? What am I, yesterday's leftovers?" More laughter.

"Naomi, please buy me a packet of the mini Snickers bars," he said, then quickly added, "nix beggings!"*no one can beg me*

They laughed yet again. Amara and Naomi looked at each other knowingly. That had gone off without a question or a hitch. Naomi wrote down the orders. She agreed to get the card from Madam before they left.

Chapter 46

The judge walked calmly to his room after breakfast, humming softly to himself. The plan was proceeding well. He was past the worst of it now. No need to leave now. With those two arrested, he could finish what he'd started, and in a few days, drive back to Nairobi and disappear. He smiled at his luck.

One thing remained before he could relax completely: meeting O'Brien Onifade. He'd offer restitution for that woman, Mrs Bakari? He never remembered the names of his marks. Soon, this family, this Manor would be just another fading memory.

He packed his golf bag, got enough cash, and necessary documents into a briefcase. He slipped the key to his suitcase into his pocket. Prying eyes would not suit him now. He left the room. Crossing the lounge, he spotted Lauren. Dropping his bags, he swept her into a kiss, impulsive, out of nowhere. He chuckled at her stunned look. He could never resist a beautiful woman. He also needed to continue the lie a bit longer.

"Come on, love," he said cheerfully. "Let's go have a game with your father."

She shook her head, explaining she had things to do with her mother.

"Then promise me tomorrow morning," he said lightly. She smiled and nodded, and he added, "Later, then."

Taking up his bag, he stepped out into the sunshine. It was a beautiful day. He got into his car and drove out through the front gate, humming again. A lesser man would have kept driving straight to Nairobi, but not him. Not before finishing what he'd come here to do, what he'd planned for months. The police had nearly rattled him last night, but the danger had passed. His partner hadn't answered, but he wasn't worried. He'd find him after tying up loose ends.

Meanwhile, back at the manor, Amara was upstairs, also tying up her own loose ends. She still wasn't sure who had committed the murder, yet one last confrontation with the judge and Naomi's official statement might tip the balance. With the manager and the housekeeper already in custody, someone was sure to break.

She organised her notes, and added them to her satchel with the two withheld letters. She was ready to hand them over to the police now. She knew they'd be angry about her deception, but sometimes, she thought, the ends did justify the means.

Downstairs, the house was returning to fragile normalcy. Madam, Lauren and Naomi sorted household matters as they adjusted to life without the housekeeper. Julius was on the farm settling affairs with Mr Okelo. The Master had left for Nanyuki Sports Club.

Julius had confessed everything to his parents, shocking them. He even apologised to Madam for his past cruelty and admitted he had misjudged her. Though his parents were sceptical about his sudden change, they welcomed his new sense of responsibility in the wake of tragedy. Their tearful reconciliation renewed Julius's purpose and gave his parents hope that his change would last. They loved him and gave him grace.

By midmorning, the house felt lighter. For the first time since the tragedy, Amara sensed peace creeping back into its walls. The moral corruption had been all but removed.

The judge was not finished. His bags stayed in his room; his documents untouched. He'd even made golf plans with Lauren. He clearly intended to stay until he got what he wanted. His arrogance toward the family he betrayed was astonishing. A true psychopath, Amara thought.

As the afternoon approached inside the manor, Amara joined the women in the dining room.

"Amara," Madam called, "come help us, we're trying to reorganise everything now that…" she trailed off.

Naomi finished under her breath, "that witch is out of here," and they all laughed.

Amara joined them, grateful for the lightness, though she still sensed restraint in Naomi's manner. There were still secrets lingering behind that silence.

Lunch was casual, sandwiches from the kitchen. Julius entered, closed the door, and reminded them of his divorce. He told them he had informed his wife of his final decisions and would drive her to Nairobi the next day. Madam suggested a driver take her instead. He agreed, relieved to avoid the 3-hour journey with her. He left to arrange a driver for the trip.

Moments later, his wife burst in, as dramatic as ever. "I'm divorcing him," she said. "He's useless, and I never loved him. I wanted you all to be the first to know." They were silent. She mistook this for defeat, smiled in satisfaction, and asked for food. They pointed to the kitchen.

Around 3pm, Amara's phone rang, breaking the lazy afternoon. It was the OCS asking her to come to the station. "Ready?" she asked Naomi. Naomi nodded, and both women got up and went upstairs to get their things, ready to leave.

Naomi followed her to the car and got in.

"Amara," she said suddenly, "is the judge coming back?"

"Yes, I believe so."

Naomi hesitated, then blurted, "Please don't trust that man. He's… he's evil."

Amara nodded, and they drove off.

The drive to Nanyuki was quick; the police station was near the golf course. Naomi asked to drop Amara off at the station so she could go shopping. They agreed to meet later and stay in touch by phone. Both got out. Amara handed Naomi the keys and entered the station, where she was ushered into a meeting room with the OCS, Detective Lewa, and Sergeant Kipsang. They greeted her warmly, and the OCS gestured to a chair. The meeting began at once.

Detective Lewa briefed her on their plan. She showed all the documents she'd compiled and admitted to withholding evidence. She produced it and received a pointed reprimand from the OCS. She expected and accepted it, knowing she deserved it. She also knew that, given the same circumstances, she would do it again. She did not say that.

Detective Lewa stepped out and handed the new information to the investigator, who had Eruya's other evidence. Given the personal nature of the evidence, the policemen did not give Amara a hard time. With her apologies, they moved on. Lewa explained that neither the manager nor the housekeeper admitted to having seen the judge that night. Amara reminded the group that Naomi would be coming to the police station that afternoon to give an official statement. Amara had sent a text to Detective Lewa and the OCS about it immediately after her conversation with Naomi, when Naomi agreed to come forward as a witness.

At the same time, over at Nanyuki Golf Club, the judge stood on the tee box of hole number 18, a short par three. Two bunkers framed the green, one on either side, leaving a narrow strip between them. Beyond lay the clubhouse lawn, with neat tables, covered by bright umbrellas, and guests sipping drinks as they watched the players on their final hole. It was a beautiful afternoon. A soft breeze cooled the air, but not enough to carry the ball.

The judge positioned himself, checked the flag at the back left of the green, and took a few practice swings. Then, with full concentration, he took a full swing and struck. He held the pose watching. The ball soared through the air, perfect, until a sudden gust of wind caught it and pushed it far left, over the water hazard, towards the driving range.

He cursed softly. It had started so well. He'd been sure this shot would land him squarely on the green, finishing the round in triumph. He stepped off the mound, scowling. He got polite, sympathetic nods from his four ball partners.

Was this an omen? The round ended badly for him. A six on that hole. His overall score had been good up to the 18th, second place, but now he'd finished last. He forced smiles and handshakes as they all left the course.

At the Veranda, the group found a table and ordered drinks. The judge calculated he had just enough time for one beer before his next meeting, ten minutes away. He'd arranged to meet Double O at 4:30 and then return to the Manor in time for cocktails at sunset. He marvelled at how much this family loved their little rituals. Tonight, he thought, he'd have plenty to celebrate. In a few days, he and Lauren would drive to Nairobi, he'd drop her off, then vanish.

He needed to settle matters with Naomi that night. He would make promises about a future he never meant to keep. Now, his only fear was exposure of their affair before his forgeries were complete.

He sat back, sipping slowly, already planning his exit. The master sat across from him, content and oblivious. The judge regarded him with as much pity as a true narcissist could muster. This fraud would destroy the man and his family, yet the judge felt nothing; they were marks, not people. Merely means to his ends.

When the bill came, he paid for the table, ordered another round for the other three and paid for that as well. He could afford to be generous. He stood, made his excuses and left. At the parking, his caddy loaded the clubs into the boot. The judge tipped him handsomely, slid into his car, and followed Double O's directions to the restaurant.

Chapter 47

At the gate, he called. Double O appeared at the entrance and jerked his thumb at an old gardener to open it. The man shuffled over, his clothes dusty, head down, hands fumbling with the rusty latch. Typical, thought the judge. The idle poor are always dragging their feet. He parked beside another car, which he took to be Double O's, and the gardener shuffled back to his broom.

Straightening his jacket deliberately, the judge smoothed his collar and prepared his best mask: charm, sincerity, remorse. These always opened doors. When he suggested restitution, it would sound truthful. Double O met him at the door, smiling.

"Your lordship, welcome, and thank you for coming."

The judge shook his hand warmly.

"We're not in court, my friend. Olumide will do, or TO," he added with a grin, amused by his own wit.

They entered the small, intimate, quiet restaurant. The places currently empty and been converted into an impromptu office. Papers were laid out neatly on a central table, and a small bar stood against the wall.

"I like to be prepared," Double O said, seeing the judges glance at the bar. "It helps to offer a man a drink before we talk business."

He poured two beers and, offering one, he gestured for the judge to sit. Down to business, thought the judge.

The judge began a long speech about regret, poor judgment, and "momentary desperation", Double O leaned back, arms crossed, nodding, his face unreadable. When the judge finally finished, Double O leaned forward, extended his hand firmly, and said,

"Thank you for that, it makes my job easier."

The judge pressed his advantage. "Let me make this right, or her and for you. Name your price,"

Double O smiled faintly. "It's a lot. There's the amount you owe, my expenses, fee, and…" he paused, meeting the judge's eyes, "…the price of my silence."

Exactly what the judge had hoped for. He grinned, signalling readiness for the negotiation.

"Name it. I can afford it," he said with sudden bravado.

As Double O wrote figures in bold strokes on a notepad, the judge leaned back, a cocky smirk spreading across his face.

"You know," the judge said, "we could work together. There's money to be made in this country. Plenty of fools with too much cash. And you know what they say; fools and their money are…"

"Soon parted," Double O finished.

The judge stood, grabbed another beer, and launched into a performance, gesticulating, pacing before Double O like an actor on stage. He recounted the con at the Manor, the family, the boy, amplifying his arrogance with each gesture.

"I don't get my hands dirty," he bragged. "Money does my dirty work. I paid that boy more money that night than he'd see in a year, one hundred thousand Kenya shillings," the judge explained, "that is approximately 1.1 million Naira."

Double O listened, shaking his head in mock disbelief.

"I wasn't observed," the judge went on. "Going to meet him, yes, maybe. But leaving? No. I walked away clean. I got my evidence, and the boy got his money. He laughed, self-satisfied.

Double O rose and clapped slowly. "Bravo, your lordship. Bravo."

The sound of boots followed. The judge turned and froze. Then turned and grabbed his briefcase.

The "gardener",actually Detective Lewa, stepped inside. Behind him came the OCS and half a dozen armed men.

The judge slowly raised his hands, fingers splaying wide. The OCS nodded curtly. A constable approached and frisked the judge efficiently, removing his keys and prying the briefcase from his grasp.

"Thank you, sir," the OCS said to Double O. "We couldn't have closed this without you.

Double O inclined his head. The room was quiet except for the hum of the ceiling fan. A few minutes later, a car pulled up outside, marking the next arrival. Sergeant Kipsang entered with Amara. The judge's eyes narrowed as she entered. She hesitated at his glare, then met it steadily.

Double O smiled at her. "Miss Amara. A pleasure. Nice to see you again," he said. They shook hands.

"Since I'm clearly not leaving," the judge said coldly, "I might as well hear why I'm being detained."

A uniformed officer pulled up a chair in front of the table. The judge sat, fists clenched, as handcuffs locked him to the armrest with a metallic snap.

The OCS turned. "Detective," he said, "your show now. I've better things to do than watch a rat squirm." He tipped an imaginary hat, nodded to the team, and walked out.

Detective Lewa leaned forward. "Let's start with fraud, shall we?"

He was interrupted by his phone ringing. He had been waiting for this call; he picked up, listened, and hung up. "Do you deny attempting to defraud this family?"

The judge started to answer, but Lewa cut him off.

"Don't bother. We've already opened your suitcase. All your forged documents are there. The boy's records match them, photos, recordings, phone logs."

He smirked. "Oh, and your Nairobi partner? He's in custody. Singing like a canary. We also have your performance to Double O, it was recorded."

The judge's tone turned contemptuous. "You can try me for fraud. That's all. I have the best lawyers. I won't serve a day in jail," he said.

Lewa smiled slightly. "There's still the matter of the boy's death, Judge. Did you kill him?" Lewa asked.

The judge sneered. "Do you have proof? My talk with Double O, is that it? I said I don't get my hands dirty. And didn't you already arrest those two servants for murder? I paid the boy. He gave me the evidence. That's all."

Sergeant Kipsang placed an envelope on the table. "The notebook and letter. Only your fingerprints and the boy's. We confirmed the one hundred thousand shilling transfer via mpesa, too."

"Thank you," the judge said coldly. "That supports my claims."

"And the cufflink?" Lewa asked. "Found at the scene?"

"I never denied being there. It must've fallen off when he gave me the envelope," the judge said.

He remained belligerent. "When I left, the boy was alive. I never went back!"

"Didn't you?" Lewa said softly. "You paid him around 11:45 p.m. But you returned, because you were seen," Lewa continued. The judge tried to rise, shouting, "I did not go back! That witness is lying!"

Lewa watched him quietly until the outburst passed.

Then he turned to Double O. "Anything to add, sir?"

Double O looked at the judge for a long moment, then shook his head. "Not yet, detective. My time will come."

Lewa nodded, turned to Amara. She said nothing, only met his eyes and shook her head in disgust.

"Then let's move him to the station," Lewa said. "He'll find it's not quite the Manor House."

He gestured to Kipsang. "Sergeant, take him."

The officers un-cuffed the judge, lifted him from the chair, and then led him to a waiting car.

When they were gone, Lewa spoke quietly to Double O and Amara.

"Thank you again, Double O. Let's regroup later today? possibly tomorrow?"

"I might come by the station with Miss Amara if that is alright," Double O replied.

"Absolutely," Lewa replied. They shook hands. Lewa started moving towards the door. "See you at the station in a little while, Amara?" She nodded.

The detective left, and silence settled over the room.

Double O and Amara sat together, piecing the story from start to end. The conversation cemented them as allies. Now they both saw the full picture: every motive, every lie, every mask on the matters of deceit and fraud.

Discussing the more serious crime, Double O disagreed with Amara when she mentioned the judge. Nothing in his past double O explained, suggested that he had the personality to take a life with his own hands. He was too careful and too arrogant to get his hands dirty, choosing instead to hire others to commit physical crimes.

Double O listened and observed Amara keenly. This young woman had a gift he thought. She was intelligent and extremely observant. She also seemed to have a very good sense of people and an instinct of their characters. He liked her. Liked that she was so tenacious and so determined to bring truth tot he forefront.

He had liked her when he first met her and despite her initial hesitation of him, she was obviously wary of the judge and his intentions with Lauren. He could see how protective she was over her friend.

Now he saw he had been right about her. Through contact with her, he had connected with Detective Lewa and now finally, he had gotten the break he needed desperately with the case against the judge. Here was a woman he wanted to keep in contact with, even beyond this case. He hoped that they would be able to find the person who killed the young man. He knew Amara would not stop until she got to the truth.

They left the restaurant in his car, heading to the police station. The same question lingered in the air between them: Who actually killed Eruya?

Chapter 48

At the police station, Sergeant Kipsang and Detective Lewa, were determined to get to the bottom of things. The manager, they felt, would be the one likely to break. If he had killed the boy, it would only be a matter of time before he admitted it. He was clearly still hiding something, maybe omitting the truth. It was the job of these two men to compel him to confess.

He was brought from the holding cell to the investigation room. It was nothing like the study at the Manor House. This room was stark: two basic chairs and a table, another chair on the far side for the person being questioned. No frills. This was the police station, and things were getting very real.

He sat facing the two policemen, handcuffed to his seat. Sergeant Kipsang and Detective Lewa both held cups of tea, notes in front of them. A recording device rested on the table between them, on. Sergeant Kipsang looked hard at the farm manager. He said, "You realise that you are going to jail, don't you?"

The manager started in surprise.

Sergeant Kipsang continued, "You are going to jail. The question is what for and for how long." He looked at Detective Lewa continued, "Right now, we have you for fraud and theft." "I think detective, we should add murder to that since it is evident that he killed the boy." Lewa nodded in agreement.

The manager almost fell out of his chair. He was frightened, shaking, and trembling. He tried to speak but could not get the words out. He looked like he was about to pass out.

Detective Lewa got up, came and sat on the edge of the table nearest the manager, and looking at him said quietly, "You know it would be better for you to confess now, if you killed the boy."

The manager managed a sputter in protest, but Lewa continued, "If you did not, and know who did, then you should tell us what you know. It will be better for you in the long run."

The manager's eyes were darting back and forth, and he was obviously battling with his conscience. Thinking he should take a chance and tell the truth?

Lewa got up to give the manager time to think. He walked to the door of the room, leaned outside, and spoke to a constable in the corridor. He then came back in. The manager looked at him warily. Lewa smiled, walking back to the table.

"Mr Aricha," he said, voice full of understanding, "even if you did commit the crime, I am sure it was not premeditated, more an impulse, a spur-of-the-moment thing, right?. He paused, "So we cannot even call it murder, can we? Again, he paused, "more… an accident? At worst." Lewa let the silence stretch. "Manslaughter?" He gave the manager a look that suggested they were on the same side. The manager nodded rapidly.

"Yes," Lewa said. "I thought so", as though confirming what had already been agreed upon. "At most, manslaughter, and based on that, I am sure you will not serve too long in prison because," he paused again "you did not mean to do it."

Suddenly, as though waking up from a trance, the manager said loudly in a panicked voice, "Me? Me? I did not commit murder or manslaughter! I never laid a hand on that boy! You cannot pin that on me." Then, just as suddenly, he fell silent.

The door opened, and a policeman brought a cup of water and handed it to the detective, who placed it in front of the manager. He drank gratefully.

Then Lewa continued, "You know, it's better to just tell the truth. So why don't you sit back, relax, and close your eyes?" The manager did as he was told.

"Okay," Lewa said, "why don't you now walk us through that night as it actually happened? Start from the very beginning..."

Lewa said all of this so quietly that the manager almost felt like he was in a trance. He thought to himself, I will go back through that night and tell it as I remember it.

He opened his eyes and said to Lewa, "Okay, you already know that I met with the boy and gave him money, right?"

Lewa nodded.

The manager continued, "This is what happened after I left the boy. I swear it is the truth of what happened that night."

He began...

"I walked off into the darkness, clutching the envelope tightly to my chest. I was smiling to myself, that had been a worthwhile exercise, and with the boy now my accomplice, I could make twice as much money each month. The family trusted the boy, and I intended to take full advantage of that.

I remember thinking to myself, 'It's true every human has a price!'

I wasn't shocked. That boy's too-good act always rang false. Kumbe, he was just as crooked as the rest of us. I walked to my house. I could not risk this evidence being found in the office. It was dark as my wife was away visiting her family.

I entered, switched on the lights, closed, and locked the door. I removed boots, my wife always shouted at me about my work boots in her clean house.

Walking into the lounge I, threw the envelope on the chair, opened the little cabinet, and took out a bottle and a glass. I needed to steady my nerves. I poured a tot or two, maybe three, of Richot.

Drink in hand, I walked to the chair, sat down, and, placing the glass on the little table, picked up the envelope. A swig of the amber liquid worked. My nerves were steadying.

I tore open the envelope, checked inside, and found nothing but the notebook; I dropped the envelope to the floor. I opened the notebook labelled Farm. Page one: a section describing the farm buildings and positioning. I turned the page hurriedly, trying to get to the good stuff. More descriptions about planting seasons, cowsheds, and cows.

With a sinking feeling, I continued until I found a section: Pigs. Here now was the good stuff, I thought.

"What the hell was this?" Descriptions of different piglets and sows; the stupid boy had even named them. I kept reading, hoping to find the "evidence."

Then I saw a section on farm machinery. Granted , I saw the boy had taken an inventory of the farming machinery and dated that inventory. As the dates progressed, he had adjusted the inventory sheets to match, I realised, with the times when Julius and I had "sold the machinery."

Now we are getting somewhere, I thought. Still, only lists, no explanations. I went back to the pig section, fearing I'd missed something, looking for codes. I refused to believe the information was as mundane as it looked. The boy must have a secret code to decipher the book.

Then I had a sinking thought: the thirty thousand shillings I had sent to the boy. I reached for my phone and checked. The latest M-Pesa message, "Your transfer to Eruya Murimi has been successful." Anger burned inside of me. I snatched up the notebook again. There had to be more. My gut twisted. I hated to admit, maybe this little fool had outplayed me.

Then fear crept in. I found myself shaking. I was very angry. I grabbed the glass and downed the brandy for courage, then stood up, shaking in fear and reeling in anger. I finally accepted the boy's treachery. I remember throwing the glass across the room. It crashed and splintered at the base of the cold fireplace. I was out for blood. There was no way this boy was going to upstage me, trick me, not me and not by a young farm hand.

"No," I said loudly as I formulated a plan. "He will have to explain himself. If he cannot be reasoned with, then he will be made to comply, and he will give me that evidence by force." I found myself saying these things out loud.

I remembered that the boy was still at the pigsty; he must not have finished his work. I turned back and walked into the side room, turned on the light, and opened a little metal safe hidden under the desk. I used it so much that I knew the combination by heart. Inside, I found a particular key. I walked to a key cabinet fixed on the wall, opened it. Finding the key labelled Room #4, I took it off the hook and put it in my pocket. I left my house.

I walked to the staff quarters. It was late, and very few staff were still awake. I nodded to a couple of passing figures and kept walking until I reached the door of #4. Seeing no one around, I used the key, opened the door quickly, and stepped inside.

Keeping the light off, I locked the door behind me, turned on my torch, and started searching suitcases, anywhere I could, looking for the evidence.

It was hard work because I had to be quiet and only had the torch for light. Then I noticed the bed had been pulled away from the window, and pulled it further.

On the floor, I found some wooden planks pulled away from the boards. Aha! Basi, I thought to myself, here we are. You thought you were so clever, boy. Umepatikana! *you've been found*

I quickly moved the rest aside and looked in the cavity beneath, an excellent hiding place. Except it was empty. I searched drawers, under the bed, and between the mattresses.

I found some notebooks similar, but they were all empty; I threw them on the floor. They clattered loudly, and I had to remember I was supposed to be stealthy. I turned off the torch and listened to see if anyone had heard. Silence.

I decided then to have it out with the boy and force him to give the money back and produce the evidence. This boy was not going to get the better of me. I needed this job and would not lose it.

Leaving the room, I locked the door, and strode toward the pigsty. I did not notice the amber light of a cigarette glowing across the courtyard. I had been seen, I later found out.

I walked to the south entrance of the pigsty. I knew I would find the boy still there, working. I opened the door silently and closed it behind me; I planned to corner him.

Walking across to the north entrance, which was ajar, I stepped outside and looked around. Then I thought I saw a figure walking off in the distance toward the little abandoned store near the river, but I was not sure.

Just then, I heard hurried footsteps coming from the west side of the pigsty.

I hurriedly stepped back inside the building and jumped into one of the empty sty's near the north entrance, crouching low to the ground. I covered myself with empty burlap feed bags, held my breath, and waited.

The footsteps came closer, and then someone entered the pigsty calling, "Boy! Boy!"

I knew that voice, the housekeeper.

She stepped back out; I heard her calling softly again, then started walking toward the east side of the building.

I quickly and quietly slipped out of the pigsty and hid behind the door.

I heard a loud gasp, a clang. Something falling to the floor, I heard grappling, then rapid footsteps as she ran past just where I was standing inside the door.

I waited until I was sure she was gone before coming out slowly, sticking to the edge of the building. I saw her run rapidly back toward the cowsheds and the river.

The night was clear; the full moon illuminated everything. It was the housekeeper for sure.

I turned and walked back toward the east side of the building, then saw something on the ground. The shovel, and automatically I picked it up, thinking it did not belong there. As I picked it, I noticed something shining on it, a liquid.

I jumped back and dropped it. What had she done? That must have been the loud clanging sound I'd heard. I continued cautiously around the corner. Then I understood.

There, huddled in a mass, was the boy with a massive gash across his head. He was dead. I started to approach and stopped. He lay against the waste pipe, his left fist clenched tight even in death. I had not heard him cry out. Death must have been immediate.

For a moment, I remembered him as he had been earlier that day, polite, quick to smile, eager to please. I felt a sharp pain inside. What a waste of a young life. The housekeeper had just killed him and run off.

Then I realised: if I was found here, no one would believe I hadn't done it? The shovel, a tool I handled from time to time, lay right there, obviously the murder weapon. Now my fingerprints were on it.

Suddenly, I was terrified. I felt cold sweat bead on my forehead and slide down my neck. Had anybody seen me come into the pigsty? Could I be implicated? I had to get away from here.

I quickly walked past the shovel and re-entered the north entrance, pulling the door behind me. I walked through to the other entrance, turned off the lights, and exited the pigsty.

Not a sound, no movement except the rustle of leaves above. The moon had hidden behind the clouds; it was dark, perfect. Again, I did not know there was someone watching, unseen.

I walked quickly to the offices. If anybody saw me going to my house, I could pretend I had been working late. I opened the office door with my key and entered; I had left the office light on earlier in the evening. I sat down at my desk, shaking and shivering. All I wanted was to be in my house and for this night to be over.

However, I had to make the fake look real. I struggled to my feet, still shaking, and staggered out of the office, locking the door behind me.

I took a deep breath, bracing myself, and tried to walk nonchalantly toward my house southeast of the office and beyond the staff quarters.

I unlocked the door and entered, then closed and locked it behind me. This time, I did not even take my boots off or turn on the lights.

I staggered in the dark to the cabinet, pulled out the bottle of Richot, opened it, and slugged down the amber liquid until I felt the warmth spread through me.

I walked to the chair with the bottle in hand and sat down heavily, trying to make sense of what I had just witnessed.

The boy was dead, and I had been there and could be accused of killing him. I had been angry enough to want him dead, but I am not a violent man, yet no one would care. I was in the wrong place at the wrong time, with a very strong motive. I chugged the rest of the drink and let the bottle clatter to the floor.

Then fear and dread crept back again: I remembered my fingerprints were all over the boy's room; what if someone had seen me go there? Then to the pigsty? I would definitely be implicated.

Oh God. What was I to do? I had seen the culprit, the housekeeper, and even heard her kill the boy. But I was afraid of her. She would spin that story so well, and if I were the only witness, she would have me in jail in no time.

How could I prove I had seen her? What would I say I was doing there, hiding in the dark? It would be my word against hers. I know how ruthless she is. I knew I could never beat her.

I thought of running: pack my things, leave in the early morning, abandon the car somewhere, empty my accounts, and disappear. For a moment, the escape seemed possible. I felt exhausted. I thought I'd take a little nap first, then put my plans into action. I slept."

The manager trailed off, depleted and tired. Sergeant Kipsang and Detective Lewa looked back at him, waiting. When he did not speak, they began.

"Let me get this straight," Lewa said. "You refuse to admit you killed the boy. You say the housekeeper did it. You didn't actually see her do it, but you heard her. Right?"

The manager nodded, defeated. "Detective, I did not kill that boy. I am not a violent man, greedy, fraudulent, yes, but not violent. I did not kill him. The housekeeper did. She's ruthless. You know she once stabbed a woman in the market?"

Both policemen glanced up sharply.

"Yes," he pressed on, encouraged. "She stabbed a young woman who went against her. That woman is pure evil." He dropped his eyes. "I'll admit I'm afraid of her," he said quietly. "But I cannot accept being tried for murder when I saw and heard her kill that boy."

He looked up again, desperate. "You do believe me, don't you?"

The two policemen exchanged a look. Sergeant Kipsang said evenly, "Thank you for your statement. We'll discuss and see how to proceed." Then he added, "You do understand we'll have to tell the housekeeper that you claim to have seen what she did, yes?"

The manager jerked upright, eyes wide. Then slowly, he nodded.

"Pray that she confesses," Kipsang said. "Because right now we have your fingerprints at the scene and on the evidence. It doesn't look good for you."

The manager began shaking again. Lewa called the constable, and they led him back to the cells, a beaten man.

Chapter 49

It was time to have another conversation with the housekeeper. Sergeant Kipsang went to the door and asked that she be brought in. She was immediately cuffed to the chair. The two policemen knew how volatile she could be; they were taking no chances. They turned on the recording device.

Detective Lewa started boldly. "Why did you kill the boy?"

The housekeeper didn't take the bait. She just stared back, lips tight, eyes hard.

"You admitted to going there with a large kitchen knife. We have an eyewitness," Lewa continued.

Still, she said nothing.

He leaned forward. "And," he went on, "we have everything the boy had on you. We've already picked up your accomplice from the market."

She looked up sharply.

"Yes," Lewa said, watching her. "We've also spoken to your former employer. He told us why he had to let you go. Something about a stabbing at his home? A staff member who was going to expose you?"

She stiffened.

"We know all about your history, your violence, your ruthlessness. So, stop wasting our time and admit to this crime. It'll go easier for you if we can say you cooperated."

Sergeant Kipsang added, "Or we can add obstruction. Don't make it worse for yourself. Maybe you didn't mean to kill the boy, maybe you saw someone else do it?"

Lewa leaned back, voice calm. "Madam, help us help you. You're going to prison, but what for, and for how long, depends on what you say today. Think about it."

The housekeeper sat perfectly still for several minutes. Then she lifted her head and said quietly,

"I'll tell you what happened. I didn't kill him," she said. "I swear it."

Lewa nodded. "We're listening."

"I went to meet the boy at the pigsty, as we had arranged earlier that evening on the bridge. He was expecting me. We transacted, and just then, I heard footsteps approaching, and I took off. I didn't want anyone to see me, least of all to know I'd been on the farm. I carried the bag stuffed with clothes, the knife, and the envelope, the evidence. I was happy. I'd paid the boy twenty thousand shillings, but knew I'd make it back soon enough, selling what I planned once the family left again.

Yes, I was pleased. The boy was in my power now. I'd start using him as my messenger. Why should I take all the risks? Twenty thousand shillings well spent.

I walked quickly past the pigsty, checking to be sure no one was about, then ran a little way down the path, veered left, and joined the main track, keeping to the shadows. At the bridge, I paused, looked, listened, then crossed fast.

As I climbed toward the Manor, I saw a figure ahead. I ducked into the bushes and held my breath. It was the night guard on his rounds. I waited until he turned, then hurried silently to the side entrance. Inside my room, I locked my door and switched on the light.

I dropped the bag on the floor, tore open the envelope, and pulled out a small notebook titled Housekeeper.

'Good,' I thought. But inside: only a Window Cleaning Schedule, nothing else. No evidence.

The boy had tricked me. He had my twenty thousand, and worse, I'd sent it by M-Pesa, traceable.

I was shaking with fury. 'Who does that boy think he is? 'He won't get away with this, not while I breathe.'

Just then, Madam called from the kitchen. I composed myself and answered, "Yes, madam, I'm coming!"

She stood by the kitchen table. "There you are. I've been calling."

"Sorry, madam, I must have dozed off," I said, head bowed.

Madam smiled kindly. "No problem. I just wanted to be sure you've ordered more milk and eggs. And tomorrow, send the guard to buy newspapers and yogurt. Breakfast upstairs at eight. Do we have enough fruit?"

"Yes, madam. I did a big shopping."

"Good. Set tea, coffee, sausages, pancakes, fruit, and yogurt buffet-style in the dining room. Miss Amara's leaving early."

"Yes, madam."

She gave more instructions for lunch and dinner, Indian the next night, then finally dismissed me with a kind word. "Dinner tonight was excellent."

I forced a smile and bowed again.

Inside, I was boiling. Sick of all the bending and bowing. Sick of these people. But it was a means to an end.

And the boy, he'd humiliated me. I couldn't let that stand.

I looked at the butcher's block. The small knife was in my room. Slowly, deliberately, I picked up the larger one instead.

Turning off the light, I slipped outside, keeping to the shadows. The night was cool and silent except for the wind and the river. My anger propelled me forward.

Crossing the bridge, I walked quickly. For a moment, I thought I saw a shadow move to my left, but I wasn't sure. I crouched, waited, then kept going. The boy would still be at the pigsty. I turned onto the narrow path to the north side. The door was open.

"Boy?" I called softly. "Boy, where are you?"No answer.

I stepped out again and swept my phone light around. A glint, a shovel near the east corner. The same one he'd been using earlier. I went closer. The blade glistened.

Blood. My stomach turned. I rounded the corner and stopped.

There, crumpled by the waste-water pipe, lay the boy. The red stain was spreading down his clothes, pooling beneath him.

I dropped the knife, which clattered on the ground. I scrambled to find it and pick it up, then ran. I didn't scream. I couldn't.

By the time I reached my room, I was trembling. I locked the door and fell to the floor, shaking. Later, because of the cold, I crawled into bed. I must have slept.

In the morning, someone came knocking to deliver milk and eggs.

That is the truth, Detective. I did not kill that boy. Yes, I went to confront him. Maybe if he hadn't returned my money, I would've stabbed him, but he wouldn't have died. People don't usually die from being stabbed. Right?"

The two policemen said nothing. She went on, defensive now. "But what about the manager? He had more to lose if the boy talked. And that judge, did you check where he was that night? Always sneaking to the farm after everyone's asleep. He's a foreigner. You can't trust him." She smiled slyly, still calculating.

The two policemen watched her in silence. She didn't seem to grasp the gravity of her situation.

"You know you're going to jail," Sergeant Kipsang said finally. "Definitely for theft and fraud. And I'm still not convinced you didn't kill that boy." He turned to Lewa. "I think we should add murder to her charges. She's handy with a knife, and you heard what was said about all the previous stabbings."

The housekeeper shrieked. "It was self-defence! They all got what was coming to them!" She struggled violently, chair rattling, but the handcuffs held.

Lewa thought grimly that she could definitely have killed that boy and spun this whole story.

He said aloud, "The manager saw you kill that boy, you know."

The housekeeper, chair and all, lunged at him. Lewa dodged. She went crashing to the floor. The constable rushed in; together they lifted her upright.

"Yes, Sergeant," he said. "Let's add murder to her charges. This one can kill."

She glared at him, venomous. “Yes, I can kill you, and that stupid coward, farm manager. But I did not kill that boy.” She went silent. Staring at the floor.

“Time will tell,” Lewa said. “Right now, you’re our best suspect.” The constable led her away.

Chapter 50

The judge remembered snatching the envelope from the boy. Turning abruptly, he strode past the north entrance to the corner and on the path left towards the river, then stopped. He turned back toward the pigsty, and instead veered left onto the faint path leading to the abandoned store. From whence he had come for the initial meeting.

He had to be sure. He would not risk going all the way to the Manor, until he was certain of what he held in his hand. He walked quietly but briskly toward the shed. He was thankful that the sky had filled with clouds, creating a darkness that offered him cover. He entered, knowing it was empty. Yet, for a moment, he felt as if someone else were there. He looked around and, without turning on the light, walked to the ledge by the window and sat down.

He tore open the envelope. Inside, he found a notebook. He checked it for anything else, but it was empty. He let it fall to the ground. Using his phone's light, he flipped through the pages. He stared, stunned. His breath hitched when he realised what he was looking at. This was what he paid one hundred thousand shillings for? How could he have been so stupid? So reckless? He realised he had completely underestimated the boy.

He began to laugh bitterly at himself. He, the master of cons, had been outsmarted by a mere boy, an upstart farmhand from the village. Uneducated and common. The laughter gave way to realisation. The danger he was in hit him hard. All the anger of that day, that evening, all the suppressed feelings he had been holding down, rose like a deluge to the surface. He could not restrain them. He could not control them, even if he wanted to. They had to have an outlet.

Abruptly, he emerged from his memories of that night. Now, in the present, where was he? His eyes darted around the dim room, the cot, the cracked wall, the faint glint of metal on the door. Was this a dream? For a moment, he couldn't tell. He sat up, then the stench, the cold, and the faint scrape of footsteps from a corridor reminded him. He in a police cell.

He looked down at himself, still dressed in his golf clothes. His shoes were gone. A pair of rubber slippers lay beside the cot. He slipped them on reluctantly, grimacing at the dirt on the floor. He smiled ironically. A cell. How many men had he sent to rot in rooms just like this? Now he was the one locked up.

His head throbbed. Shaking the slippers off, he lay back down on the cot and closed his eyes, trying to piece the fragments of the past days together.

They had finally caught him. The fraud, the double-dealings, the lies. It had been a good run. He had taken risks before and always escaped unscathed. But this time, he thought bitterly, a stupid young idealistic farmhand had gotten the better of him.

Anger welled up in his gut. He closed his eyes again, letting his mind drift back to that night…

He did not remember how he left the store, only that he did, walking with blind, burning fury toward the pigsty. He entered through the north entrance, saw it empty, stepped out again, and walked toward the east. He remembered leaving again, walking past the north entrance again. Somewhere, faintly, he heard the soft rush of the river. He would later realise that it must have been when he crossed the bridge. He did not remember how he reached his room. He entered, closed the door, and went straight to the bathroom, where he started vomiting violently, barely reaching the bathtub in time. His dinner lay there, evidence of his collapse. He crumpled to the floor and lay there cold.

He remembered that when he woke hours later, a horrible stench filled the air. Wrinkling his nose, he dragged himself slowly up and saw the mess in the tub. He was horrified. What had possessed him? He remembered his walk to the pigsty, but not how he got back to his room. His hands began to tremble; his whole body followed.

He had attempted to steady himself. He had to get ahead of this fear. Fear of what? This horror. He must regain composure. Regain control. He took a deep breath, then tasted bile in his mouth. He went to the sink, scooped water in his cupped hands, rinsed, spat. Again and again. He washed his face, trying to drown out the images. The water was cool on his skin. His heart still raced, but his breath came easier. The chill in his bones remained, a chill he felt would stay with him for life.

He was not a violent man. He would have paid someone to do violence, but had never done it himself. In the past, he had set things in motion, and a man had died, but that had been distant, brought about by money and intermediaries. No one could trace that crime back to him. Or could they?

A cold dread crept in as he remembered Double O, the lawyer turned investigator. His blood curdled. Was that why he was in Nanyuki? For him? Then he shook his head. No, Double O had spoken of an old woman, the one he had swindled. That was different. Double O had no idea of his other crimes.

He exhaled slowly, relief settling over him. That, he could fix. He would offer restitution, with interest. Agree to pay Double O's fee. He was still a wealthy man. This last deal would make him wealthier still. After that, he'd retire, perhaps to the Mediterranean, buy a villa, and enjoy the spoils.

The thought gave him courage. The night's horror was already fading. He needed to finish this con and then disappear. He remembered Naomi, his suggestion that she join him. He grimaced at the thought. He remembered locking his door.

He remembered taking out his leather flask. He uncapped it. He sipped. Slowly. Deliberately. The liquid slid down his throat. LOUIS XIII COGNAC. Limited Edition. The kind that costs $5,000 a bottle. The taste of wealth, refinement, power. Yes, this was who he was. He liked the finer things, and he would have them, no matter the cost.

He remembered sitting on the bed and taking another slow sip. The warmth spread through him, steadying his hands. The boy's life, he thought, was not worth half of his.

He replaced the flask, rose, and went in to clean the bathroom. He scrubbed the tub and wiped his shoes. He stripped carefully, showered and brushed his teeth, and set his alarm. By the time his head hit the pillow, he was asleep.

Now, in the present, he found himself back in the cell. He remembered all of that, and that was all. Yet the police were telling him he had killed the boy. How could that be? He frowned. Because it never happened.

He sat up suddenly, a smile spreading across his face. They could try him for fraud, perhaps even attempted fraud, but not murder. A good lawyer could destroy that case before it even began.

He, Judge Tunde Olumide, Esq. , a killer? Absurd. He who drank the finest cognac, wore Italian suits, and could twist any truth to his advantage? Let them do their worst. Even Double O. He would face the fraud charges and win. He had been in tighter spots than this. He smiled to himself and lay back down, eyes closing slowly, the smile still there as he drifted off to sleep.

Chapter 51

The interrogation room at the police station again. Detective Lewa braced himself. Today was proving to be a very long day, though a necessary one. They needed to get to the bottom of this matter. Yet, all they seemed to be doing was going around in circles.

From the three main suspects, all they were able to bring home were cases of fraud and theft. Nothing close to murder. Each said they did not do it. Yet, each had means, motive and opportunity.

They all accused each other. The judge accused the two servants. The housekeeper accused the manager or the judge. The manager said it was the housekeeper, swearing he had heard her do it. None of them was a credible witness. If one of them did not actually confess, or unless more incriminating information arrived from an outside source, this case might end up another unsolved "accident."

Now they needed to tackle the judge yet again. They had brought him in from the restaurant, where the sting had been successful. At least they could legitimately arrest him for attempted fraud and bribery. But he was a very cool customer, and neither of those two crimes would be enough to take him, let alone keep him, in jail.

Based on the conversation with Double O, there was enough evidence to extradite him back to Nigeria to face charges that seemed to have more teeth. Still, Detective Lewa's sense of justice demanded that he find the person who ended that young man's life. Something had to give.

As he sat there, he remembered the phone call from Amara last night about a new witness to the events of that night. He had responded accordingly and set some plans in motion. Now, new evidence had been brought forward, they wanted to confront the judge and see how he reacted.

The judge was as arrogant as ever when he was brought in, still in his golf clothes and slippers. He looked around the interrogation room as though he could smell something bad. It appeared that he had been sleeping, because his clothes were rumpled and he still had sleep in his eyes. What an arrogant man, he was so sure he could beat any rap the police had on him, that he could take the time to sleep. He sat across from Detective Lewa and Sergeant Kipsang. Contempt and amusement flickered on his face.

The judge could tell they were clutching at straws and that it would only be a matter of time before they set him free. He wondered whether the family would let him back into the Manor, but figured not. He did not care. He could not continue with that con anyway, so he needed to regroup and reorganise himself to take on the next "project" that would come his way.

Turning on the recording device, Detective Lewa spoke then. "Your lordship," he said mockingly, "I hope you had a good rest in the accommodation that was provided to you? I'm sorry, it is not what you are accustomed to."

The judge looked at the detective, knowing he was trying to bait him, and said, "I can make do, thank you, and yes, I needed that rest. I was tired after playing eighteen holes of golf, and after all that's happened these last few days."

He looked away, amused and bored. He already knew the most they could do was take him to court. They would attempt to mount a case against him for attempted fraud, but with a decent lawyer, the judge knew he would not spend a day in jail beyond his present situation.

He turned to Sergeant Kipsang and asked for some water. Lewa nodded, and Kipsang got up, went to the door, and asked the constable to bring the judge some water. He sat back down.

Detective Lewa, looking at the judge, said, "Your lordship, I am begging your indulgence again." He said "your lordship" as though it was nastier and smellier than chicken droppings. The judge knew the detective was mocking him, baiting him, hoping he would lose his temper and say things he might regret later. This was not going to happen. So the detective wanted to play games, the judge thought, well, let's play games then.

He said arrogantly to the detective with a flick of his wrist, "Carry on, Detective. What can I do for you? You know I am always happy to aid the police in any way possible."

The detective gave him a mock bow and continued. He went back to asking him about that night. The judge, after his dream, or whatever that was, in the cell, was more confident on his movements. He looked the detective in the eye and repeated that he had only gone the one time, that he had taken the envelope from the boy after sending him 100,000 shillings via M-Pesa, and then returned to the Manor.

He knew he had just lied, but what was one lie in the thousands, possibly more, that he had told and would continue to tell in his life? Lies were like breathing to him, so another lie did not matter.

Also, he thought with irritation, why were they harping on about that boy as though he was important? So he had died, there were millions of others in the world to take his place, but there could only be one Judge Tunde Olumide esq. He mattered, his life mattered, not the life of that little upstart who thought he could outsmart him.

He smiled to himself. The little upstart had outsmarted him and conned him out of 100,000 Kenya shillings, something not easy to do. But there was more where that came from.

Detective Lewa, seeing his smile, asked him sternly if he thought the matter was funny. The judge looked at him with fake innocence and explained that he had not been laughing at the detective's questioning; something had just occurred to him that made him smile.

"Please, Detective, continue with your questioning."

The detective then said something the judge had not at all anticipated, though, in retrospect, he should have. "I have an eyewitness who saw you return to that boy."

The judge rolled his eyes once more. "What, another servant? Farmhand? The watchman?"

To all of these, Detective Lewa shook his head. Then he said quietly, "This person has graciously given us a complete statement of their movements that night, and in it is a clear indication of you having returned to the pigsty to confront the boy again. Do you want to hear it?"

Though his heart was pounding, he faked boredom, saying, "I am happy to listen to the statement. I am sure it is full of falsehoods. But firstly, let me ask: what time do you serve dinner here?"

Detective Lewa looked like he could knock the judge out of his chair, but being the professional he was, he said quietly, "Why don't you listen to the statement first? You may lose your appetite and not feel so hungry after it."

The judge sat back, waiting to be bored with more mundane information; Detective Lewa pressed play on a second recording device on the table, and suddenly the judge heard Naomi's voice. His blood ran cold. This he had not expected.

By the time the recording was completed, the judge realised finally that this was the end. Everything had finally come crashing around him, and he had no escape. Between this damming statement and the evidence from Double O, he could not see a way out.

He sat perfectly still. His face drained of all expression. He tried to speak, but words failed him. He opened his mouth, then closed it. He looked like he was gasping for air, but there was no sound. He looked down at his hands, palms down on the table in front of him; he did not dare look at the detective or the sergeant. He stared, only at his hands, his shoulders slumped. For the first time, probably in his life, he had nothing to say.

Detective Lewa looked at the judge with contempt and said quietly, "*The truth will out.*"

Then he and Sergeant Kipsang stood up, took the recording devices and their notebooks, and walked out of the room.

Outside the room, as the door was closing, the judge heard Detective Lewa say to the constable, “read Mr Olumide his rights, place him in custody, AND”, he emphasised, “put him on suicide watch.” The door closed. The performance was over.

Chapter 52

Naomi noticed a man watching her in the supermarket. She had seen him in another aisle and thought he was shopping too. Now he stood still, looking directly at her. When he realised she had noticed, he quickly turned into another aisle.

She felt a sudden surge of fear. She had been afraid ever since that fateful night, but could not fully articulate who or what frightened her. One of three people had killed Eruya. She knew that much. She had seen all three at the pigsty that night. As a witness, she knew she was at risk.

What if one of them had seen her too? What if Amara had said something to the wrong person?

She moved quickly toward the checkout counters, feeling safer among people. Her shopping list was nearly finished. Whatever remained could wait until tomorrow. The chocolates and sweets were near the front. Walking as nonchalantly as possible to the front of the store, she grabbed three bags of mini Mars and two bags of mini Snickers bars.

She saw the man again. Her pulse quickened. She moved faster. Relief swept over her as she found a queue with only one person ahead. Almost immediately, a woman and her two children joined behind her. All she needed to do was pay, dash to her car, and drive straight to the police station. She would be safe there.

At the register, Naomi's thoughts raced. Why the anxiety? She scanned the aisles. No sign of the man. No one else seemed to pay her any attention. She realised then that the fear had always been there. She had simply stayed busy, keeping it at bay.

Was this what Eruya had felt on his last night? Afraid, but not knowing exactly of whom?

The cashier gave her the total. Naomi paid quickly. A shop attendant offered to help with her trolley. She accepted; he was in uniform and familiar. He helped load the bags into the boot. Naomi scanned the parking lot for the man but did not see him. She tipped the attendant, got into the car, locked the doors, and drove off. As she rounded the end of the building toward the exit, she saw him again, leaning against a wall, watching her, speaking on his phone.

Naomi panicked. The police station was minutes away. She pressed the accelerator, grateful Nanyuki was a small town. Roads were clear. She drove into the police compound, parked, grabbed her bag, locked the car, and ran inside.

She approached the officer and asked for Amara or Detective Lewa. After giving her name, she was told to wait. She sat near the desk and texted Amara. Surely, no one would harm her in a police station. Then her heart stopped. The same man from the supermarket walked in. She was about to flee when Detective Lewa appeared, greeted the man, and spoke to him quietly. The man nodded and followed him.

"Good afternoon, Miss Naomi," Lewa said kindly. "I hope you haven't waited long."

She shook her head, unable to speak.

"I'd like you to meet Sergeant Kamau."

Relief washed over her. She gave a brittle, hysterical laugh, then stopped herself. "Sergeant Kamau? Thank God.

I thought you were stalking me. I saw you in the supermarket and assumed the worst. I'm sorry. I've been on edge."

Lewa smiled gently. "I understand. Shall we?"

She followed them. Breathing easier now. Inside the interview room, Sergeant Kipsang was waiting. He stood and greeted her. Lewa offered her a drink; she chose water. Sergeant Kamau stepped out to get it. Once seated, Lewa thanked her for coming. He told her that Amara had contacted him after Naomi confided in her. Lewa had arranged immediate protection; Sergeant Kamau had been nearby the whole time.

Naomi nodded. "Yes. I was scared. I knew that if anyone realised I was a witness, I could be in danger."

Lewa explained the next steps: recording, transcription, and signing. He offered to have Amara or a female officer present. Naomi declined but asked if she could change her mind. Lewa agreed.

Naomi settled into her chair. She closed her eyes. She wanted to make sure she remembered everything that had happened that night. She held her hands on her lap. Took a deep breath. She looked at Lewa. "I feel terrible about what happened to Eruya. He did not deserve it. I realise it's important for me to tell you what I witnessed that night."

She stopped and looked at Detective Lewa. "I hope that what I tell you will help your investigation."

She stopped. Closed her eyes tightly. Opened them. Placed a fist firmly on the table.

"I swear to tell you the truth of what I know." She breathed out shakily. "May it help bring justice to Eruya."

She smiled at the detective, who smiled back. She took a deep breath and nodded. He nodded and turned on the recorder. She began.

She told of her meeting with the judge at the abandoned store, how she had gone there to confront him, to force him to tell the family about their love and his intention to take her away and build a life together.

Naomi paused, closed her eyes, and was deep in thought. When she spoke, it was as if she were back on the farm, reliving that night.

"Earlier that evening, I had felt as though I were floating. The judge's last words as he ushered me out of the store still rang in my ears."

"Later, darling. Remember, I'm yours. Go now."

"He had never spoken to me so gently. So lovingly. His touch had felt like silk. In that moment, I had felt cherished. Special. I remembered thinking: So this is how love feels."

Naomi was smiling as she relived that memory. Her mouth curved, her eyes grew distant.

"I walked back toward the Manor, barely touching the ground, basking in the warmth of his words and kisses. I did not bother to hide. If anyone saw me, they would assume I was with a farmhand. They would never imagine it was the judge.

"Crossing the bridge, I remembered thinking: if I saw the leopard everyone whispered about, I would hug it. Everything deserved love.

Inside the Manor, all was quiet. I wandered through the lounge, touching the furniture, imagining the family gathered as the judge declared his love for me. I imagined walking toward him, past their shocked faces, and taking his hand.

My uncle and aunt, speechless. Julius, stunned. His wife pleased, another heir displaced. Amara staring in disbelief. Lauren broken, running out of the room, humiliated.

At the time, I felt no shame or remorse. They deserved it.

I wanted to hold onto that feeling of euphoria, so instead of going to my room, I went to the judge's. I removed my shoes, entered quietly, lay on his bed, breathed in his scent. When it wasn't enough, I opened his wardrobe, burying my face in his clothes.

Then I saw the suitcase. I opened it without knowing why. Inside were documents: title deeds, seals, stamps, and the names of my aunt and uncle. Then I saw several sales agreements, for the manor and a few other assets belonging to my family. For each one, the seller, Tunde Olumide Esq., the Judge.

The truth hit me with brutal clarity. I realised I had been used. The affair, the secrecy, the timing, all of it had been a cover for fraud. I laughed bitterly, then cried. I had been a fool. And like Lauren, a pawn.

Then I understood why he got so angry at my disclosure and threat. I was jeopardising everything he had planned for months. My cousin, like me, had just been a pawn in his little game. I even more so. He liked the pleasure of the underhandedness, having me behind everyone's back. While professing to love Lauren.

I had bought into it all, stupidly thinking that he genuinely liked me, maybe even loved me. The sex was real, but love? Like he had professed earlier that night in the abandoned store? I shook my head and laughed again at myself as angry tears ran down my face. How could I have been so blind?

Then I got angry, so angry all I wanted to do was hurt him, make him pay for the treachery. I am a fighter. I wiped away my tears and became determined. He would not get away with this. He would not hurt me and escape the consequences. I might be vindictive, vengeful even. Deep inside, I knew I owed my family a lot. They had given me much. I certainly did not want them hurt, let alone destroyed. I decided on a plan.

Who the hell did this Nigerian devil think he was? He wasn't even that handsome. Our lovemaking had seemed fantastic only because I had faked my screams and sighs for his ego. Men like him needed to believe they had satisfied their partners. So I let him believe what he wanted. In truth, I found more pleasure with some of the farmhands.

Now that I understood what was really going on. I was determined to right some wrongs. I would not let him get away with this. I would bide my time that week, and at the right moment, divulge all I knew, in as public a way as possible. I would make sure he never showed his face before that family again.

I went back to the suitcase. First, I took a picture of the items' positions inside, then reached in and found all the pertinent documents, quickly scanning each one. I took pictures of the seals and stamps, including their inscriptions, then carefully replaced everything using the initial photo as a reference, arranging the items exactly as I had found them.

I looked around once more. Slowly, quietly, I backed out of the room, shutting the door gently behind me. I ran on tiptoe to where I had left my shoes. I decided to go back out through the Veranda and across to the farm. I was angry enough to want to confront him about what I had found. Pulling up my black hoodie, I ran across the bridge. I hugged the hedges and the darkness, then veered left in the direction of the abandoned store. I hoped he would still be there.

I heard footsteps coming toward the store, and, having second thoughts about confronting him, I did not go inside. Instead, I walked quickly past to the north of the little store and crouched down out of sight, waiting.

It was the judge. I knew his scent anywhere. Before, I had savoured his masculine cologne; now it made me want to gag. I restrained myself and waited. He entered the store, and within minutes, I heard the rip; later, I learned it was an envelope. I could feel his anger emanating from him as he growled and cursed harshly under his breath. In the quiet, each whisper was like a shout. Whatever he had found in that envelope, he had not liked.

Suddenly, he got up, and I heard him walk out of the store, striding aggressively up the hill toward the north side of the pigsty. I decided to follow him quietly, stopping whenever I got too close, lest he turn and see me. He seemed oblivious to everything around him, walking with such determination. Though I could not see his face, I could see, even from a distance, his body heaving with rage.

I saw him walk briefly into the north entrance of the pigsty then out towards the east. I quickly ran behind him and entered that entrance. I hid against the wall next to the door. I heard his footsteps a moment later, and my heart dropped. If he had come back into that entrance, he would have seen me standing there.

He did not. He walked past, heading west past the pigsty, veering left toward the main farm path and down toward the river. I did not follow him."

At this point, Naomi stopped speaking. Tears were streaming down her face; she was shaking, breathing heavily and wringing her hands. Detective Lewa paused the recording device. He looked at her and said, "Miss Naomi, are you okay? Do you want to stop?" He was concerned.

Naomi tried taking hold of herself. She was losing control. Her heart was pounding as she relived that night. She realised that she had not allowed herself to remember the details before. She remembered now. Now, as she told her story, she felt it all, every emotion, every scent, every smell. She looked at Detective Lewa and shook her head over and over again, trying to get control of her emotions.

The policemen watched the anguish in silence. Eventually, Naomi got control of herself enough to look up at Detective Lewa and say, "Can you please get Amara for me?"

As Sergeant Kamau was getting up, the door opened, and Amara walked in. Naomi stood up from her seat and ran to Amara, grateful that she was there for her as she had said she would be. They embraced, both crying uncontrollably.

They stood there hugging, giving each other grace and power. Amara rubbed Naomi's back and soothed her, saying, "It will be okay, Naomi. All will be well. Be strong. I am right here with you."

Sergeant Kamau pulled another seat next to Naomi's and the two women sat down. Sergeant Kipsang got Amara's attention and handed her a box of tissues. Settling down once more with Amara at her side, Naomi attempted a smile.

Amara asked, "Would you like me to stay here with you?"

Naomi nodded. She blew her nose, wiped her face, and, looking at the policemen, said through her tears, "I am so sorry. I do not know what has come over me. I don't usually lose control like this."

She inhaled and exhaled a few times, trying to calm herself down. She reached for Amara's hand again, sat up, and, taking a few more deep breaths, she looked at Detective Lewa and nodded.

Detective Lewa began recording again.

"I remembered waiting in the dark, then I quickly ran, as fast as I could, not toward the main path, but back toward the abandoned store. I ran to the right side of it and crouched where I had before, listening, watching. Heart in my throat.

I heard footsteps and crawled backwards. From there, I could see the pigsty. But even if someone looked toward the store, they could not see me. I saw the housekeeper striding into the north entrance. I caught the glint of something in her hand. My heart beat so fast I thought it might burst. I was terrified, yet curious.

She walked in through the north entrance. Immediately, she walked out and towards the east corner. Moments later, I saw her flying out of there as though chased by demons. She had something glinting in her hand. She ran down the path toward the river, and I heard her bounding across to the other side.

Then, as I was about to move, I saw movement in the north entrance of the pigsty. What was happening? Was everybody awake and about? I stopped, watching.

I saw a man. In the moonlight, I recognised his gait; it was the manager. He had a slight limp, I knew well. He walked to the east of the pigsty, picked up something, looked at it, and then quickly dropped it back. He rounded the corner, then came around it again rapidly, entered the pigsty, and I saw him shutting the entrance door, running across and exiting through the south entrance after turning off the lights.

I sat there, shivering in the dark and the cold, and asked myself what on earth I had just witnessed.

When I was sure everything was quiet again, I stood up and made my way into the store. I could not trust my legs to take me across the bridge to the Manor. I did not need to turn on the light; the full moon illuminated the entire room.

As I walked in, I noticed the notebook and torn envelope on the floor. Instinctively, I reached into my pocket and drew out a handkerchief. Using it, I picked up the book, then the envelope, slipped the book inside, and placed them both into the large front pocket of my hoodie.

I sat down; it was all too much. I bent forward and covered my eyes with my hands. I sat there for a while, twenty minutes, an hour, maybe two, I was not sure. I was not asleep; I was just, trying to take it all in. So much had happened that night. One thing I was very sure of was that the person I had been at the beginning of the evening was not the person I was now, and would never be again.

I saw the people around me with new eyes. I appreciated my situation more than I had ever allowed myself to before. I thought of my family, their love and protection of me all those years, and I felt ashamed. I thought of Amara, such a true friend to the family, and of my hatred of her, which I had to admit was rooted in jealousy."

At this, Naomi gave Amara an apologetic smile and squeezed her hand. Amara returned the smile and said, "It is okay, Naomi. I understand."

Naomi continued telling them how she burst into tears, and through those tears, she finally experienced loss, acceptance, and understanding. She felt the sorrow for Eruya, the family, even for Amara, whom she knew had shared a special bond with him. She remembered, she cried uncontrollably until she had no tears left.

"I wiped my face, then got up and left the store. I felt tired. Heading back to the Manor, I crossed the bridge, and walked up to the house, entered again through the Veranda, took off my boots at the door, and carried them inside. I walked quietly to my room, entered, shut, and locked the door.

I put the envelope in a special hiding place I had found, knowing it was important, though I did not know why. I placed my phone on the bedside table and threw myself on the bed fully clothed. I remembered crying myself to sleep."

Naomi paused. The room was quiet, and time stood still. Detective Lewa paused the recording machine.

Finally, Naomi gripped Amara's hand and looked directly at her. Amara squeezed back and smiled encouragingly. Naomi looked at Detective Lewa and said, "I have left out a very crucial part of what happened that night."

He looked at her, nodded, and turned the recording device back on. Naomi continued.

"I said that I had followed the judge to the pigsty and hidden inside. The truth is, I had seen and heard something while there. After he walked towards the east side of the building, hiding just inside the door, I could see him through the window. He walked to the corner of the pigsty, and I saw him lift something from the wall. I realised later that it was a shovel. I saw him raise it and strike. Three loud thuds.

Then he turned back from the corner, and I heard a heavy clanging sound as he dropped it. He walked right past me, heading towards the river. He was not running or looking bothered. He walked with determination, not looking back.

I stood there frozen, but once I was sure he was out of sight, I ran out of the pigsty and moved to my right. I saw a shovel on the ground where he must have dropped it, something on it gleaming in the moonlight. I walked past it and rounded the corner. In horror, I understood the reason for the three thuds and knew without a doubt what it was gleaming on the shovel.

Eruya was crouched, huddled against the wall leaning on the waste-water pipe, dead.

I almost fainted, gasping for air. I had never seen a dead person before. Blood was trickling down his clothes and pooling on the floor.

I could not believe it. I saw it all. I heard the judge pick up the shovel, saw him raise it and strike three times. I heard the thuds, then the clang as something was dropped. Finally, I heard his footsteps as he walked right past me on his way back to the Manor.

The judge killed Eruya. And I witnessed it.

I remember standing there shaking, trying to make sense of what I was seeing, what I had just witnessed. The realisation hit me so hard that, again, I almost fainted. What sort of monster was this judge to so brutally take a life and then walk away as though nothing had happened? He had not even run. He just walked. I looked directly at him, though I doubt he even saw me. He was not shaking. He seemed steady, controlled. His face, as I remembered, illuminated by the moonlight, had no expression at all."

Naomi, in a tired, resigned voice, continued with her statement. "After seeing Eruya dead, I somehow found the strength to go back towards the abandoned store and, hiding in the dark, saw the other two as I told you before. The rest of the night was as I had earlier stated."

Naomi fell quiet, realising that this was the first time she had allowed herself to fully relive the horror of that night. Suddenly, she felt drained, tired, very, very tired, and she leaned heavily on Amara. Both women wept. Detective Lewa stopped the recording, and the men quietly left the room, giving the two young women privacy to grieve.

Epilogue 1

Amara and Naomi sat in the interview room. Minutes dragged into what felt like hours. Both women had endured so much. When the final clue to the mystery was revealed, a wave of new feeling overcame them; it was as if their hearts and souls were finally free, free at last to truly grieve for Eruya. With the case solved, a heavy weight was lifted from their minds, making space for grief.

Both women let themselves go. After a box of tissues, countless hugs, and plenty of tears, they knew it was time. They had to leave, face the rest of the world with the final truth.

Detective Lewa had instructed the officers to leave the women alone and not disturb them. When they eventually walked out of the room and into the bathroom to wash their faces, a constable met them. He informed them that Detective Lewa wanted to see them, or, more specifically, Amara, before she left the police station.

Naomi understood. Frankly, she did not feel capable of doing anything more at that point. Quietly, she said, "Amara, I'm going to wait in the car, if you don't mind."

Amara nodded and watched Naomi walk slowly down the corridor and out through the main door to the car in the parking lot. She then turned and followed the policeman to Detective Lewa's office.

When she entered, she found Detective Lewa and Sergeant Kipsang in deep discussion, which halted upon her arrival. They both stood to greet her and offered her a cup of tea. She opted for water. The constable left the office and closed the door behind him.

Detective Lewa eyed Amara carefully. She must have looked a mess: eyes bloodshot from crying, nose red from repeatedly blowing it, face worn from the emotional toll and resolution. Trying to keep herself together, she sat up, forced a sad smile, and said, "At least now we finally know." The officers nodded.

Detective Lewa quietly outlined the next steps, including returning to the Manor, where the OCS would brief the family. He thanked Amara for her help and asked her to bring Naomi back to the police station the following day to review and sign her statement.

Amara stood. "I'll see you at the Manor then?" she asked, glancing at her watch. "Around 5:30 p.m.?" They nodded. Rising, they all shook hands, and Amara left to join Naomi in the car. Before setting out for the manor, she phoned to ensure that Lauren and Julius would prepare everything for the meeting and inform their parents.

Naomi was sitting in the passenger seat. As Amara got in, she looked at her long and hard, then offered a tentative smile, which Naomi returned. Amara started the car, reversed, and drove from the police station toward the Manor. The women did not speak much during the drive, both lost in their thoughts.

Amara was physically exhausted and emotionally drained. Nevertheless, tomorrow, and for the rest of the week, she would still need to complete the tourism work that had brought her there. She reminded herself that she had taken time off to help the police conclude the investigation and bring justice for Eruya.

Driving slowly through Nanyuki, the end of the railroad. Amara thought sadly that for Eruya, it had indeed been the end of the line. Tears slid down her cheeks. She remembered him smiling, hopeful, full of life and loyalty. That same loyalty, she thought bitterly, had cost him everything. He sacrificed it all for this family.

Wiping her tears, she forced herself to focus. She had listened to every interrogation. Spoken with Double O at length and learned the full truth about the man who had called himself a judge. Now she had to face the family. Finally, they would know everything, the status of the case and the fate awaiting those involved.

She dreaded what was coming. The weight of truth pressed on all of them in different ways: Lauren would be devastated. The master and madam, deceived and robbed. Julius would be confronted with his own failings. Naomi would have to face the family who had given her everything and admit her betrayal. None of it would be easy. Amara took a deep breath and braced herself, steeling for the hard evening ahead.

"The truth will out" Eruya had written in his final message. And so it had! Using the breadcrumbs he had left, the police investigation, her help and Naomi's testimony, had uncovered it all.

As Amara turned through the Manor gates, dusk set in. The grey and indigo now softened into a blaze of orange and deep burgundy on the horizon. It was a beautiful evening, especially for a day that started laden with shadows and secrets. Today brought resolution: an end to doubt, freedom for the family, and, finally, justice and peace for Eruya.

The OCS and Double O had arrived first. She assumed Detective Lewa and Sergeant Kipsang would follow shortly. They had agreed to brief the family together, a final official act before handing the house back to its owners. At dusk, the family always gathered on the Veranda. Tonight, that ritual would hold a higher purpose.

As Amara approached the front entrance, turning off the engine, she looked at Naomi. "Go on inside and upstairs. I'll help the staff unload the shopping and join you."

Naomi smiled in relief and walked into the house and up the stairs. She met Imma at the door. Imma briefly returned to the kitchen and then came back out with Felicity. Together, they headed toward Amara's car. Seeing Amara, Felicity hugged her, took the car keys, and told her they would handle the unloading. Amara smiled gratefully and went inside.

She hurried upstairs, sad but resolute. Amara freshened up quickly. As she left her room, Naomi was waiting for her. The women hugged. Holding hands, they walked downstairs and out to the Veranda, where the visitors and the rest of the family were gathered.

The judge, of course, was in custody, and the vulgar wife had left with a driver, early that morning for Nairobi.

Amara greeted the family. She nodded to the OCS and Double O, then exchanged brief smiles with Lewa and Kipsang, who had just arrived. Both she and Naomi took refreshments and sat down next to Lauren and Julius.

Sergeant Kipsang opened with a short prayer. Then the OCS stood. He thanked the family for their grace during the investigation and the way they received his officers. He spoke of closure, justice taking its course, and the charges already confirmed: theft and fraud for the housekeeper and manager, and fraud for the man they knew as "the judge."

Pausing, he added that it had been proven that the judge had killed Eruya. A gasp of horror rippled through the family. Naomi lowered her head further as Amara tightened her grip on her hand. The OCS paused, allowing the truth to sink in. Then he formally introduced Double O and sat down.

A murmur passed through the group as Double O stood. He explained that he was a lawyer turned private investigator from Nigeria, pursuing the man they knew as a judge; a seasoned con artist wanted for multiple crimes. He confirmed that police in Nairobi had arrested an accomplice. Through a plea bargain, this accomplice would provide crucial testimony. Then came the final truth: the "judge" had never been a judge at all. Not even a lawyer. He had left school at sixteen but possessed a brilliant mind and a dangerous talent for deception.

Lauren turned grey; she looked ready to pass out from shock. Noticing her distress, Double O said gently, "The entire Nigerian bar was fooled. He was that good."

He went on to describe his year-long pursuit of the man's frauds and the suspicious deaths linked to him. Those cases had now been reopened. Kenyan and Nigerian authorities would work together to ensure justice was finally served.

He thanked the family for their patience and singled out Amara for her cooperation. With a small nod from her, he explained that he first met her at a golf tournament in Nairobi and, upon realising the connection between her, Lauren, and the judge he was pursuing, he reached out. Though Amara was initially hesitant, they exchanged numbers and agreed to share information.

Amara turned to Lauren. "I wanted to protect you," she said softly. "Something didn't feel right." Lauren squeezed her hand. "Thank you."

The OCS stood and thanked the family again. He said the officers, including Double O, would leave now to give them privacy. Detective Lewa would return the following day to collect items from the judge's room, which was to remain sealed.

They all rose. There were handshakes and quiet words of gratitude. Amara noticed Detective Lewa step aside to speak quietly with Naomi, who nodded. The master, madam, and Amara walked the officers to their cars to see them off. When they returned, the master and madam embraced Amara and said simply, "Thank you."

They agreed to meet for dinner at 8:00 p.m. to make plans for the next few days.

Epilogue 2

Dinner was a sombre affair; each person lost in their own thoughts. Everyone at the table bore a measure of guilt. They faced with dread the role each had played in Eruya's demise. All wondered which signs had gone unnoticed, which choices could have changed the outcome. None was spared that burden. They accepted the truth now, questioning how it came to this, a young life cut short.

The Master, on his own compound, his own staff, his farm manager and housekeeper. Closer to home, his daughter and niece were at the mercy of that man. He shuddered at the thought. He was supposed to be the protector of this family, and all the while, he had been oblivious to what was obviously happening, until the devastating outcome.

He made a resolution to be more present with his family, pay more attention, and not assume all was okay. He looked at Julius and Naomi and realised he had neglected both and relegated the responsibility to his wife, who already had too much on her plate. Things would have to change immediately. Moving forward, he would be the head of that family in the way he ought.

Madam blamed herself particularly. She was the one who had instigated the audit and encouraged young Eruya to come forward with his proof of the wrongdoings. How could she have exposed that young man to such danger, caring only that she got to the bottom of things, not acknowledging how exposed he was and protecting him from his final demise? She had set things in motion, and that motion had taken

Eruya's life. She felt morally and emotionally responsible. She would probably never be able to fully forgive herself.

Julius felt complicit in the madness that led to that fateful night. Eruya had been trying to protect that which he should have been protecting. He hurt deeply at the thought that the young man had loved this home and family more than Julius himself had. If he had been the sort of son he was supposed to be, he would have found out what Eruya had found out and put a stop to it, long before that fateful night.

Now he was determined to spend the rest of his life living up to his rightful place. He would make whatever changes he needed. Earning his family's trust and finally becoming the son they could be proud of.

Lauren marvelled sadly at how she had got it so wrong. She had met this man, spent time with him, enjoyed his company, believed his lies and cons. She had exposed her family to a dangerous criminal who eventually killed an innocent boy. All because she could not see beyond the façade. Double O had said it wasn't her fault, but she felt it was. To compound it, in exposing her family, she had given this man access to documents and personal details by leaving her parents' room open, again exposing the whole family to risk and ruin. She had set things in motion with her naivety that led to Eruya's death, and she would have to accept that and maybe, in time, learn to forgive herself.

Though Lauren had not been in love with the judge, she had liked him a lot, and she had completely fallen for his charm, accepting him for who he said he was without question. Truth be told, she resented Amara's obvious reserve somewhat, feeling that Amara was being unfair and not giving the judge a fair chance. Now she knew better. She needed to wake up and make braver choices. She was resolved.

A lot had happened, and Naomi felt that much of it was her fault. She had not brought the judge into the family; however, in her desire to spite them, she had allowed someone, dangerous to almost destroy them. She had been so caught up in her own sense of injustice that, even though the warning signs were there, she had done nothing to stop it or alert others to the danger of this man. She was, however, very glad that her testimony was what had provided the police with the final piece of the puzzle. Finally, thanks to her observations, the question about who killed Eruya could be answered, and justice would be served. Finally, she could give back to the family that had already given her so much.

Finally, Amara. The heaviness she felt was real. Had she not suggested that Eruya observe and document what was going on on the farm, he would not have ended up in such grave danger. She had encouraged him, even given him guidance, not knowing that all of this would culminate in his death. If she had known that was going to happen, she would have willingly only shared coffee with him. He would still be alive today.

Her heart was broken. She had thought she was being a good mentor, encouraging a young man in the art of observation. Unfortunately, this time, that observation led to him knowing too much about very dangerous people, and one of them took his life for what he knew.

She would always miss him. She knew she could not undo the situation or change it, but she was changed, probably forever. Going forward, she would be careful how she advised people and what she allowed them to expose themselves to. Amara had always thought that truth was everything, that knowledge was power, and that it should be sought at all costs. Now she knew better. She was sadder and wiser.

They all sat, barely eating or speaking as they absorbed what had happened. During that dinner, the Master and Madam stated that the next night they would hold a short prayer service at the north end of the pigsties, near where Eruya had fallen. They would hold it in the evening at 5 p.m. and invite all the farm workers and Eruya's friends in Nanyuki. They asked around the table for help to organise it.

They turned to Amara and asked her to reach out to Eruya's friends and invite them. They also asked her and Julius to work on the logistics and programme for the event. Lauren and Naomi were to work with the staff to get refreshments for everyone after the short service. The Master would reach out to the OCS and his team, and he and Madam would arrange with the church to send someone to conduct the service. They all nodded in agreement.

Amara made a mental note to invite Double O. In her dealings with him, she had found a mutual respect and instinctive trust. somehow she know their paths would cross again.

The role he played in the investigation and the information he shared were instrumental in revealing the judge's true character and bringing him to justice. She decided that while he was in town this week, finalising with the police, she would reach out and ask him to have a coffee with her. She felt she could learn a lot from this man.

Additionally, the Master and Madam shared that they were resolved to visit the boy's mother. They would ensure his sacrifice had not been in vain: they would pay for the funeral, support his family, and place his savings, including the money taken from the three culprits, into a trust. Julius offered to work with them on that and assist with all the arrangements. They all agreed they would attend the funeral as a family.

After dinner, they all cleared up and headed to bed. Naomi had officially moved upstairs, so after locking up and saying goodnight, they headed to their respective rooms and straight to bed.

At 4:30 a.m., Amara woke as usual, dressed quietly, made her coffee, and slipped outside with her satchel. She crossed the bridge to the farm, followed the path past the buildings, through the grove of trees, and up the hill. At the top, she sat and waited.

Only then did she allow herself to think, to breathe, to feel. She smelled the dawn air, rich with earth and morning dew. When the sun rose, it came with a gust of wind carrying the scent of wildflowers and honey from the mountain. Amara breathed deeply, letting it fill her lungs. As the first rays appeared over the horizon, she waited in anticipation. The light touched her legs first, then her hands, and finally her face.

She bowed her head and whispered a prayer for Eruya, asking God to let him rest in eternal peace, and asking him to forgive her, and to know that she had fulfilled her promise to him. Now he could truly rest.

Just then, a strong gust of wind swept past her, this time toward the mountain, and she knew in her heart that all would be well. There, in the first warmth of the day, Amara made peace with herself, knowing that finally, the truth had set them all free.

Acknowledgements

My heartfelt thanks to, my beta readers, and my tribe, for your honesty, encouragement, and belief in this story. I could not have done it without you.

Erugak, I see you!

About the Author

Thandi Noah is an African storyteller whose work is inspired by the people and places she encounters along her travels.

Drawing on her background in hospitality and her gift for observation, she crafts narratives shaped by lived experiences, cultural intersections, and human connection.

Her Amara Travel Mysteries explore diverse cultures and locations, revealing how everyday relationships can unravel into unforeseen, and sometimes devastating, consequences.

Stay Connected

To learn more about Thandi Noah and connect with the world of the *Amara Travel Mysteries*, visit:

thandinoahauthor.thandishaven.com
(News, behind-the-scenes notes, and future releases)

What's Next

Amara's journey continues.
Her next adventure in Lamu is already taking shape.

A Small Favour

If you enjoyed this story, consider leaving a review where you purchased the book.
Reviews help readers discover new voices, and they mean more than you know.

www.ingramcontent.com/pod-product-compliance
Lightning Source LLC
LaVergne TN
LVHW100513110826
845146LV00002B/616
* 9 7 8 9 9 1 4 9 4 0 6 4 0 *